PUNKTOWN

PUNKTOWN

Published in the United States by Prime Books
An imprint of Wildside Press

www.prime-books.com

Hardback ISBN: 1-894815-74-2
Paperback ISBN: 1-894815-75-0

PUNKTOWN

• • •

JEFFREY THOMAS

PRIME BOOKS

OTHER BOOKS BY JEFFREY THOMAS

As Author

Aaaiiieee!!!

Godhead Dying Downwards

Letters from Hades

Monstrocity

Punktown

Terror Incognita

As Editor

Punktown: Third Eye

CONTENTS

INTRODUCTION BY MICHAEL MARSHALL-SMITH 9

A BRIEF HISTORY OF THE CITY BY JEFFREY THOMAS 13

THE REFLECTIONS OF GHOSTS 17

PINK PILLS 33

THE FLAYING SEASON 47

UNION DICK 59

WAKIZASHI 71

DISSECTING THE SOUL 85

PRECIOUS METAL 91

SISTERS OF NO MERCY... 101

HEART FOR HEART'S SAKE 107

THE BALLAD OF MOOSECOCK LIP 127

FACE 133

THE PRESSMAN.. 141

THE PALACE OF NOTHINGNESS 145

THE RUSTED GATES OF HEAVEN 155

IMMOLATION 159

UNLIMITED DAYLIGHT 175

THE LIBRARY OF SORROWS.. 191

NOM DE GUERRE 205

For Scott Thomas and Thomas Hughes
– fellow citizens

And with loving appreciation to Rose of the nimble fingers

. . .

Through me you go into the city of grief,
Through me you go into the pain that is eternal
Through me you go among people lost.

– Dante Alighieri
Inferno, Canto III

Some things are hard to classify, and I am glad about that.

In a world where there is a niche and a shelf for everything, where books have a genre stamped on their spine, where everyone thinks of themselves as a double-shot latte or single espresso kind of guy or gal and you can go to a Tower Records and find the 'unique' lost in a row of similar products, it is rare but delightful to find things which truly seem to stand by themselves: stuff which appears to have been carved from a different rock to the rest of creation. When you find it, you pick it up and stare, entranced, feeling as though the doors of perception have been nudged wider. 'Hard to classify' means something that may, for just a little while, make you feel alive.

This is one of the reasons this publisher is to be congratulated. Jeffrey Thomas describes a world that some will see as futuristic, but which feels more as if it is located one step to the side. But remember what I said about being unique. Thomas' stories need no support, no vision or visualisation, no backup. They contain a world in themselves, stored in fragments and glances and details, and together they create a whole even greater than the sum of their parts—while remaining, individually, stories of great impact, a collection of which anyone would be proud to have written just one tale.

Some, like *The Flaying Season* and *Face*, are quietly devastating in their portrayal of human emotions; others are just as poignant in their evocation of feelings which—while technically alien (*Wakizashi*)—seem to find plenty of room to breathe in human heads. Some—like the superb *The Palace of Nothingness*, one of my favourites—are elegiac, and fade like smoke; others are sharp nuggets of well-twisted plot—try *Precious Metal* or *Immolation*. Some take great ideas and turn them until they bend to the oddest shapes, like *The Reflections of Ghosts*. And there are yet others which are so good and so strange that it's impossible to imagine them coming from any other writer in the world—which must surely be the highest accolade of all.

Yes, there are parallels and hints of other marvellous worlds, like the sound of footsteps heard around a dark corner in a Punktown backstreet: a waft of M. John Harrison's *Viriconium*, of the early work of Geoff Ryman, of Paul McAuley's more Brit-SF *Fairyland*, of Lovecraft's crawling chaos and Conrad Williams' *Nearly People*, sometimes even the whisper of the sensibility of a curdled Ray Bradbury, a damaged clone of his, perhaps; one who has been abandoned somewhere dark and damp and left there until stories have begun to grow on his skin like a fungus.

But these writers speak of different places, and place is of the utmost importance here. Jeffrey Thomas sounds like no-one else precisely because he writes of a place no-one else has been, and yet which can feel like home.

The best fiction, particularly that in the more imaginative genres, contains this sense of place. Without a genuine environment, stories often dissolve into so much juxtapositioning of elements and archetypes, of beginnings, middles and ends. This is true of fiction in general, but doubly so of stories of the fantastic. Only when the writer communicates a strong idea of the *place* in which tales happen, do they seem to come truly alive—and in *Punktown*, the place is utterly palpable. The geography may be fetid and crumbling, but it is concrete. It is there between every line, an adjunct to the thought and behaviour of every character. You can hear it, feel the damp in the walls, smell the distant cooking of local food you would not understand at first, but might come to like. In *Bad Land*, his masterful account of the attempted settling of a place almost as alien and mysterious as Thomas' world (the 'great desert' of the American West), Jonathan Raban remarks how our fantasies of other countries are inherently flawed, carrying with them the smells of home, and small details—whether the light switches go up or down, for example—which render the fantasyscape merely that. The landscape of *Punktown* is not diminished in this way. It comes entire. Thomas doesn't actually specify whether you flick a switch up or down to turn on the lights, but you feel that if you were suddenly transported there, you would know. Your hand would reach out, and it would be done.

The place houses the stories, but the place is also the story. Thomas' Punktown is a character just as much as Drew the clone artist, MacDiaz the cop who cannot forget in *The Library of Sorrows*, or the heroic Magnesium Jones. And gradually—as the stories progress and you come to pick up more about the Choom, little hints of their lives and history before the humans, and also about the other species and races who inhabit this strange city, the snippets of their history and culture and life—it becomes increasingly hard sometimes to remember that *Punktown* isn't real. It feels it. It feels like a place to which you could go.

The only question is whether you'd want to. And actually, I would. I want to go there, meet these people, see these things.

I'm going to Punktown.

Luckily, if you turn the page, you can come too.

London, July 2003

A BRIEF HISTORY OF THE CITY: SOME WORDS ON PUNKTOWN BY JEFFREY THOMAS

A single image could not have spawned the entire concept of Paxton, the city better known by its citizens and by myself as Punktown, but I think an image did help to put that last critical bolt into Frankenstein's neck, while the majority of the monster had been piecing itself together subconsciously to that point. One summer afternoon in 1980, my father was driving me somewhere or other, and in a passing car I saw a woman whose long hair appeared to me to be growing out of the shadowed sockets of her eyes. I interpret perfectly ordinary things in such a way, perhaps only to startle myself needlessly. But this shocking visage became the Tikkihotto, one of the alien races living in an otherworldly city, the basic conception of which I had by the time we arrived home. The title was inspired not by the punk music of the times, ironically, but by a disco song whose lyric was, "Won't you take me down to Funkytown?" I guess I initially misheard it.

I saw Punktown as being an opportunity to satirize society in a manner as grotesque as my interpretation of that woman in the car. I would attempt to caricature humankind in the often obscure but always unsettling way Bosch did in his paintings. After scribbling down some basic notes on the planet (Oasis), major races (such as the indigenous Choom), etc., I invited my friend Thomas Hughes and brother Scott Thomas to join in my universe by contributing Punktown-related stories of their own. Tom moved his action to the neighboring city of Miniosis, centering around the recurrent character of the irresistible and enigmatic Domino Diamond. Scott wrote several short Punktown novels to complement my own. None of these early efforts have been circulated to publishers as of this writing (with the exception of Hughes' first Domino Diamond story, which is included in the anthology *Punktown: Third Eye*), but over the years I continued to set novels and short stories in Punktown, in between writing other stories that settle more comfortably in this genre or that than my Punktown pieces do . . . which can all be considered science fiction, due to their futuristic setting, but which can also be considered horror, noir, gangster fiction, romance, or any combination of these from one story to the next. Such is the freedom I find when I walk on her streets.

By 1995, I had published a few short Punktown-based stories, the best of these being *The Reflections of Ghosts*, sold to Ann Kennedy's *The Silver Web*. (My favorite of my own stories, its appearance in this book is its sixth in print . . . plus there's a group who hope to turn it into a graphic novel, while I've also learned of an English teacher who had planned on using it in her class until the school forced her to change her literary selections!) Not long after my appearance in *The Silver Web*, Ann Kennedy's future husband Jeff VanderMeer informed me that he wanted to put together a chapbook of my stories for his Ministry of Whimsy Press. I sent VanderMeer a good many of my stories, both those set in Punktown and those that weren't. It was Jeff's idea to go either one way or the other with the chapbook . . . either all horror, or all Punktown. I chose, as I'm sure he'd hoped, to stick to Punktown.

Over the next few years, the original concept of the collection as a black and white saddle-stapled chapbook with three stories mutated into a beautiful trade paperback with brilliant cover art by one of my favorite artists, H. E. Fassl (this favorable evolution thanks I'm sure to the Ministry's success with their award-winning release of Stepan Chapman's novel *The Troika*). *Punktown* appeared in May of 2000, and was received to wide acclaim, I'm not too humble to relate. *The Library of Sorrows* was accepted for a "Best Of" dark fantasy anthology which unfortunately never saw print, but *The Flaying Season* was selected by Ellen Datlow for the 14th edition of St. Martin's *The Year's Best Fantasy and Horror* (with four other *Punktown* stories making the Honorable Mentions list). I could have died happy the day I first saw it in my local Borders.

Several years after the original appearance of *Punktown* from the Ministry of Whimsy Press, I set about expanding the collection into a meatier edition. Sean Wallace of Prime took on the project, but also very kindly gave me and Delirium Books the opportunity to publish this expanded version (with the additional addition of one more story, not included here) in a 26 copy leatherbound, tray-cased edition (*Punktown Ultra*). There is also a German-language limited edition of *Punktown*, published by Festa-Verlag, with more stories than the Ministry of Whimsy version but less than this version, featuring cover art by H. R. Giger, who also signed each of the books—but I'll get back to discussing this edition before I confuse us both too greatly.

Not all the new material included here is brand new, to be accurate. A few pieces were cut for reasons of length from the original collection (*The Ballad of Moosecock Lip, Union Dick*). A few are reprinted from my Punktown City Limits web site (which has since been lost in the aether), or magazines like *Knightmares* (where my first published Punktown story, *Sisters of No Mercy*, appeared in 1992). *Pink Pills* and *Nom De Guerre* were lost ideas given life for this edition. Therefore, the nine stories from the original *Punktown* have been supplemented by eight stories and one poem. (Also especially for this edition, I have added subtle connections between each story, to link them sequentially in a tenuous fashion. Some elbows are now rubbed by the citizenry.)

This, however, does not constitute the definitive collection of my Punktown-related fiction. That could simply not happen, so long as I'm still breathing. Also, the short fiction has been joined by novel-length Punktown work like the forthcoming *Everybody Scream!* and Prime's *Monstrocity*. I may not want to live in Punktown, but I'm sure I'll continue to visit it for the remainder of my writing life.

I want to thank Janet Fox for having created the late and great *Scavenger's Newsletter* . . . without it I'm sure far fewer of my stories would have seen print, including perhaps in *The Silver Web*, and therefore perhaps in a book called *Punktown*.

And I especially want to thank Jeff VanderMeer, without whom I'm not sure a collection of my Punktown work would ever have been brought together. To him I award the key to the city.

THE REFLECTIONS OF GHOSTS

There was no question; the dead thing in the gutter was one of his clones.

It was naked and fetal-curled like a withered spider, rain drops bursting all over its white skeletal body. Its face was turned up to the sky, lips folded back from a frozen gnash of black teeth. Its flesh was ossified, like stone, pitted all over and cracked black at the joints and around the neck and jaw. The black eyes were like holes where spikes had been.

Drew thought it was beautiful, lying there, like a cast figure from Pompeii. He looked up around him as he sipped from his lidded coffee. Across the street was the Chrislamic Cathedral, a looming metal structure of jagged black spires and stained glass windows all red in webs of black steel. On this side was a row of warehouses, half of them empty and sealed up, a few converted into housing for the cheap labor teams who worked in the warehouses that were still operating. It was a nice setting for the corpse; a quiet street, a lonely street. As lonely a street as anything could hope to die in.

He was tempted to move the creature just a few feet to be more directly opposite the cathedral. In that way, it would seem even more like some lost soul denied its salvation. But no, the thing had chosen to die here, not there, and while Drew was the artist, he decided to respect its choice.

He walked the rest of the way home quickly. Along the way, he passed a group of four Vlessi, an infrequently encountered race. Their inhuman appearance and probably fictitious reputation as blood-drinkers unnerved him somewhat, but when he was past them he gave them several looks over his shoulder, intrigued with their forms, making a few mental notes for possible use in his art.

The lift to his loft was not functioning again today; it merely squealed painfully and shivered until he shut it off. The metal steps he took instead clanged under his heavy boots; some of the staircases he mounted were inside the old warehouse, some outside. Dirty rain water trickled between the filthy white ceramic tiles of the building's skin, to which the external staircases were affixed like the skeletons of immense parasites. He heard a woman crying behind one window he passed. Wasn't aware someone had moved into the trashed third level. Maybe it was a ghost. He used to think ghosts lived on the roof of the old sealed-up factory across the way—at night they would often move about in the rain, a softly glowing blue—until he finally realized that it was someone's holotank sending out a scattered signal on stormy nights. That would explain the frequent shootings. Movies. Drew had thought it was the ghosts living out their deaths.

His loft comprised the entire upper floor. Its narrow balcony ran the length of the building, and on warm nights he would sit and listen to music as he stared out at the city lights of this Earth-established colony called Paxton—or, more commonly but not necessarily with more affection, Punktown. Sometimes he would sketch out there. Though he worked with more three-dimensional mediums, he was adamant that every artist should be able to draw, as every surgeon should still know how to stitch a suture.

The balcony furniture was piled and tipped over now for the winter, and the rain slanted into his back as he struggled to unlock his door. The illumined code buttons were flickering, and he was about to dig out his key when finally the big metal door grated open three quarters of the way before jamming in its track. He slipped inside, hit an overhead bank of sickly greenish lights, and punched the internal door key. The door slid shut with a mournful metallic groan.

The overhead lights were sputtering now, too. Maybe the storm interfering with his illegal power tap-in. Well, that was the price he had to pay.

He didn't remove his overcoat. With it still swirling around his legs, weighted with the rain, he went directly to a series of metal shelves lined with large jugs of liquid and powder, labeled with markered tape. He pulled down one without a label, screwed off the cap to sniff the contents, flinched back from the fumes. This was the one.

With the jug slung from one finger, through the handle like a trigger guard, he clomped back across his loft to the door, and returned to the torrents.

The downpour was picking up strength, but he doubted the water would interfere with the sealant. It was, after all, water-proof.

The clone was still there. No being had carted it away, no animal had come to dine. It had no stench. How long had it been dead? Did its fossilized skin seal in its decay? The plastic sealant would do that, much better.

He poured the clear, sap-thick fluid directly onto the corpse, unmindful of a few wildly varied vehicles which floated past or splashed by through the wet street. He was careful not to let his feet get near the stuff as it began to pool around the figure. He wanted to pour the sealant on so heavily that the clone would be impossible to remove, glued to the street, until someone finally went so far as to chisel it free.

Only a little sealant left, so he poured that on just to kill it off and tossed the jug into an alley between warehouses. He nodded, smiling at the figure, which glistened as though varnished. He thought it might be interesting to spray-paint his signature on the sidewalk near it—he had, after all, tattooed and branded his signature onto a few of his clones before setting them loose—but was afraid that someone might think this was some ordinary mutant, and he its murderer.

Of course, there were always the clones in progress at his studio to prove the actual situation.

He was getting soaked, was anxious to get back and take a hot bath, make a fresh tank of coffee. He left his dead offspring behind him, still satisfied with the way it had died and the way it would continue to exist as a work of art even in death.

. . .

He always kept full a large coffee tank that had once belonged to a local art cinema; its smell was a comfort and the aquarium burbling soothing. This brew was a little old, several days, so he drained it to mix a new one. He had already bathed, changed into clean sweat pants, a black T-shirt and kung fu shoes. Inspired by his discovery earlier that evening, he was anxious to get to work. There was a paying job in progress.

Was that it now, sloshing in its chemical bath? This also gave off a nice burbling, though the chemical stink was unpleasant, so he usually kept the partition drawn, as now, and the vent fans on. Like fetuses with troubled dreams, the clones often tossed and turned in their amniotic baths.

This one, as usual, was for a wealthy client. One clone took weeks, sometimes longer to create, but one sale would pay a month's rent and keep Drew in food for himself and materials for his work.

At first he had been naive about his sales. He had thought the clones he sold were exhibited in cell-like terrariums, perhaps, like exotic animals, or freely moved about at parties among the guests, to be examined up close, Well, yes, both of these were true. But a friend, Sol, his contact with the wealthy, had once attended a party where one of Drew's clones was given as a birthday gift. The thing had been chained all night to a faux marble pillar. At the end of the night, it had been taken out into the brightly flood-lit yard and made to swallow a tremendously expensive ring. Then, the young man whose birthday it was had been given a knife so that he could retrieve his ring, his other present. His young friends had howled and hooted, cheering him on as he began to carve and dig and chase the scrambling thing. Sol had told Drew that the youth had been disappointed when the thing finally vomited up the ring as it died. But the youth gutted it anyway, threw the offal at his hysterical friends, chased his girlfriend around the pool with the thing's head before finally tossing the head into the pool amid roars of approval.

Drew had not known how to feel about all this, at first. For one thing, obviously, it was his artwork being destroyed, like a canvas slashed to ribbons.

But also, the clones were an extension of himself, weren't they?

The most important thing to do with each clone, no matter what its final form would be, was to obliterate its resemblance to him. He did this through a multitude of means; chemical infusion, dyeing, branding, tattooing, scarification, burning, removal of limbs, addition of limbs, surgery, molecular tampering, genetic manipulation. He did not mean for the creatures to be self portraits. They must not look like him, or else that was merely nature and science at work, not an artist. He only used his own matter as a kind of clay, because it was available to him. And, if it ever became a legal problem (he had lost his art grant once he began making his clones), he could use the defense that it was his own body alone he was tampering with, and he could do anything he wanted to that. The ethics of cloning and the rights of cloned life forms were cloudy enough topics at this time that he felt reasonably safe in his activities. Just so long as it was only himself he cloned.

Just as important as the physical obliteration was to obliterate the mind, so that it also bore no resemblance to his own. He achieved this, too, by various means, some crude and brutal, some utilizing more finesse, but always rendering the clone a shuffling sub-idiot at best, not even capable of serving canapes off a tray at one of those upper-scale parties. It was another legal defense—he was making nothing more human than a starfish, in this way—but also, he did not want his mind to be duplicated in something so wretched. Something that might feel horror at its own condition.

In the end, he acclimated himself to the more sadistic uses of his progeny. The snuffed clones, the tortured clones, the hunted clones and gang-raped clones. Target practice for darts and arrows, Sol had heard—summer yard games. They were not himself. They were certainly not anyone else. He need mourn them no more than he mourned the skin cells he was constantly shedding, the fingernails he clipped. And if his art was destroyed, well, it was now another's possession to do with what they wanted. The money they paid to own and sometimes kill part of him kept the main part of him alive.

And with that money he could create the clones that mattered most to him; the ones he turned loose into the world when finished, to wander the streets of Paxton/Punktown wherever their mindless minds took them. Some naked, some clothed for winter, some beautiful in their way and others hideous, like the four he had turned out last Halloween, to his great amusement.

But for all the clones he had turned out over the past three years, since he had begun, he had never seen one of their dead bodies before tonight. Oh he had heard of the fates of a few. Murdered by a gang, struck by a hovercar. He imagined most starved to death or froze. He had heard that several had been taken into homeless shelters. It always intrigued him to wonder where his creations had disappeared to in the vastness of the city. Once he had been thrilled to see one of them still alive after a year, eating a bird in a little courtyard park. The thing had looked up at him without recognition, its flesh permanently dyed a vivid red and spiral brands raised on its forehead and both naked pectorals, like some lovely demon. Even if people did not venture close enough to see his branded signature, even if they never knew Drew's name, even if they thought the thing was a painted madman, a mutant, an alien being or a true demon, they would marvel at it, and even if Drew never saw them marvel, he was gratified knowing that they did. Whether people gazed in admiration or horror, he knew they gazed, and in gazing at his creations they gazed at him, their creator.

Even though he turned them loose, he was always connected to the beings; though he disowned them, he owned them each and every one.

Coffee in hand, he moved around the partition to check on his work in progress.

In aquarium tanks atop a work bench and against the walls here and there, indistinct organic forms hung suspended in gurgling solutions of violet liquid. Some were embryos, though in one tank he had grown a copy of his head alone like a living bust; he meant to offer it for exhibition just like this to a local gallery, hooked up to life support in its womb-like container. He knelt, said, "Hello, Robespierre." He tapped the glass, watched the eyelids flicker as if from a dream. He had suppressed growth of hair, eyebrows and lashes to keep its resemblance to a minimum, but for the sake of impact had left the thing as human-looking as possible.

More sloshing; he looked up to see a swell of violet fluid pour over the side of the main bath, run down its side. He sighed, rose, took up a mop as he went to peer into the tank he had dubbed "Narcissus's Pool."

Drew couldn't help but grin at it. At her.

Where he had suppressed hair in the disembodied head, he had encouraged it here; long dark hair stirred lazily around the clone's face like a sea plant. He had not distorted or marred her face, had instead achieved great change through skillful genetic work. It was not a surgical sex change, but something more subtle and true. This was, for all intents and purposes, an actual female version of himself. Even nature in her genius could not achieve such a thing; an identical twin of the opposite sex.

He rolled up his sleeve, slipped his hand into the bubbling violet fluid. Took one smallish breast in hand and kneaded it, as if he were molding the breast out of clay. He ran his thumb over the nipple, coaxing a reaction. It took several minutes, but at last the nipple began to harden. And so, in his way, did Drew. He grinned more broadly, and watched her eyes move in REMs beneath their thin lids. Soon he'd awaken this sleeping beauty. And he did make an awfully fetching woman, if he had to say so himself.

He let his eyes trail down her body to the flaring of her hips, then to her shadowy patch of hair. Back up to the breasts which he had kept on the modest side, resisting the temptation to make them more bountiful. He didn't want her to be a caricature.

Yes, she was lovely. It was a pity that he had already ruined her mind. What kind of woman would he have been in that sense, he wondered?

Though he had not, admittedly, obliterated her mind to the extent that he usually did in his creations.

. . .

In the section of his loft that he thought of as his living room, on the wall above the sofa in fact, Drew had suspended the one clone which he constantly kept on personal display. It had a human enough head, but he had suppressed the formation of eyes, for he did not want anything to be perpetually gazing at him as he went about his work and his life, or dozed on his couch. But the thing did grunt or wheeze, sometimes. It was hooked up to a life support unit hidden behind the couch. A keyboard was on a side table; when the rare friend visited, Drew could amuse or tease them by hitting keys to inspire movement of the limbs or the face of the crucified thing—mostly just electrified muscle spasms and jerks.

Its chest was opened up in two wide sheets like a spread cowhide, the flaps of a dissected frog belly, spiked to the wall. The ribs showed through a translucent membrane, as did the nest of fat bluish intestines.

The first time he had seen the thing, Sol had said, "Drew-man, I think you must really hate yourself, to humiliate your own body like this. It's masochistic. You create yourself so you can destroy yourself. It's a kind of suicide, isn't it?"

Drew had laughed. "It's art, that's all. I just choose to use flesh as my medium. People always have. Tattoos and brands, scars and piercings. Flesh as canvas; only it hurts less to do it to a clone of me."

"Yeah, see, that's it—a safe way to punish yourself."

"Whatever you say."

"You can't have kids, you told me, right? You don't produce sperm. Is this some kind of perverse reaction to that? Are these your children, created in hatred of a body that can't make the real thing?"

"Sure," Drew had replied, "why not?"

"Is it because you hated your father, and he hated you?"

"Yes, that's it exactly." Drew wagged his head, then. "You read too much into my stuff," he told Sol. "These aren't me. They aren't meant to represent my emotional or psychological state. They're all an Everyman; they aren't a personal expression. Hey, I just like the way I make them look. It's a matter of aesthetics, that's all."

He dried his hand, smiling at his reflected face in the liquid of the tank. Speaking of aesthetics: this one was going to be a big hit, that was for certain. She looked so pretty, he doubted that they would treat this one as a pinata. If it were me, he thought, I'd fix her up a room and keep her around as a pet for lonely nights.

He still felt a crawling arousal. He would have to go relieve it himself. Drew and his last girlfriend had broken up three years ago. She had appreciated his art less even than Sol. Lack of understanding was something he had learned to deal with.

But lack of companionship was harder.

. . .

The rains had stopped today, and the streets were dry. Of course, the corpse in the gutter was still there, and its decomposition had been effectively sealed up and suffocated. But in his zeal to affix the thing to the pavement, he had used too much of the sealant, and it had turned a discolored yellow in drying, it was so thick, like a layer of dirty wax painted over his creation. But there was something far worse than that. Some kid, some punk, had spray-painted a witty remark on the body. An obscenity. It was a desecration of his art. Here he himself hadn't autographed it, and some worthless insect had sprayed a joke on the thing as if to sign his own name to it. Furious, Drew glanced around as if he expected to find the kid lurking in an alley, snickering. He saw no one. Could he remove the paint with a solvent? He must try. If that didn't work he'd spray the whole cadaver another color to mask the vandalism. Or maybe he'd have to chisel up the thing and dispose of it, rather than leave it here like this—its lonely beauty, its statement, muddied.

Its lonely statement. Yes, all right, Drew thought. He did seek emotional expression through his work. But it was a universal palette of emotion he worked from, not a personal one, he thought. He painted in broad, archetypal strokes of color and meaning. Every clone of himself was merely another Everyman—body debased, mind burnt away and spirit enucleated.

. . .

Drew sighed, pushed himself back from the monitors before him. Against one section of his work area's wall was his computer center, its screens glowing like aquariums of exotic knowledge, bundled cables trailing across the floor or up the wall. Drew had excelled in college. He could have been a doctor, according to every family member, friend and girlfriend he had ever been criticized by. But medicine was for mechanics. He was an artist. The same knowledge could be turned on its ear. The same ear could be turned inside-out to make a new flower of flesh; ugly or lovely, it would be a miracle of one man's imagination, not a miracle of nature's mindless engineering.

She was ready to be born from her artificial womb.

He rose from his chair, took one more sip of coffee, and went to her.

First, he drained the violet liquid into a recycling system, where it would be purified for the next creation. When the tank was sufficiently dry, he raised the platform on which his clone lay. Her face was serene, her arms at her sides and her feet pale as those of a corpse on a morgue slab. But Drew inserted a tube into her mouth, down her throat, as if to undo her embalming. There were discs adhered to her chest, and he tapped the keys of a device on a rolling tray beside the tank. A jolt went though the woman's wet, glistening flesh, and her back arched violently. Again. Again. She was like a fish drowning in air. Like a sleeper gripped by a terrible dream.

But at last, a beeping came from the portable unit on the tray, and Drew smiled. It was the sound of her heart stumbling to life.

A few minutes later, her eyes opened. She looked up into Drew's face with a dull, fish-like expression. But her eyes followed him as he moved across the room to pour himself a fresh coffee. He noted this with satisfaction. He had wanted to keep her an animal. But not the usual starfish. For this creature, a product of his highest artistic refinement, a little more seemed called for than the usual shuffling zombie.

When she began to sit up, he set down his mug and rushed to her, took her arm to help her. He swung her legs over the side of the platform, eased her to her feet with one of her arms slung over his shoulders. She was heavy, awkward, but he walked her to a stained love seat. Along the way, she turned her face to gape at him. He grinned back at her. "Hello, my beauty," he whispered. He was as proud as a father, or a groom carrying his wife across the threshold.

· · ·

As he went through his bureau to find her some clothes she could wear, just some sweat pants and a T-shirt maybe, he watched her crawl on hands and knees across the room. She stopped at the foot of the sofa, and gazed up mutely at the flayed, crucified creature on the wall. As if it sensed her, the blind thing moaned.

Drew frowned, wondered if perhaps he had left too much intelligence in the female clone after all. He couldn't have her crawling all over his apartment, learning to walk, perhaps. Getting into things. Maybe he could sedate her, but anyway, Sol would be picking her up in a little over a week, so it wouldn't be a problem long.

Her rear was to him, bare, the dark cleft inviting, her drying hair spread across her back. Jesus God, what was he waiting for? He knew it was inevitable. He couldn't be embarrassed about his desire, could he? After all, it would be no more than his usual masturbation, would it?

Drew set aside her clothes, moved across the room, knelt down behind the clone. He began to rub her back; so smooth. He cooed to her, soothing baby-talk, as if to a kitten. She looked around at him, perhaps at the sound of his zipper. He pressed against her, and something like a drugged, foggy wariness—not quite alarm—came into her eyes, but he was slow, easy, did not want to harm her, had no intention of raping her. If she found it pleasurable, too, he would be ecstatic. It would prove him all the more successful.

He could not determine how she felt about it. She did not resist as he pressed her into the sofa cushion, wrapping his arms around her, with her bottom spread against his belly. Their pallid skin tones matched precisely, and though she was so different from him, he saw something on her face that unnerved him, interfered in his pleasure so that he had to look at her back instead. Her head lay on the sofa, on its side, her eyes staring without apparent emotion. And on her temple was a small mole, just a dot, really, exactly like the one on his own temple. Something so tiny, so unimportant, that all of his clones must have possessed and yet it had never consciously called attention to itself before. But now . . . now . . . it seemed to glare, like another eye, staring back at him.

. . .

He kept her in bed with him in the nights that followed, as much to be aware of her movements as to enjoy her flesh. He didn't leave the apartment much, afraid that she'd get into his equipment like a curious toddler, but that was okay, too. Sol called. Drew told him that the clone had come out well, and that was all he said. He did not tell Sol that yesterday he had dressed the thing and found a perverse delight in taking her out for a hot dog sold by an automatonic street vendor.

He did not tell Sol that last night he had awakened in the dark to feel the clone's face nuzzled in his neck as she slept, her arm draped over his chest.

As much as he enjoyed the sensation, he had pushed the thing off him gently.

Tonight, he would sleep on the couch. She could have the bed. After all, she was only to be a guest for a few nights longer.

But later that evening, he called Sol back.

"This client, Sol . . . what's he have in mind for this clone? Is it for a party?"

"I don't think so; just a wealthy couple buying some artwork for themselves."

They had requested a female—that had been their idea. At first, they had wanted a clone of a woman they knew, but Sol had informed them that Drew only did clones of himself. But Drew had been inspired, rose to the occasion. The work of art they sought would be all the more special, valuable, for having been made a woman in this manner.

He pressed Sol. "Don't you know anything about these people? Are they going to exhibit her in a showcase? Bring her out at parties? Take her to bed—what?"

"Drew-man, I don't know. That's not unlikely. Even some of your most grotesque pieces have been used for that. Why, isn't she capable? Drew? Is there a problem with that?"

Drew glanced over his shoulder at the clone as she knelt on the floor staring at a movie on his old 2-D VT. "They aren't going to . . . hunt her or anything, are they?" he asked. "Tie her up . . . burn her with cigarettes? Strangle her while they rape her? That kind of thing? Can you find out?"

"Look, I can't do that. What's the matter?"

"Can they wait a few weeks? For another clone? This one . . . I've become too attached to. It's my finest work of art. I can come up with another one, just as nice." Just a little more like a starfish, though, he thought.

"Look," said Sol, "make another clone for yourself, then, but we have a deal, and I have a deal with them, and it's too late. Sorry. Don't make me disappoint them, Drew—they're looking forward to this. And you need their money a lot more than I do, remember."

Drew glanced again at the clone. Yes, it was true, he could make another one. And he could make that one more intelligent, not less intelligent. Intelligent enough not just to snuggle, an adoring dog, but to love him as a true woman.

But then wouldn't she also leave him, as other women had? Criticize his art first, and then leave him?

Whether he made another clone for himself or not, he had yet to decide, but he must give this one up. And maybe it was for the best. She made him too confused. She made him feel more alive than he cared to. It was all right for his clones to starve, freeze, die in the street. But for him to feel the ache of his own solitude . . . that was more of a burden than he cared to carry. Better to keep his suffering in those extensions of himself, safely distanced.

As he shut off the vidphone, Drew saw that the woman had twisted around from the VT and been watching him finish with Sol. "Hi, there," he said, smiling uneasily like a guilty teen caught making plans by an eavesdropping mother. The woman only stared back at him, her dark eyes narrowed slightly and blinking. She looked like a person trying to remember a dream.

. . .

A heavy thump awakened him.

Over the top of the partition, the monitors and tanks of his work area cast a blue and violet glow on the ceiling. But that was the only light. The artist felt as though he floated in a dark void, a black womb, listening to the burbling of his coffee and his chemicals. A computer chirped like some night insect. Rain pattered on his balcony outside.

That was all normal enough, but something was amiss.

A sound of movement, from the living room section. As of something— crawling. Dragging itself across the cold bare floor in the deep gloom.

Drew realized then what was amiss; the woman was gone. No warm body against his, as there had been these past nights, her skin sticky from the sweat of her exertions. The previous night she had kissed him on the mouth before he could begin to make his advances. Had she become programmed? Or had her adoration evolved from the dog-like? She had begun to moan when they were entwined, these past couple of nights, and responded more enthusiastically to their love-making; writhing, clutching him, even riding atop him last night.

With only two days remaining before he had to give her up, Drew had again begun to doubt that he could part with her. Even if he had the ability to create a dozen more like her. They would be a dozen women like her. But they would not be her.

He sat up in bed, stared into the darkness. He wanted to call her name but hadn't given her one. She seemed to be crawling toward the bed. Yes, he decided, she was. Had she fallen in the dark, hurt herself? Without waiting any further, he reached out blindly for his beside lamp . . .

But as he did so, he felt her fall against the mattress. He reached instead to her, took hold of her arms, pulled her up. "Are you all right?" he asked, not expecting an answer.

She gave a deep groan.

Her arms seemed thinner, like those of a starving child, atrophied. And her breath was sickly. And her chest, as she fell upon him. It was hard and bony . . .

Drew cried out, tried to push the thing off him, but its wide flaps of skin covered him like a blanket, lent weight to the pathetic creature as it lay atop him. Its face pressed into his neck in a terrible mockery of the woman, but Drew knew that it wasn't her. Instead, it was the crucified thing, somehow. Somehow it had fallen, its spikes torn free.

He pushed it off the bed with one panicked surge, terrified suddenly that it would suffocate him with its manta-like body. It thudded to the floor, and he thrust his arm out for the lamp.

It came on and he leapt from the bed, backed across the room. He saw the abomination trying to push itself up. The eyeless head lifted as if to sniff him out, its twisted mouth working, drooling. It trailed the cords of its life support.

He looked around to the wall where it had been suspended, and saw the woman there, standing before him.

She was naked. As lovely as ever, her thick hair half obscuring her face like a primal thing, a savage innocent. His beast. His pet.

But under one arm, she held his decapitated head.

And across the sofa cushions lay every one of his embryos, his future clones. All were dead already but for one, wriggling its tiny limbs like flippers.

Under her arm, Robespierre had rolled its eyes up, lips quivering as it died, disconnected from its tank.

Drew felt fury rising up in him. But along with that, a vertigo of horror and revulsion, disorienting him. Paralyzing him. His eyes dropped to the spike in the woman's other hand. One of the spikes that had affixed the crucified being to the wall.

She came forward then, the head under one arm and the spike rising up like a dagger.

Drew raised him arms and cried out, "No!"

The woman lunged past him and fell atop the back of the blind, half-flayed thing as it sought to rise, plunging the spike into the base of its neck.

The three collapsed as one; the woman, the head, the sightless creature. Only the woman rose, but she lifted the head in her arms again. Now it was entirely motionless, as were all of the embryos reverently lined up on the sofa.

"What are you doing?" Drew asked the woman, lowering his arms slowly. "What have you done?"

For a moment, she gazed at him. Her face was nearly blank. And yet, he knew his own face well enough to interpret sadness there. Despair. And self-loathing. He had seen those things often enough in the mirror to recognize them now.

She turned, and moved to the door. Tapped the keys to open it, as she must have seen him do. From the inside, it did not require a code, and the door ground painfully open most of the way. Where was she going, nude, with a human head cradled like an infant? She had no weapon now, yet Drew was still almost afraid to follow. But he did.

"Wait!" he called after her.

As he slipped out through the door, into the mounting rain, he saw the woman standing at the balcony railing, gazing out at the city lights. Maybe searching for the ghosts he had seen.

"Hey," he said to her, holding out his hands. "Come back inside. Please. I won't send you away. I promise you."

She half turned to look back at him, rain water streaming down her face. He saw her lips move slightly, as if she were trying to mold words.

"Please stay with me," he told her.

The woman turned back to face the night. With a solemn kind of grace, she stepped over the low railing.

"Hey!" Drew said, lunging forward. And he saw the woman leap out into the dark, wet air, his own disembodied head still clutched in her arms.

Drew yelled for her to stop, even as he watched her white form plummet. He fell against the railing, looked down. Saw her pass through the yellow light of a lower window as she fell. Then she passed out of the light, and he lost sight of her altogether. He heard a heavy thump, and it was like he had heard his heart drop, severed, to the floor of his chest.

He pounded down the stairs, some outside the warehouse, some inside, until he reached the street. It was cold as the surface of an iced lake beneath his bare feet. He welcomed the punishment of the sensation.

He moved to her side, knelt there.

"Oh, God," he murmured. "Why . . . why did you do that?"

He moved the wet hair which obscured her face, afraid at what death might have done to alter it, evil sculptor that it was. The drop had not been so great as to disfigure her. With her head turned on its side, she merely appeared asleep. She was beautiful, even in death. A beautiful work of art, bleeding in the gutter.

Tenderly, he shifted the hair at her temple. Though it was too dark to see it, he lightly touched the tiny mole there. A birthmark that united them.

Drew did not leave her in the gutter. Gently, he scooped her slack form into his arms, and began the long climb back up the stairs.

He went to the bed, rested her there. Again, he cleared wet strands of hair from her face.

He had taken the head with him, and now he gathered the embryos, the heavy grotesque corpse of the crucified being. In addition to these, he went into his laboratory of a work shop and collected organic cultures and growths which the woman had missed in the darkness.

He deposited the woman and all the rest of his brood into the tank in which she had been grown. But instead of pumping in the violet amniotic solution, he took down two jugs of chemical from his metal shelves.

With a mask over his face, he poured the contents of one jug and then the other over the figures in the tank. He quickly stepped back from the billowing fumes. Inside these clouds, the bodies in the tank were indistinct shadows. They appeared to have all become one tangled, deformed being. But the limbs shortened, the shadows began to fade away, leaving only the vapor . . . which the vent fans sucked out into the night air to be dispersed like the ashes of a pyre.

Watching the last fume tendrils rise to the fan, Drew mourned the woman. He mourned himself.

He felt like a ghost of himself . . . as though it were he who had committed suicide.

PINK PILLS

The tiny ball rolled playfully under Marisol Nunez's fingers, as if they chased it in circles, around and around, but with no way for it to escape her flesh, or for her fingers to catch hold of its slippery perfection. It was perfect, wasn't it? She was the lumpen, disorganized mass of pulsing membranes, writhing organs, fluttering valves. She was the oyster and her tumor was the pearl.

Sitting on the train, she rested her jaw in the cup of her hand and no doubt looked merely exhausted after a long day of work, which she was, but there was more than exhaustion below the epidermis of her thoughts. The fingers of her cupping hand kneaded the base of her jaw, on the right side. It was almost a sensuous, soothing motion, only partly conscious. She had discovered the ball there last week. She had cried on that night. This evening, her eyes were dully dark and more distant than the train's last stop. A young man, holding the overhead bar, his crotch swaying near her face, looked down at her and told her she was pretty. She ignored him, and thankfully he got off at Rumford Park. But after he'd gone she belatedly and internally answered him: "Am I? Will I be? A year from now. Or less?"

The hovertrain continued on . . . burrowing through the guts of Paxton, a vast city established by Earth on the planet Oasis but since colonized by numerous other races as well. Even the Chooms, who had lived here before the first Earth people, had come to refer to the city by its nickname of Punktown.

Along the glossy, reptilian tiles of the tunnels snaked cables and conduits and sewerage pipes in a complex circulatory system, a convoluted digestive tract. Some pipes, cracked or burst, released billows of steam the train plunged through, as if they flew through clouds. She saw some wires raining molten sparks onto a maintenance catwalk. By the intermittent service lights, she saw the huddled shapes of people sleeping or dying on those narrow walkways. A train passed them the other way, and in the windows she saw streaking faces so smeared and haunted she couldn't tell whether they were human or alien. Across the walls of the train's interior ran animated advertisements in endless loops. A trailer for the latest serial killer movie. An ad for a gun store chain. An ad for a drug to alleviate depression. An ad for a drug to squelch addiction to other drugs. Kill and cure. Yin and yang. Whatever made you feel balanced. Vicarious violence. A pistol under the pillow or a hand full of pills. Were those to preserve one's own life or take it?

The subway train whispered to a halt at the underground stop for Mercy Hospital.

Marisol pressed her smooth forehead to her window to watch the boarding and departing of passengers. One day she would be debarking here. For the last time.

She pitied those she saw leaving the train, as if they had stepped off Charon's barge. And these passengers boarding . . . they must be those who had been grieving over the dying, or those granted a brief reprieve from their own deaths. Death was inevitable. It was nothing unique, special, or else every morsel of steak she devoured would be a tragedy. Though maybe it was. And I'm only twenty-six, she thought. I'm only twenty-six and I've never been married. She had never miraculously grown another life within her. Except this bastard pearl . . . this immaculate misconception.

Marisol watched an elderly man cross the platform in a slow, ungainly fashion, and her heart cowered behind her rib cage. She followed him as he mounted the few stairs to enter her train. She flinched back from the window, and in so doing, confronted directly her wide-eyed reflection. It was as if her own reflection was what had inspired this expression of horror. But she was so pretty, as that passenger had said. She was small, doll-like. An explosion of dark tendrils gathered back into an unruly ponytail. Huge blackly lustrous eyes under arched heavy brows. A small, almost haughty pout. And skin like ivory. All the gifts of blind Nature. Not engineered, not cosmetic. Accidents, purposeless. Flukes. But the tumor; she could almost sense a sentience to it, a sinister cognizant determination. Like a demon that meant to possess her. Replace her.

Marisol turned slightly in her seat to watch the old man enter her car; afraid to see him this close, but masochistically unable to resist.

He had the same sort of tumor that her PCP (primary care physician) had diagnosed in her . . . but his was in its advanced stages. It grew squarely between his shoulder blades, bent him like a hunchback under its weight. They could grow anywhere. She had looked at photos on the net. One child, eight at the most, had one growing in the orbit of his eye. A pink sphere as big as a tennis ball, swirled with white, like a pink planet viewed from space, streaked with clouds, glossy as if made from marble, like an orb broken off the pinnacle of a grave monument. But the thing was, you never grew more than one of them. Just the one. But the other thing was, it could not be excised (exorcized, she thought). At its base: a nest of filaments so widely spread throughout the body, so intricately interwoven like ivy through a trellis, so blended into the nervous system even on a microscopic level that they were impossible to weed out except, with great effort, postmortem. To sever the parasite at the base would kill a live host. Its ingenious design, a sort of self defense mechanism, had led to some calling it an alien life form, a sort of being, but it wasn't, her doctor had assured her. It was mindless. And that made it more frightening. It could not be reasoned with, appealed to.

Even her tumor, as small as a marble, would already have rooted its poisonous arms like those of a jellyfish into her own body, pretending they belonged, invading her tapestry with its own thread, becoming one with her new self. Wired into her complex nerve web and thus, through that, into her brain.

Why can't it be screened out with teleportation? she had pleaded. This is why, said her PCP, though his explanation was too vague or too technical for her to assimilate.

Why can't it be poisoned in such a way that its nerves die but mine stay alive? That can be done to an extent, her PCP told her, to delay the process . . . sometimes for many years . . . but not all the tendrils die and they ultimately regenerate. And it wasn't possible in every case; in some, the disease advanced much more aggressively than in others.

Marisol was lucky she was no longer a temp; she had full insurance through work. She was scheduled for her first poisoning treatment—at a clinic, not Mercy Hospital, not that place yet—in two and a half weeks. But even by then, how much further would the pearl have integrated itself with her body?

The elderly passenger was too doubled-over to hold the overhead bar. With an impatient sigh of disgust, a young man in a five-piece suit stood up from his seat so the old man could use it. He half lowered himself, half fell into it.

His tumor was like a cannon ball that had been fired into him, sunken deeply but halfway breaking through the skin, pushing aside his loose collar, exposing part of itself to a few gawks, mostly from children, but most didn't even glance at it. It wasn't an uncommon ailment. There were worse things in Punktown, and people didn't bother to look at most of those, either.

Bigger than a cannon ball, though, bigger than a pink bowling ball dropped from a height into gelatinous flesh. It was as big as a basketball, easily. She had seen a photo on the web, a dead woman on a slab, naked, with a vast belly as though pregnant but it was in fact a tumor, almost entirely free of her skin, glossy smooth and even beautiful, hard as bone, and this tumor weighed two hundred pounds. Most didn't live long enough for them to get that large. Thank God.

This man, she realized, didn't have use of his left arm; it was folded at the elbow, clenched up tightly against his chest. And every half minute, his tongue spasmed between his lips. That crushing weight on his spinal column, but the real damage done on a microscopic level.

The old man lifted his eyes and met Marisol's.

His eyes were very tired. And though he was so old, and his tumor was visible where hers was not, not yet, and he was a man and she was a woman, they recognized the same look in each other's eyes as though reflected, and he smiled at her sympathetically. His smile was as bad as the doctor's confirmation had been. Marisol denied, if only for this moment, any fellowship between them. She tore her eyes off him, wanting to cry, to scream, but too numb . . . as if, already, her nervous system had been hijacked and reprogrammed, shifted from her control.

. . .

The tech who scanned her prior to her first poisoning session was youngish, and offered Marisol his first name: Jay. Jay Torrey.

"How do you catch this thing?" she asked him as she lay back on the scanning table, dressed only in a flimsy white gown through which Jay's scanner would be able to see. And through which, thus, he would be able to see. He would see beneath her very skin. See *inside* her. Her voice trembled with her vulnerability and she wished Jay wasn't so cute. It made her feel so ugly. He would see to the rotting core of her. Even the sexiest lips, hugely magnified in lipstick ads, looked to Marisol as creased and repellent as an elephant's anus.

"They haven't figured out yet," he told her, standing near her bare feet, adjusting controls on his scan console. "But it isn't confined to human races. It first appeared on Anul. In fact, the doctor who'll be administering your poison session today is from Anul. They seem to be the most adept at fighting it."

"Some people say the Anul brought it with them. That it's their fault."

"Shh." Jay smiled over his shoulder at her. "Don't be prejudiced, now. You've just been reading too many conspiracy theories on the net."

"I'll tell you another one, then," she said. "Some people think it's a secret weapon from an enemy race."

"Nahh. It works too slow, in most cases. It's too unevenly spread through the populace. Can't be a bioweapon." He gestured at her feet. "I like your toenails." As on her fingernails, she had a photo of one of her own eyes reproduced on each nail. Her right eye on all the right finger and toenails, her left on all the left. It was a current fad. "But it makes me nervous that you're looking at me like that," he joked. He cupped his hands over the ends of her feet as if to blind those unblinking eyes. His palms lightly touched the tops of her feet; she took this as flirtation, and it both excited and dismayed her.

"Some people decorate their tumors when they break the skin," Marisol noted. "They paint them. I saw a guy a year or so ago who painted a face on his."

"It must help them deal with it. Make a little joke out of it. Some levity to lighten the load."

"Yeah? I think it's sick, myself."

Jay had seated himself to commence his scanning, though his body blocked the screen from Marisol's view, for the most part. She tried to lift her head to look but he cautioned her not to move. What she glimpsed didn't make much sense to her, anyway. Were those her cells or the cells of the tumor's lattice or both, blended on a nearly molecular level, like linked chains in the mesh of her composition?

"Has your PCP got you on pinks?" Jay asked, without looking around.

"Yeah. One a day." It was a pill, pink in color like the tumors that had been nicknamed "orb weavers," after the spider with its intricate web. The pill was a small dose of the same poison with which the Anul doctor would infuse her body after Jay had completed the scan for him. "For what it's worth," she added. She wished she didn't sound so bitter. He'd think she was too gloomy. And then she asked herself why she should care what he thought. What were the chances that he would be interested in a diseased woman? What were the chances that she'd even let him be?

"Everything that helps, even in some small way, is worth trying." The young tech swivelled around to smile at her. "There. I'll go send in Dr. Fald now. Any more questions before I do?"

"Not that immediately comes to mind."

"I have a question for you, then. Do you like films?"

"Films?"

"I was hoping you might go to one with me, sometime." His grin became embarrassed. "I know it's not professional of me to ask you, but . . . I understand if you'd rather not . . . "

He'd seen within her, seen the hard seed of corruption that even she hadn't seen, and yet he was still asking her out . . .

In a small, uncertain voice, but without hesitation, she found herself telling him she would.

. . .

During the poisoning session, Marisol slept. And dreamed.

In the dream, she was walking barefoot through a vast factory, wearing only that thin hospital gown. She was following a great conveyor belt along its river-like course through the chambers of the factory, through billowing steam clouds jetted from valves, through walls of buzzing and clanging noise, through nearly unlit hallways as silent as a subterranean labyrinth of tombs. At the beginning of the conveyor, naked people had been standing in a queue and were stepping up onto the slowly moving belt, then lying back upon it with their feet together, their arms at their sides. Some of these people looked quite normal, but in most, their orb weaver tumors were bulging beneath their skin, or even broken bloodlessly through the skin to expose their hard smooth surfaces like the enamel inside a conch shell.

The conveyor carried these bodies onward to a point where guillotine-like blades whooshed in from either side, severing heads from necks. The belt, the floor, the walls became splashed with explosions of blood . . . but no one as they neared the swinging blades sought to scramble free . . . and the decapitated bodies did not flinch or convulse. It was as if the procession was passively sedated by the pink pills they had been handed back when they were waiting in line.

The headless bodies were transported into an enclosed area that Marisol could not see within, so she continued along outside the covered conveyor, padding along a narrow catwalk because the floor had dropped away, lying she couldn't tell how far below because of the gulf of blackness. Toward the end of the covered section of the belt, ahead of her she saw white shapes being ejected out of a chute to plummet into the void below. As she drew nearer to the chute, she saw what these ejected forms were. Headless, bloodless corpses. And each had a black hole drilled into it, but the hole was in a different spot in each cadaver. Also, the hole might be very small or a gaping crater. She knew what had been extracted through these holes, even before she saw the conveyor emerge from its enclosing cover.

On the belt now, the blood having been sprayed from it, rested orb weaver tumors where the bodies had once been. Some were so tiny as to be nearly invisible, while others were too large for a person to get their two hands around. One, she guessed, had to weigh at least as much as she did. And all so perfectly round and smooth—could anything be more perfect?—glossy pink with white striations like cirrus clouds.

The floor returned. Marisol stepped off the catwalk and followed the conveyor until it entered another closed section. From within it came a deafening grinding sound, so high-pitched she imagined her ears would soon trickle blood. Despite the cover over the belt, a fine pink dust misted the air, which Marisol couldn't help breathing in. She knew it coated her lungs.

The belt was drawing toward its terminus, passing through the bodies of various loud, vibrating machines . . .

At the end of the belt stood a queue of nude people, old and young, male and female, human or nonhuman. Marisol stripped her light gown up over her head, then added herself to the end of the line. She turned her head to watch the belt again. From the last of the machines through which it passed, she saw what the belt now carried forward, its final product. Evenly spaced, tiny pink pills. Like the others in line with her, she reached out and took one, popped it into her mouth and swallowed it dry.

She could feel the forests of tendrils emerge from the pill as soon as it hit her belly. And she saw that the belt did not end, after all. It had completed a circle as perfect as the tumors were round. It was an endless cycle.

The man in front of her in the shuffling line wasn't human. From the rose pink hue of his skin and his bony mallet-shaped head she could tell he was an Anul. He turned his head around to look down at her. The tumor that had broken through the flesh of his shoulder, as big as his head, swivelled in its socket as if to look at her, too. "Miss Nunez?" he said.

. . .

"Yes?" she said groggily, slitting open her eyes, and seeing the face of Dr. Fald leaning over her.

"Your session is finished. How do you feel?"

"Tired," she grumbled.

"You can convalesce in here for a while, and then a nurse will be in to assist you and check you out of the clinic."

Dr. Fald had no tumor, as in her drugged dream. Because she had never seen an Anul up close before today, his face hovering so low over her own face disturbed her greatly; she wanted to push it away or at least close her eyes again. The being's huge head, supported by two thin necks, was like that of a hammerhead shark, but with no eyes at its ends; no eyes visible at all, in fact. At the base of this bony mass, which was thinly coated in a shiny pink skin, was an imposing lipless mouth filled with rows of oversized molars in a constant, skull-like grin. The offworlder did not wear a translator clipped to its uniform, but Marisol wore a common translation chip in her skull which deciphered the being's speech as if telepathically.

"How did it go?" Marisol mumbled.

"Well, it appeared to go well, but we can never be sure, Miss Nunez . . . the orbs are an inscrutable foe. But the poisoning should inhibit its development . . . "

"Are they closer to finding a cure for this, doctor?"

"Research is proceeding—slowly. But don't give up hope. We'll keep you around until they do." The death's head grin grew wider in what was meant to be a smile. Marisol wished he would stop. She closed her eyes.

"Thank you, doctor."

. . .

"The Anul religion says all nonbelievers will be cast into the void," Marisol said.

"*All* religions say that," replied Jay, while munching a mouthful of native Choom salad. It was garnished with crunchy black beetles which Marisol had refused to sample.

"I've been reading about them on the net."

"I've worked closely with Fald for a few years now. He's been very good to me."

"I'm not suggesting . . . " she let it trail off.

"Suggesting what?"

"That he wouldn't be nice."

Jay munched quietly some more, as if studying her. Marisol wondered if he was staring at her jaw, if he could see the little ball pushing against her skin now. She could swear it was bigger than it had been last week, on their first date. She resisted the impulse to reach her hand up to it.

Jay said, "Don't tell me you read that urban legend on the net."

"What urban legend?"

"You tell me. The one about the Anul . . . and the orb weavers?"

Marisol poked at her own Caesar salad, keeping her eyes averted from his. "I read something. It was an eyewitness report . . . "

"It's just a rumor. Based on bigotry . . . xenophobia. I know which one you're talking about. I knew you'd read it . . . "

Her huge eyes lifted, glowering darkly. "Don't make fun of me, Jay. How do you know it's not true?"

"I'm sorry, Mar, but it's ridiculous. And I've read variations on it, differing only slightly . . . I get mass net-messages about it a couple times a year. It's always something about this woman, or this man, who's wealthy enough to go see this incredible specialist from Anul. The Anul is so skillful he can remove the tumor without killing the host; he can't promise that a new one won't grow back in its place, but he's buying the victim a lot of time. When the patient wakes up after his operation and poisoning session, he's all alone and he goes out into the doctor's rooms to look for him or his assistant. He opens a door and sees a room like a morgue, with several dead bodies covered in sheets and one who's uncovered. The dead woman, or man in some versions, has a hole in her where her tumor was removed. And there stands the Anul specialist—caught by surprise. In his hand is a good-sized tumor. The patient doesn't know if this tumor is his own tumor, or if it came from the dead body, but one thing is for sure . . . the Anul doctor has bitten into the sphere, and is crunching up that mouthful between those big teeth of his with this awful . . . grating . . . grinding sound . . . " He chewed a little of his salad for emphasis.

"I told you, don't mock me, Jay. This isn't a funny matter. Maybe if you had a tumor you'd take things more seriously, like I do. Maybe you'd be more open-minded about where it comes from, how it can do what it does, how it can't be filtered out by teleporters, how . . . "

Jay dropped his smile and reached across the restaurant table to take her small pale hand. "Marisol . . . I'm sorry. Believe me, I don't take it as a joke. I don't."

"The Anul brought it. How do we know that they didn't do it on purpose?"

"As a food source? I'm sorry but it wouldn't make sense, Mar . . . they get this disease themselves. And we don't know for certain they brought it . . . "

Marisol curled her own fingers around his. "Jay . . . you know this thing of mine is going to get worse, sooner or later. The poisoning only slows it, and it doesn't even work every time. We don't know how far from a cure we are." She swallowed nervously. "How are you going to feel about me later on? When it grows? When it breaks the skin?"

He crushed her hand hard in his, as if desperate. "We're going to fight it, Mar. Trust me. I'm going to protect you."

"Protect me? How can you protect me? Dr. Fald?"

Jay let go of her hand, and lowered his own eyes as if now he couldn't bring himself to face her. He scooped a beetle onto his fork but only rocked it there, did not lift it to his mouth. "Do you have a pen?" he whispered.

"A pen? Yeah . . . why?"

"And paper? Or I can use a napkin . . . "

"I have paper. Hold on." She pulled her bulky pocketbook into her lap.

After she produced the stylus and a notepad, and handed them to him, Jay leaned over the pad intensely and began writing rapidly in a crowded, tiny script. He shielded it from her gaze with his free hand like a little wall. While she waited, Marisol glanced around her at other tables. She caught a Tikkihotto woman staring at her, and again fought the urge to clap a hand over her jaw. The Tikkihotto woman was human in appearance except for the translucent, floating nests of tentacles that sprouted from both eye sockets. Did they enable her to see what others could as yet not discern?

Marisol felt Jay slide the pad against her hand. She took it, turned it around so that she could read from it. Jay Torrey had written:

"I can't tell you anything aloud, because they make me wear a chip in my head. The chip can hear what I say, and they can listen to it. Stop taking the pills your PCP gave you. They're either a placebo, or something designed to make the orb grow faster. I have pills you can take instead. They're very effective in keeping the growth arrested. But you can't tell anyone about any of this or we'll both be in danger."

Marisol tore off the sheet, pocketed it, and began to write in turn. She wrote:

"Who are you talking about? Who are you working with? Do you mean Fald?"

Jay read her questions, and answered by scribbling: "I can't tell you. But it's big. There's a lot of money made by people for the treatments and medication they give. There are too many cures for other diseases—no one gets rich if no one is sick. This is an industry of death. Don't ask any more about it. Just take the pills I'll give you tomorrow . . . and throw those others out before the growth in you advances too fast. I can only hope that Fald's session with you was real. I can only hope he didn't make matters worse instead."

Marisol read this last bit with her mouth gaping open, and snapped fearful, enraged eyes up to meet his wordlessly. But she wrote in a jagged hand: "You let them do this to others, and you don't warn them like you're warning me, do you?"

Jay wrote no reply to that note.

. . .

On the vidscreen of her home deskcomp, Marisol saw the face of Dr. Fald's nurse, Miss Banal. She was an Anul as well, indistinguishable from him right down to the vast smile. She could easily imagine those teeth grinding up the ossified mass of an orb no matter what Jay might say.

"Would you like to reschedule your next appointment, then, Miss Nunez?"

"No. I'd like to cancel it."

"But it's six months away. May I ask why you wouldn't want a follow-up exam?"

"I expect to be away from Oasis by then. On Earth."

"Ah. Well, Dr. Fald has an associate on Earth, named Dr. Olad. Where on Earth will you be?"

Marisol digested that for a moment. Earth too, then? "I'd rather not make a follow up appointment at this time. I'll contact you if I change my mind." Before the nurse could protest any further, Marisol broke their connection.

She tried calling Jay again. There was no answer, so she left another message. Then, she shook from a vial one of the pills he had given her to replace those her primary care physician had prescribed. It was pink, too.

For a few days after he had given her the new pills, Marisol had not wanted to see Jay. Yes, he had confided in her . . . placed his trust in her. Yes, he was trying to protect her. But she was disgusted with the idea that he would never have warned her, had she not accepted his offer of a date that day when she first met him. Disgusted that he had warned no one other than her . . .

But she was still attracted to him. And anyway . . . these new pills wouldn't last forever. If he was going to be motivated by selfishness, then so would she.

. . .

Marisol read, on the net newspaper she subscribed to, that a suspicious person had been seen lurking in the foyer of the apartment house where Jay Torrey had lived. This loiterer had been a Vlessi. The Vlessi were a related but separate race that lived on the same world the Anul did; little was known about them but they were rumored to be a race of vampires. When his roommate discovered his body, Jay Torrey had been drained of blood . . . besides having had his head lopped off, and placed like a centerpiece atop the counter of their kitchenette.

Marisol did not attend the funeral, for fear that whoever might have learned of Jay's betrayal would be there, waiting for her to show her face. Had Jay confessed anything before he was silenced? Marisol bought a telescoping stun wand that could be adjusted to a lethal setting from a teenage boy who lived several floors below her in the same apartment complex, whom she'd heard could supply stolen weapons. She took to carrying it with her, especially when she was crammed into a train with so many strangers on her way to or from work.

. . .

With what little money she had left over from her disability pay after she paid the rent on her new, tiny flat, Marisol printed flyers that she handed out every afternoon in the train station nearest her boarding house. The flyers were printed on pink paper. She would often see this pink paper, crushed into balls, lying carelessly on the floor around trash zapper units. Most people would not even accept the sheets when she thrust them at them. Most people shunned her, wouldn't even befoul their eyes with her.

There were several different versions of the flyer, each more strident than the last. On the most recent, she had added a photo of Jay's severed head, taken from a net site where crime scene photos were posted for the entertainment of the masses. A mother had scolded her harshly, once, for trying to hand one of these sheets to her young daughter.

When she was still beautiful—before the pills Jay had given her ran out—people might have stopped to listen to her. Her eyes were as large and dark as ever, if less lustrous. But people only saw the ball and chain she carried. The tumor, polished as a sphere of pink marble, that had erupted from the side of her jaw, weighing her head at a grotesque angle. Pushing down against her shoulder, throwing her entire carriage off so that she limped along crookedly. Her voice was a half-strangled rasp from her half-crushed throat. The ball was only too visible but the invisible chain was wound all throughout her system.

Taking a break from standing at the foot of the escalators leading up to street level, Marisol stuffed her stack of flyers into her backpack and shambled over to a concession stand to buy a bottle of water. She inadvertently bumped a man in line and the man's girlfriend or wife drew him aside, hissing to him, "Tom, watch it—that might be contagious!"

A smile quivered at one corner of Marisol's mouth. It made the corner of one eye quiver as well. How uninformed people were. Superstitious. It was not a plague. It was barely organic, except on the surface. It was a machine, she thought, a great hungry machine. She bought her water, but as she was unscrewing the cap, the sweating bottle slipped through her fingers. Numbly, Marisol stared down between her feet, watched the contents of the bottle gush out . . . mesmerized, making no move to stoop and retrieve it. The man and his girlfriend walked away briskly with their own purchases, perhaps afraid that if the puddle spread to their shoes, it might convey the plague to them like pus from a lanced bubo.

A hand lightly took hold of Marisol's elbow and she flinched. Who was touching her? Didn't they know she might be contagious? Slowly she twisted around to face the person, who stood close behind her, looming over her so that she had to tip her head back like a child.

"You need help," a voice cooed gently. Marisol couldn't tell if the being wore a translator, or if it were the chip in her head that deciphered the Anul's words. She didn't know if the being was a male or female. A doctor or not.

Vaguely she thought of something in her backpack that she should take out just then. Something that might help her. She slipped her hand into the bag, and her fingers hesitated only a moment on the tubular shape of the telescoped stun wand. Then, uncertainly, they crawled on to her stack of flyers, and she withdrew one of these . . . extended it to the Anul.

Accepting the flyer graciously, then grinning more broadly, the Anul went on, "Why don't you come with me?"

Marisol did not protest. She did not speak or resist, as the pink-skinned creature led her away.

THE FLAYING SEASON

The flukes, as the great beasts were called, had skins of malachite, swirled green and black and smoothly sheened, which the Antse people flayed from the carcasses inside ceramic block garages or hangar-like structures with scrap metal roofs, and their watery yellow blood would run down the streets of the neighborhood into grates, and dry to a crust along the gutters when the season of flaying was over.

Kohl had once watched a team of Antse capture a fluke; she had never been able to watch more than once. The swollen, tadpole-like form had been called out of its dimension into this one, lured by means she didn't understand, but the Antse themselves had settled in this Earth colony from that same place conterminous with this one. Before the whole of its body had even passed through, the Antse had hooks in its flanks, cords around it, had lodged barbed metal pikes in its various apertures, which fluttered and snorted in pain and distress as the rest of the body, thrashing back and forth in empty air ten feet off the street, was hauled out with a jarring thud. The huge creature had squirmed, flailed several cord-like forelimbs, but the Antse had quickly finished it without much marring its hide.

Now Kohl drew the shade when a fluke was caught in the street below, put on music to drown out the sounds of slaughter, some jangly fast-tempoed middle eastern music to distract her. But it was hard to avoid the spectacle of the flaying season altogether, in this neighborhood of Punktown that the Antse had congregated in. The Antse hung out vast sheets of malachite hide to dry like laundry, rustling in the night breeze, smelling like tar either naturally or due to some tanning process, beautifully translucent when the sun was behind them. And then, the Antse applied those skins to their own bodies, adhering them by some means Kohl had never witnessed nor comprehended, so that the normally smooth gray skins of these naked settlers were covered every inch by the tightly form-fitting leather of the flukes. The Antse would then resemble skeletons carved of malachite, for the next season, until for whatever reason—religious, she assumed, which she found explained most unexplainable behaviors—the flesh was peeled or shed pending the next flaying season.

To be fair, perhaps the skins kept them warm during a cold season in their own world, though the flaying season occurred in summer, here. But the effigies had to have a religious meaning. Even now, a cup of tea in hand, her music turned low, Kohl stood at the window gazing across at one of these fleshy mannikins swaying in an early evening breeze. It hung from a pole protruding from a second floor window, just over the heads of those who might pass below. There would be dozens throughout the neighborhood, now it was flaying time. It was a loosely anthropomorphic figure, hewn from the translucent white flesh beneath the lovely hide of some fluke. To be fair, the Antse ate this white meat. Though Kohl did not eat meat, or wear animal flesh, she knew that the customs were not by any means peculiar to the Antse. But the mannikins were more a mystery to her than the wearing of fluke flesh; the Antse were secretive about the meaning of their customs, if not shy about the products of their customs being seen. These suspended totems were filled with thick spikes and long thin nails, and bound in strings of something like barbed wire, so that they were like suffering saints carved from God's own underbelly.

Birds would gingerly land among the forests of cruel thorns to pick at them. Stray dogs would find scraps of them fallen to the street. When they crumbled or smelled too much they were replaced with new effigies, until the flaying season was over.

Kohl regarded the hanging figure opposite her window, and it seemed to regard her back, spikes for eyes.

. . .

The neighborhood was tightly packed buildings in every color of gray, their night flanks slick with rain but abruptly bleached with strobe lightning from the sparking of the old shunt lines on which carriages flashed to and from the Canberra Mall. Kohl had just returned to her neighborhood on one of those shunts; she worked at a coffee shop in the mall. Her clothing had smelled too strongly of coffee; she had never thought she would ever have too much of its scent. She had showered, made a cup of tea (she had never imagined she'd grow tired of the taste of coffee, either). Kohl could only just afford these four small rooms (bath included) in this neighborhood, but once had had a better job. She had been a net researcher for a large conglomerate, its head offices on Earth, and she had clear memories of the job. She did not, however, have memories of being raped in the parking lot of the company. That was all she knew of it: that she had been raped in the company parking lot. She had been traumatized by her rape. The men had never been caught. She had become so troubled, so afraid to venture from her apartment, to go out at night, even to go to work, that she had lost her job.

But that was for the best, the doctor she ultimately consulted assured her. She should start life anew, put all the nightmare behind her. And yet it was he who really put it from her mind. Her attack had been delicately, precisely burned from her memory. It had been burned from the entire record of thought that followed the incident itself, tracked stealthily by complex brain scan. Even her memories of her physical wounding were gone, so that she did not know what the men had done to injure her in the course of the rape itself.

She stood again at the window, again with tea, in her robe, and watched the rain course down the pane. A shunt whooshed from the distant mall, and the sparking burst lit the face of the tenement opposite. The effigy glared in at her, its spikes looking all the blacker in the flesh made bright—almost luminous— by the stark flash. Then, a ghost, it was gone, and Kohl stepped back from the window, dropped the curtain. Setting aside her tea, she opened her robe and gazed down at her body. Smooth, white, the small neat dent of her navel the only scar, looking like a deep puncture. What had the shadow men done? How much had she been repaired?

Jazz played almost inaudibly. Kohl resumed her tea drinking, wandered back to the bathroom, where the mirror was losing its obscuring mist. Her reflection regarded her. Hair, dyed dark red, in wet tangles . . . the thick black makeup she favored washed away, making her eyes look stripped, she felt, weak and faded. Why did she like to dye her hair, and paint her lips a dark brown shade? Had her husband liked her that way, found it alluring? All memory of him was gone, but was it possible that the scan, the burning, had left behind clues to their relationship? Might she like a certain film director because her husband had originally introduced her to his work? Might even the jazz she was listening to be from a chip he had bought her? She tried to remember purchasing this one and found that she couldn't.

A shunt passed and the shade lit up, then went dark again like a closed eyelid.

. . .

"I love the smell in here," the customer said, a smile in his voice behind Kohl's back as she prepared him his mocha cappuccino. She set it before him, rang it up. He dumped all his change in the tip cup, as if to impress her. "Quiet night in the mall, huh? Everybody home watching the big game, you think?"

"Big game?" Kohl asked without interest.

"Never mind," the man chuckled. "That's how I feel about it, too. Much rather read." He lifted a bag from the book store a bit further down the main hall. "You like books?"

Kohl pushed a stray strand of hair out of her face, then regretted it, as the man might take it as a gesture of flirtation. "I read on the net," she replied blandly.

"Aww . . . you don't get that smell of paper. You can't sink down into a bath tub with . . . "

"I do, sometimes; I have a headset." But she regretted discussing her private life. Especially referring to any activities that involved her being naked. Thankfully, a new customer had just entered the shop, and was perusing the bags of fresh beans. Kohl prayed for her to hurry up and approach the counter.

"Well," the young man sighed, taking up his coffee, "time to head home before the game gets over and all the drunks leave the bars, eh? You be careful yourself, tonight."

"Thanks," said Kohl. She was careful, leaving the mall every night, waiting for a shunt. She had bought nightvision glasses that looked like regular sunglasses, and carried a small pistol in her shoulder bag.

She watched the man leave, a bit surprised that he had dropped his flirtation without asking her out. Had the new customer made him self-conscious, or had it never been his intent to ask her out? Or even flirt; perhaps he had only meant to be friendly. Whereas a minute ago Kohl had resented his attentions, now she felt a bit disappointed, she was surprised to realize. He had been an attractive man. Intelligent, obviously, probably sensitive.

But wouldn't her husband have been those things, too, if those were qualities that attracted her? And he must have shown a darker side, in time. Maybe he had cheated on her, become a drunk. Beat her. Even raped her. He must have hurt her badly, if she had returned to her doctor and paid him to obliterate all memories of her husband, after first divorcing him, after first removing all photographs and vids of him, after changing her name and moving to a new neighborhood where the nonhuman immigrants did not find her attractive, even with her red hair and brown lips, did not trouble her.

Kohl even felt insulted, hurt, that the man had lost interest in her, or never really had it in the first place. But it was for the best, no doubt.

An hour later, and her shop closed up for the night. She sat on a bench in the main hall reading a magazine. A young woman with her head forced to one side by a huge "orb weaver" tumor stopped to hand her a flyer, which Kohl tossed into a trash zapper beside her after a glance when the woman was far enough away not to see. A group of teenage boys drifted past, eyeing Kohl and making lip-smacking noises. She slid one hand in her shoulder bag as she continued to read, but a security robot came rumbling along, dented and covered in graffiti, and rolled after the boys, urging them onwards. Kohl removed her hand from the now slick grip of her pistol.

Her sister was late, but at last here she was: Terr, so pretty, with her thick black eyebrows and perfectly shaped head shaved down to a mere dark stubble. She kissed Kohl lightly and they began to walk the half closed mall.

"Traitor," Kohl said, nodding at the coffee cup Terr carried; not her shop's brand.

"Sorry, couldn't wait . . . "

Kohl asked how Terr's wedding plans were going. Her fiancé seemed like a nice enough man; attractive, sensitive, artistic. Kohl worried about her sister but was afraid to darken her enthusiasm in any way. She just wished her sister had known the man longer.

"How are you doing?" Terr now asked her in turn, as she drove Kohl to a restaurant where they planned to have a late meal and a few drinks.

Kohl stared straight ahead through the windshield at the night city; buildings so black they seemed windowless, like solid obelisks, others lit brightly but no more warmly. One great scalloped Tikkihotto temple was of blue stone and lit with blue floodlights and struck Kohl as particularly lonely-looking. Some local journalists spoke of the exciting blend of cultures in Punktown (they of course preferred its true name, Paxton), the fascinating ethnic melting pot. Kohl felt that the buildings were not a rich diversity but a silent cacophony, disharmonious, so many unalike strangers forced to stand shoulder-to-shoulder.

"Terr," she asked in a dull voice, "did you like my husband?"

"Jesus, Kohl!" Terr said. "Jesus!"

"What?"

"Are you trying to get us in an accident?" Terr composed herself, sat up straighter at the controls. "You know I can't talk about him. You asked me to never talk about him . . . or the other thing! You paid a lot to have that work done. Why would you even want to know?"

"I don't know, I just . . . it bothers me . . . sometimes."

"It bothered you when you knew; that's why you wanted to forget. First the rape, then him. You were hurting, so you wanted to take away the hurt. You're gettng your life back now, so don't walk backwards."

"I'm just curious, sometimes. How can I not be? Does he still live in town? Has he ever asked you where I am? Did he hurt me . . . physically?"

"Shut up, Kohl. I'm just honoring what you made me promise before, so shut up."

"Just one thing, Terr. Please. Did he hurt me? Physically?"

Terr said nothing; wagged her head.

"Please, Terr. Just that one thing."

"No. Not physically. All right? Happy? Not physically."

"How, then? Why would I leave him? Or did he leave me? Maybe he wasn't bad to me, but good to me, huh? Maybe that's why I wanted to forget him . . . because I loved him so much . . . "

"It doesn't matter either way. It doesn't matter if I liked him or not, if he's alive or he's dead. You wanted this, and I gave my word, and that's that. Move along. You were purged clean, you have a fresh start. You should concentrate on getting your old job back or suing those bastards and forget about the rape and your marriage."

"I was married two years, and dated him before that. Three years gone. I remember work, in that time, but not him. I remember the dental work I had in that time, but not him. It's just . . . strange, Terr."

"I'm sure it is. But not as strange as being raped."

Kohl was quiet again for a few moments. Then: "Sometimes I try to remember. I think a song will remind me, or a smell, or . . . "

"That's not possible. It won't come, so don't wait for it. Memories physically alter the brain. Your brain was physically altered to erase all that. You will never remember, okay? It's as gone as if it never happened . . . like it should be. It's the closest we can come to going back in time and making things so they never were. I'd like to go back and touch up a few painful memories myself, sometime when I have the money. Not Dad altogether, but just the times he teased me; he could be really sadistic, the way he teased. And some stuff from school; that too." Terr nodded, her intense face underlit by the vehicle's dash displays. "It's a good thing to forget. Life hurts too much."

"I know," Kohl conceded softly. "It's just . . . it feels funny to have . . . holes like that. Three years. Even . . . even the rape. It's something important that happened to me . . . "

Terr glared over at her sister. "It's a horrible thing that happened to you! You learned nothing from it, gained nothing from it, you don't need it, so forget it, you hear me? You forget it!"

"It's a hole. It feels more scary, sometimes, not knowing how bad it was! Sometimes I imagine one nightmare and sometimes another. My husband, too. I try to fill in the hole and it scares me!"

"The doctor can only do so much. The rest is up to you. You aren't trying hard enough. You have to move on, and don't look back. You know, Dad used to tease you a lot, too. Probably damaged your self-esteem. You should go back and have that stuff cleaned out, too. That might help. You know?"

"It wouldn't be a real memory of Dad! It would be a censored version!"

"It would be the way he should have been," Terr muttered.

"I remember when we were kids, you and me got in a fight and you started strangling me with your hands until I couldn't breathe, and I got really scared. Maybe I should get that erased, too, huh?"

"We were just kids!" Terr snapped. "But if it still bothers you, hey, by all means do so."

"I wouldn't have anything much left," Kohl murmured. "We waste so much time sleeping. It feels like losing so much more time . . . "

"Bad time. You don't need it. It's better this way. How can it not be?"

Kohl watched the moon lower over the spires and monuments of the city's jagged silhouette. It was a three-quarter moon, and looked to Kohl as if someone had taken a big bite out of it.

. . .

Kohl had originally moved here at the end of last year's flaying season, and now she could tell with relief that this year's time of slaughter was nearly finished.

It was a few months early, but she guessed that the Antse year was shorter. The gutters stopped running with blood, and the effigies were not replaced; were left to fall into ruin and wither and mummify in the hot sun.

She was more willing to walk in the neighborhood now, and one Sunday in the early evening made a trip to a corner market. On her way back to her apartment, she paused at the front of a building. She had stopped here before.

It was an old, crumbling brick structure, native Choom, predating colonization. But there was a fossil in its brick that was not an ancient one. It was the mummified figure of an Earth man; a teleportation accident had fused the poor soul half into the gray brick. There was a painted arrow above his head, like a marking made on the street to indicate where a water pipe awaited repair, as if such were neeeded to point him out. The half of him that showed had never been claimed or removed, however. His clothing was mostly torn or worn away, and his one hand was gone, probably taken by young pranksters like whoever had spray-painted genitals where his own had withered.

His whole right side from crown to foot was lost in the wall. Half of his head absorbed into the brick so that only a skull socket and half a lipless grimace remained. A few strands of gray hair stirred in the languid summer air.

Kohl reached out and lightly touched his shoulder as if to comfort him in his solitary, silent anguish. Then, self-consciously, she looked around her, and there was an Antse male watching her from a window in the brick building itself, his face so close and his deeply recessed eyes so fixed on her that she started. Whether he was merely curious or found a cruel amusement in observing her sentimentality, she couldn't tell from the apparition's skeletal face aswirl in green and black. But he withdrew immediately upon being spotted, as if embarrassed himself, and despite their being of such radically different races, his furtive actions led Kohl to wonder if he might even have been surreptitiously admiring her.

Disturbed by this thought, she hurried on toward her apartment before it could grow dark.

. . .

"Hello again," the good-looking young man said, leaning on the counter. Had he lurked outside the shop until he saw that no one else was inside? "How about a mocha cappuccino, extra large?"

Kohl smiled faintly and turned her back on him. Reluctantly.

This was the third time this month he had come in here. The second time, she had been secretly gratified to see him again. But then, after they had chatted briefly and he had left, doubts had begun to surface. Even fears.

What if he knew her from before her treatments? What, in short, if this were her husband, who had succeeded in seeking her out, tracking her down? Her husband, who had somehow learned that she would not recognize him? Her husband, who was finding a perverse satisfaction in courting his ex-wife again, as if for the first time, who wanted to show her that she could not escape him as easily as that . . .

Her eyes flicked to her shoulder bag, resting on the back counter. Her pistol was in there. If he tried to come around the counter . . .

Placing the coffee before him, Kohl asked, "So what are we going to read now?"

"A collection of short stories by a twentieth century writer, Yukio Mishima." The man showed her the book. "He committed suicide by ritual disembowelment."

"Yuck," Kohl chuckled nervously, accepting his money. "Well, enjoy it."

"You should read him . . . he's great." The ritual dumping of change into her tip cup. "Well, see you next time, huh?"

"Right. Bye."

Kohl watched him leave. And that evening she closed up the shop fifteen minutes early, rushed down to the book shop, and bought a volume of the Mishima stories. She brought it home that night to read, beginning on the shunt ride. There might be some clues in it, even that he meant for her to catch. Something that might indicate his true identity, his true intentions.

Whether he was her husband. Whether he was one of the rapists, even, from the parking lot . . .

. . .

"Yes . . . I remember that," Kohl said to the vidphone, her right hand absently riffling the pages of the Mishima collection. "Dr. Rudy did inform me of the option to have the memories recorded in case I changed my mind . . . at an extra cost. But I didn't think I'd ever want that, at the time, and I wanted to save some money, and so . . . "

"So you opted not to have those patterns recorded," said Dr. Rudy's receptionist, her face turned from the screen as she examined another monitor.

"Right," Kohl said. "But I was hoping . . . I wondered if maybe he records these things anyway, and saves them for a while after the procedure in case someone changes their mind." Kohl tried to joke, "Or wants their mind changed back."

"No, that isn't Dr Rudy's system, I'm sorry. And even if it were, it has been over a year now since your first session. But no—" the woman swivelled back to face Kohl "—I gave it a look anyway and I don't see any indication that he ever made a recording of what you had removed. I'm sorry."

Kohl smiled, shrugged. "That's okay . . . I didn't really think he would have. I was just wondering. Thanks anyway."

"Sorry I couldn't help you."

"It's not important. Thanks again." Kohl tapped a key, and a screen saver replaced the woman's face.

Kohl more consciously thumbed through the Mishima book now. One story, "Patriotism," detailed in agonizing, loving detail the double suicide—called shinju—of a Japanese military officer and his wife. Particularly the man's disembowelment; Kohl could almost imagine that Mishima had penned it while cutting his own belly open, writing down his observations. Picturing the slicing, the bleeding, made her so light-headed as she read the story that she had to set the book down for a few moments to calm her breathing.

What might the young man be suggesting to her, through this book? Was he indeed her husband, obsessed with her, having tracked her down at last . . . and now suggesting that they perform this most devoted of romantic acts together? Die united in the ritual of shinju?

Kohl lifted her gaze again to the vidphone's mindless swirlings of color. How carefully had that receptionist really checked? Should she try to talk to Dr. Rudy himself?

What if Rudy had kept the recording for his own purposes? His own entertainment? Even now, might he be watching Kohl and her husband on their wedding night, through Kohl's eyes?

Might he be watching her rape in the parking lot, finding excitement in it?

The concept so horrified her that she was startled. But men were like that, weren't they? In polls they freely admitted they would rape if they thought they could get away with it. That it was their foremost sexual fantasy. Men hungered, men consumed. She thought again of the staring Antse in the window, his face the face of all men, stripped of the deceitful flesh, the facade of civilization, leaving only the gaping eyes and Death's head grin.

The night fell. Kohl played music. She made tea. She went to the window.

Tomorrow she would return to work. And she would bring her gun, as she always did . . . though lately she had taken to carrying it in her dress pocket, rather than her shoulder bag. And if the young man came in again, she would point the gun at him and demand that he reveal his identity.

If he were a rapist, she would shoot him in the face. And if he were her husband, she would shoot him in the heart, and then she would shoot herself in the heart, because shinju meant "inside the heart." And then she and her husband would be united, linked again forever in death. They would be whole.

A shunt passed. A burst of sparks illuminated, for one second, the flesh scarecrow suspended from the window opposite . . . now barely recognizable, a bundle of tattered scraps, all but fallen away.

UNION DICK

The Earth colony Paxton—unaffectionately nicknamed Punktown by its citizenry—was a melting pot for the crimes and perversions of a thousand planets and a dozen dimensions, and the bar called The Lop-sided Grin was a vivid manifestation of that condition.

The waitress who brought the two men their bulbs of anodyne gas through the smoky steam of that melting pot didn't prove to be human until directly on top of them, due to all the geometric implants under her skin, stretching her face into a multi-faceted gem of living flesh. Only her eyes retained some of nature's symmetry. Oh well, give her some more time.

She no doubt found the puffy, ravaged and spoiled handsomeness of Yolk's face unimpressive, as his wounds were naturally acquired, not a selected artistic deformation. Yolk was a union dick, and had acquired most of his wounding—both physical and otherwise—during the riots that had become the Union War. Yolk had fought on the side of the workers, and was a decorated hero. His recruitment and training as a detective for the PLO—Paxton Labor Organization—had been a tribute. But that had been twenty years ago. Yolk wasn't the hot-blooded and inspired angry young man he had been then. He was just angry . . . and even then, in a very tired way. Twenty years in Punktown could sap the enthusiasm of the strongest do-gooder, and Yolk had never been a saint; nothing more than a common worker with a natural sense of justice. Then again, maybe that wasn't so common . . . any more than justice was natural.

His table-mate was Scurf, an informer with the syndy. The rest of Yolk's ravagedness had come from trying to keep the syndy out of the PLO as much as possible over the years. That had made Yolk a lot of enemies in the union, and kept him from any further tributes of career evolution. Yolk had no use for the syndy but for the type of function Scurf served him, and even then he felt no great love for the man.

Yolk squirted a tiny spray of gas against the back of his throat, coughed softly and mumbled, "Proceed."

"Proceed," Scurf mimicked. "All right; what it is, is . . . I heard some weird things are going on at Mangaudis Crystalens, down in Industrial Square. Ever visited?"

"Six years ago; hazardous material threat to employees. We called the Health Agents in and they slapped a fine. Standard dung. Proceed."

"Well nobody has said anything too definite, but my ears tell me the employees aren't really operating the processes. I think it's a dildo plant, these days."

Yolk nodded; this was getting to be more common. Since the Union War, all Earth-operated colonies on Oasis were required to enforce the mandate that in every plant and factory, every institution of manufacture, the robots and fully automated processes did not out-number the amount of blue-collar workers, except where conditions were too dangerous.

Well, manufacturers had found many ways around this sort of mandate. They saw to it that the conditions *were* too dangerous, sometimes. But a more frequent method was to make two or three processes appear like one process to union inspectors. Also, sometimes employees would appear to be operating machinery when in reality they were working at dummy machines—or at least, at bogus controls on actual machines—which did absolutely nothing . . . some workers aware of this, some laboring away in ignorance. In some plants, Yolk had even seen employees who sat and played cards, napped, watched VT; in essence, did nothing but fulfill the company's organic quota. The reason for all this was that it was often more economical for plants to pay live workers to do little or nothing while still keeping processes mostly automated.

It could be ethically tricky to prosecute or fine under such circumstances, but if proven, many of these tricks could be considered a defiance of union mandates. Many couldn't, as when two or three processes were so ingeniously linked that they did, in the end, constitute one process. But hiring employees to sweep the floor of an automated plant for two hours and play cards for six was considered an "inappropriate application of workers, degrading to their contribution as individuals, as members of society and as members of the union." So the plant would be fined, and those workers would sweep for eight hours instead, in effect. Now proud workers.

Yolk squirted his gas twice more before grumbling his thanks to Scurf, and transferring Scurf's fee of fifty munits from his union-issued credit card to Scurf's. That was what the union had provided the card to him for, primarily. Let them pay their money to the syndy.

On his way to the steps leading up to the street Yolk passed a booth crammed with teenagers who were laughing and babbling loudly, incomprehensibly. If more aware of their surroundings they might have taunted him as he passed, smug in their youth—smug until Yolk jerked one of them up from his seat and cuffed him back into it. They were lighting the spray from their gas bulbs and using them as mini-torches, seeing who could endure the pain of flame on the inner arm longest. The loser would have to empty the remainder of his bulb down his throat in one shot. Could they be considered masochists when they were too wasted to really feel the pain?

They were urinating in their pants and didn't even know it; Yolk could tell by their stink. The girlfriends with them were most impressed with the entire display: it demonstrated the seriousness of the boys' commitment to pleasure.

"Idiots," Yolk mumbled to himself as he trudged up the steps.

. . .

Yolk needed no warrant to proceed; as a union-affiliated operation, Mangaudis Crystalens had to be prepared to invite union technical inspectors and investigators without a moment's notice. This way no time was allowed for the speedy alteration of unethical practices. So Yolk met his wife Vita for lunch in the lounge of the office block she worked at on Corporation Avenue in the business district, then drove straight toward Industrial Square, further from the center of town. His acidulous grumbling unrest, nurtured in The Lop-sided Grin, had been somewhat soothed away by the hour spent with his wife. She was his closest friend and greatest security in life. Pretty, sexier than pretty, and sweeter than both. Hard to believe anyone in the business district could be considered sweet, or even truly sexy, but she was a jewel, and he was grateful for her beyond expression. Three years married already. She had even dug up the fossil remains of his soul, he felt, over the past four years that he'd known her. She'll be struck by a hovercar some day, he thought, driven by some gassed-up punk. She was too good a thing to last.

The Mangaudis building was no sprawling affair, and pretty standard in design from the outside; it looked like a giant art deco radio. Yolk announced himself and showed his badge at the desk. The head of personnel came to meet him within a minute. She shook his hand, presented herself as Nancy More.

Miss More was young and attractive, but the tightness of her smile made her prettiness as unpleasant to Yolk as the feigned hospitality and interest in her voice. On a woman like this, her long black-nyloned legs were merely emblematic, about as sexy to Yolk as the perfect suit a man in her position would have been wearing. Yolk despised personnel directors.

"I received an anonymous tip today regarding possible labor violations, so I'd like a tour of your company. Can you summon your shop steward?"

"Mr. Cobb is on vacation these next two weeks, Mr. Yolk, I'm sorry."

Cobb—Yolk remembered him now from six years ago. A corrupt little alcoholic bastard who thought everyone he dealt with was too stupid to see through his transparent lies and cheating—in other words, a stupid man himself. Bad union reps paved the way for the tricks of unethical manufacturers.

"Please summon Mr. Mangaudis, then . . . if he isn't on vay-kay, too."

"He isn't," Miss More said with a dab of chilly disapproval for his insolence. "I'll go buzz him."

"I'll come with you," said Yolk. No sense taking the chance that they might stall him while an alert was sounded to alter the state of things, order nappers back to phony stations.

Mangaudis appeared promptly. He wore a beautiful charcoal gray suit, was as good-looking as Yolk remembered him. Attractive graying at the temples. His pale skin, however, looked like chalk against all the gray—bloodless. His immaculate neatness and softness of tone made him seem like a robot mannequin to Yolk. Yolk couldn't imagine color on the man, or even inside him. He gave the detective a firm friendly hand squeeze and a creepy smile. His eyes were flat.

"Wherever did you hear that we were betraying the union's trust, Mr. Yolk? Our plant has a fine shop steward who . . . "

"Yeah, real fine. I'm surprised my people didn't kick his sodden ass into the gutter after that business six years ago . . . "

"A small spill, Mr. Yolk . . . it happens every day."

"So do rape and murder. You remember an employee of yours named, ah . . . Clora . . . ah . . . " Yolk forgot her last name. "Anyway, she was there when you had that little spill. I ran into her in a theater lobby last year. I can't forget a face, especially when half of it is burned off and the victim doesn't win enough restitution for full reconstruction . . . "

"Mr. Yolk, I hardly sprayed that individual in the face myself, and you can take up the matter of her settlement with our former insurance company. We don't deal with them any more. Now please, the matter at hand . . . what is it?"

Yolk liked the man a whole lot better now without that creepy robot smile. "You tell me."

"There's nothing to tell."

"I'll take a tour of the entire premises with you, then."

"As you like. No doubt you'll find something to fine me for. The union has to make its money, after all, to keep ex-heroes like yourself employed."

Yolk definitely preferred Mangaudis this way: openly hostile, no more fake friendliness. Perhaps he was a human being after all, deep down inside. "Maybe if you'd bribed the Health Agents more last time you wouldn't have had such a big fine. But then money lost is lost, no matter which way it blows, right?"

"I suggest you watch your accusations, Mr. Yolk . . . they aren't very professional. And I am recording this conversation for legal purposes."

"Fine—except that you can't use any of what I said before you notified me of that fact. So, shall we get on with it?"

"Of course. This way." They moved down a corridor.

Yolk thought he remembered some of the plant, but he saw so many places it was hard to recollect what he'd seen six years ago. White-garbed middle-aged women with hair coverings like cafeteria workers inspected lenses with the aid of computer-enhancement screens. Living workers were not necessary here, but where were they really irreplaceable? This entire plant could have been automated, if not for the Union War. Yolk watched the women for several minutes, keenly trained eyes absorbing the process. He had warned Mangaudis not to describe the way machines and their operators functioned here unless he asked him, so that his perceptions could be less easily distracted and misled. If necessary, technological inspectors would be called in later under Yolk's command and direction.

Shipping and receiving offered little that required close scrutiny, as was always the case. In fact, it was in this area that most live employees were situated in such plants.

"How many employees?" Yolk asked, leaning his head into a cafeteria. Empty; no card players.

"Seventy-five," the company president replied proudly. Then he gave the amount of work space in the plant in terms of square feet, plus the number of individual mechanical processes as defined under the codes of the union.

Yolk turned to smile at the man crookedly. "And how many of those are office workers, sir?"

Mangaudis narrowed his eyes ever so slightly. "Fifteen. But that still leaves sixty live plant employees."

"Well, that was what I was asking you about, not about paper pushers. Of that sixty, how many are in shipping-receiving, and how many mop the floors and change the toilet paper?"

"Eight in shipping, and two non-tech maintenance people."

"So you have fifty machine operators . . . actual plant staff."

"Still within union ordinance, Inspector Yolk. We have an even hundred union-defined mechanical processes . . . therefore, half of those require live operation as dictated." Mangaudis had stressed the word "dictated."

Yolk held his hand out to indicate they go on. "Proceed."

They passed two gliding robots in a broad hallway. These were the primary technical maintenance team. Seeing to the needs of their brothers. The one with a head nodded to Yolk but he didn't nod back. Its feelings wouldn't be hurt.

"Ah, we have some innovative processes up ahead, Mr. Yolk. Something new. My own idea . . . realized, of course, by my fantastic technical designers, and some I brought in just for this job . . . "

Sounded to Yolk like Mangaudis was trying to smooth him in advance for something he was going to see. Prepare him.

The hall gave into a large circular chamber Yolk instantly recalled as being the site of the hazardous waste leak six years ago. Only now it had become a mad circus.

It didn't present live beings operating machinery so much as it seemed a weird symbiotic relationship between machine and organism.

"What the hell is this?" Yolk hissed.

Mangaudis gave his creepy bloodless smile. He wasn't just proud—he was gloating.

A man walked a tread mill attached to the side of one machine like a mouse in a wheel, this action causing huge gears to turn. The machine was covered in colored lights and computer screens. It was a bizarre mating of high tech and the Industrial Revolution. And there were others that were similar. A rowing machine connected up to one process, a bicycle to another. Two teenage boys in white sleeveless undershirts, muscular and sweaty, pushed up and down on a see-sawing bar as if driving an old railroad handcart. One man stood turning what looked like the arms of a clock face as tall as he was.

"Are you out of your mind?" Yolk snarled at his host. "These are the most blatant dildo operations I've ever seen!"

"Ahh, that's the beauty of it, Mr. Yolk. They do appear fake, don't they? But they aren't. I heartily invite your finest engineers to come down here and inspect these processes. They are all generated by live labor. Without it they won't even function."

Yolk looked again, coming deeper into the room. A young Choom woman, native humanoid to the planet, smiled her huge dolphin-like grin at him. She was reclining in a rowing apparatus, watching a VT set mounted to the side of her machine. She removed her headphones at Yolk's gesture. "Don't you get tired?" he demanded.

"It doesn't take much pressure. And we rotate every fifteen minutes. We stay in good shape. It's a great new idea, huh? We call this the Gym."

Yolk glanced about. He counted twenty-two people in the vast silo of a room. A buzzer sounded. Most of the workers rotated to the next set-up. Some rested altogether in a small adjoining cafeteria. While they worked, many were watching VTs, or listening to music, or chatting. Some processes required a bit of strain, but most very little. One device was like a fixed pogo-stick, another was a plush rocking chair. Yolk realized he was wagging his head. Mangaudis came up beside him.

"They're happy workers, Mr. Yolk. Fair pay. Good benefits. And look . . . video, music, social interaction, hard work and physical exercise, all in one package. Very innovative, wouldn't you say?"

Yolk gritted his teeth at the man. "It's a farce, Mangaudis. It's a blatant bloody farce, and you're flaunting it right in my face. You probably couldn't wait for a union dick to come see this madness. You're making fools of us and these people."

"These people are quite content."

"How long has this been going on? I'm gonna have that bastard Cobb's rocks for this!"

"Shh, Mr. Yolk." Mangaudis tried to take the detective's elbow but he jerked it away. "Mr. Yolk, there are no violations here. I had trouble with your people once before. Believe me, when this was designed I was most careful to see that there would be no conflict with union mandates."

"This is your revenge on us, isn't it, Mangaudis? That's what this is. A very imaginative . . . and very contemptuous . . . revenge on all the offices that dare to tell you how to run your business, and spend your money. Am I right? And worse than that, it's revenge on the people we force you to hire, isn't it? Isn't it? You're mocking us, and humiliating them. And you love it."

"These are contented workers, Mr. Yolk. You heard what Eti over there said. She likes it in the Gym. This is the ultimate in the life of live workers. It's work and play at the same time."

"It's a sick joke, and I'm going to bring it down." Yolk strode back toward the door, his long coat billowing out behind him. But he spun around again, and spoke so loudly that workers at their stations glanced up at him. "This isn't a gym, it's a torture chamber!"

"I don't see that at all, Mr. Yolk. Honestly."

"It's a torture chamber of the spirit! You're killing the dignity of life in here!"

"You accuse me of warped fanaticism, Inspector, but I contend that it's you who are the fanatic. Listen to yourself. Torture of the spirit. You missed your calling; you should have been a priest, or a poet. Face it, Mr. Yolk, you're simply a tech-hater."

"I don't hate technology, slime-wad . . . I just hate the bastards who use it against us." And on that note, the union dick stormed off into the plant unescorted. Mangaudis didn't pursue him to show him out; Yolk was a fanatic, and worse, an armed one.

. . .

Inspectors were brought in, the Gym thoroughly investigated. No violations were charged. The live workers truly were generating the power to the machines, or else aiding them crucially in their functions. In the ensuing weeks, the investigation of Mangaudis Crystalens was leaked to the press, and the Gym was described by the media as an innovative new approach to live labor, just as the president of the company had described it. On VT they showed Mangaudis proudly presenting the various work stations. Three in a row were arcade-style video games that were designed to link into the functions of various machines. He explained that he had a new idea for a miniature bowling alley, one or several lanes, ideas for other stations that would add a bit more recreation amongst the more physical activities. Yolk interpreted this as caution on Mangaudis' part that no one viewed the Gym as something out of a Dickensian workhouse. Which, to Yolk, it was no matter how many bowling lanes or video games or billiard tables Mangaudis introduced.

"A Bizarre Genius with a Unique Vision," claimed the cover of a magazine that showed a grinning Mangaudis seated at one of the stations in the Gym. A creepy grin, thought Yolk.

"Drop it," Vita advised him gently. "You did what you could. He's a sick bastard."

"I feel like a fool."

"Drop it before you feel more and more like one. We can't always beat the devil, love."

"When do we ever really?" he grumbled.

After work hours he sat with employees from Crystalens in a bar nearby. He asked them how those who worked in the Gym honestly felt.

"Well, it's not what I went to school for," admitted a pretty woman with a shaved head who'd told him her name was Terr. "I got laid off from my last job so I can't be picky. But for now, it pays the bills . . . and it's actually pretty fun."

"Hey, what's the problem?" laughed a barrel-chested man in his early twenties as he worked on his fourth beer. "You keep rotating through all these stations so it isn't boring. We have a good time in there. The pay isn't great, but it isn't too little . . . and look at what we do. It keeps me in my social substances." The man raised his glass to Yolk.

"And you're proud of what you do? You feel important, running around like a rat in a wheel?"

"Hey, it's as important as anything, right? What do I care about proud of what I'm doing, so long as I don't hate it. How about you, friend? Do you like what you're doing?"

Yolk just glared at the sweaty-haired red-faced man and polished off his own drink. Apathetic moron, he inwardly cursed the worker. All of you. You care less about your degradation than I do.

They were ignorant, he countered in the workers' defense. Manipulated. They couldn't see their exploitation for what it was . . .

The case was closed. Yolk felt guilty that there was nothing more he could do . . . and also guilty for being the one to bring the Gym out into the open. To be imitated soon, he was certain—here and maybe on other colonized worlds.

It was less than three months after his investigation of Mangaudis Crystalens that Vita was murdered by two Choom youths for drug money in a subway ladies' room.

. . .

They were unemployed, Yolk argued with himself. Maybe if they'd worked in a place like Crystalens they wouldn't have had to kill his love for their "social substances." Places like Crystalens were good so long as they provided jobs of some kind. And his union was effective for seeing that people were employed there, even though in a farcical manner.

But all this desperate reasoning was not enough to prevent Yolk from buying the black market explosives.

He spent the last four paychecks on them. Five packets of a material like green clay, each merely a half pound. The dealer had assured Yolk that, while crude, the stuff he'd bought was more than sufficient to level an entire building. Yolk thanked the man, considered shooting him and taking his money back from the syndy scum. But hey, he was just doing his job.

There was no second or third shift at Mangaudis Crystalens, but a guard robot—a shadowy melding of tank and insect—could be seen moving about in the lobby through Yolk's night vision binoculars, these a relic left over from distant battles, when robots like that guard and mercenary strike-breaker troops had been the iron gloves on the soft white hands of those like Mangaudis. Yolk crept around the outside of the giant art deco radio like a guerrilla.

He knew what to do. He was a hero from the Union War, and had brought down more than one factory in his time.

The cool night air felt good rustling through his hair and against his skin. Through his pain, he felt alive. Young again. He pushed the rolled-out worms of explosive clay against the base of the building, in one place pressed a ball of the stuff into a pipe vent. No wires necessary: it was a smart material, its ameba mind and very stability at the mercy of a special radio code from the tiny transmitter device in Yolk's coat pocket.

When all the clay was spent, Yolk stole back to his distant car and sat in it with the window open. He sipped a beer he'd brought with him. He dreamed for a few minutes that Vita—rare, jewel-like Vita—sat there beside him. But he was alone.

They don't care, he thought. The workers in the Gym. Those jesters. Those organ grinder's monkeys. They didn't even care that Mangaudis was making fools of them purposely. To spite the union officials, and to spite the workers themselves. How much did the union really care? They made their dues . . . that was what counted. They were just another operation, weren't they? Like a legalized syndy. So why should he care?

If he went through with this he was a criminal. The Union War was over. It was lazy, apathetic peace time. Vita had always been proud of him for his sense of justice and fair play. "You're a good egg," she always joked. He'd be a criminal . . .

They don't care, his mind repeated. They made their substance money. They were no more ashamed of themselves than the scum who'd killed Vita for their substance money. They didn't care about themselves, let alone the whole of society. They couldn't respect others when they didn't respect themselves.

The device was in his hand, his thumb hovering over the button, and he was like a man contemplating a change of VT channels, like a man contemplating a rocket target . . .

They don't care. Go home. Do what you can in the union. It was all one could realistically hope to do. One must accept one's limitations. Like Vita had said, you couldn't always beat the devil.

Yolk started up his vehicle.

Yes, go home. Fireworks wouldn't bring Vita back. Fireworks wouldn't wipe the creepy smile off every bloodless face. The car lifted to the two feet it floated off the ground. Just go home. They didn't care if Mangaudis wanted to take his vengeance out on them.

The hovercar glided quietly across the empty parking lot, into the silent street. Its passing stirred an empty wine bottle to roll away . . .

Well, maybe I want revenge on you, too, Yolk said to the workers in his mind. Because you don't care. And I'm sick of caring for you.

He glanced back over his shoulder and pointed the tiny device in his hand.

And the night burned briefly with his anger . . . until the robot fire engines came, and a few straggling human firefighters drank coffee while they watched them extinguish the flames.

WAKIZASHI

On the walls of the L'lewed's cell were blown up photo print-outs of his three victims. Soko stared up at them while waiting for the L'lewed to appear from his container like a lazy genie loath to stir from his lamp.

One photo showed a plump young woman, a human, face down in the long grass of a neglected park corner. She wore only socks. A second poster showed a naked woman curled on her side as if sleeping in the cave-like mouth of a drainage tunnel, in the same park. The third photo was just a woman's face, apparently a morgue shot. Her eyes were open and her mouth was a huge mysterious smile; she was a Choom, native to this Earth-colonized world, humanoid except for that vast mouth which looked like a wound carved back to her ears. But none of the three women bore visible wounds; the L'lewed had committed his cruelty within their bodies.

The L'lewed had a computer in his cell, on a desk below the posters. He had net access, and it was from this—specifically, a site called TrueCrime—that he had called out the photographs of his victims. Soko wondered if their families were aware that their loved ones were displayed this way in the cell of the being who had murdered them. Still, he doubted the families could do anything to violate the L'lewed's rights to extract information and to decorate his cell. He could only be asked by the warden to remove the posters willingly, and the L'lewed had told the warden that he had hung the posters so as to remind himself of the terrible acts he had committed, that he might haunt himself with these ghosts, and repent for his sins.

Soko turned his attention back to the prisoner's container, which sat in the center of the floor. There was no bed in the cell, the prisoner resting in this device instead. More than a bed, it was his life support. When he had been a foreign diplomat living in the embassy of his people, here in Paxton across from the park, he had been transported about in this device by a human aide. That man was now jailed in this same penitentiary for being an accomplice to the ambassador's crimes; he had carried the genie's lamp on his back into the park to seek out appropriate victims for his boss.

Soko heard small grinding sounds, mechanical, such as a very old clock might make before it gonged out the hour. There was a central cylinder, and fused to its sides, two smaller cylinders—all three a brassy-colored metal. From the tops of the two smaller tubes, nozzles now arose. Following that, a spiral iris in the main cylinder swirled open. Peripherally, Soko saw the other human in the cell with him step forward a little with anticipation.

Though he doubted the L'lewed would ever attempt violence, he rested his hand on the pistol holstered at his hip. Like all the guards at the Paxton Maximum Security Penitentiary, he carried a handgun which would not allow itself to fire if it sensed it was being held by anyone other than the guard to whom it had been issued. (During one escape attempt, a prisoner had chopped off a guard's hand and kept it curled around the gun he'd stolen, but the gun sensed the hand was not alive and would not function as hoped.) But the L'lewed would not attempt to steal his gun: protected by diplomatic immunity, he was to be returned to his home world as soon as conditions permitted the opening of the portal which gave access to that other dimension in which the L'lewed's planet existed.

The prisoner began to emerge from his cell within the cell. It was like watching a child's play putty stretched almost to the breaking point, as from both of the side nozzles a string of taut flesh-colored matter extended into the air. These pseudopods adhered themselves to the ceiling, as if to hoist out the rest of the being. From the middle cylinder there arose something that reminded Soko of the egg purse of a shark or ray: a squarish, featureless package of flesh with two horn-like limbs at the top, and two at the bottom. The pair at the bottom remained mostly inside the device; Soko wasn't sure what might be at their ends, just how much of the being remained in the container. The two top horns, somewhat flexible, wavered subtly in the air like feelers.

There was a grille in the front of the major cylinder. From it came a voice, soft and whispery and sifted through a sand of static. It was the L'lewed, translated.

"Hello, Officer Soko. And my guest?"

The other human smiled, and nodded in greeting. "Ambassador Rhh, I'm David-Paul Friesner, the newly appointed spiritual liaison here at P.M.S.."

"As I had hoped," whispered the device on the floor, the thing of putty hanging above it like some leafless vine grown from a coppery vase. "A pleasure."

"I'm here in response to your request." Friesner smiled, but he made his expression politely pained. "It's a difficult request to fill, but . . . "

"You must be able to find someone with a terminal illness, who might want the money I offer, to give to her family. Someone who would like to end their suffering . . . "

"Well, in fact, after discussing the matter with the warden, we've gone another route with your . . . problem. Um, we have a number of people in this facility who have received a death sentence. I myself don't approve of the concept of execution, but there are inmates waiting to die, nonetheless. The warden has personally asked a dozen of them whether they would be willing to . . . assist you in your . . . ritual . . . in return for the money you offer from your personal account."

"And your results?" The feelers swayed like underwater plants.

"Well . . . uh, there was a lot of concern, actually. Of course, most of those on death row are hoping to have their sentences commuted. But also, there was concern about pain. The warden told them . . . ah . . . told them that drugging them for pain was not possible, as it would deaden the . . . death throes . . . "

"The Vibration," the L'lewed corrected him.

"Frankly, that's where I see the potential for the greatest public . . . disapproval."

"But did you find an individual willing? Did any of them express interest?"

Soko turned to watch the other man's face. He couldn't believe that any man would agree to being murdered by another prisoner, especially in the manner the L'lewed killed their sacrifices.

"Yes . . . yes, there was one. He's a Waiai; if you're not familiar, a very humanoid being. His name is Oowoh Kee. He killed five human teenagers who lived in his apartment building. They had apparently raped his wife in the laundry, and yet she couldn't identify their faces because the Waiai are blind. That is to say, they use a sort of radar in place of sight. In any case, Mr. Kee's act of vigilantism was deemed first degree multiple murder, and hence his sentence. After all, two of the boys were only thirteen."

"And this man . . . this Kee . . . wants the money for his wife."

"Yes. He's willing to do this. Even without being drugged."

"What a courageous man," said the L'lewed. With something like a sigh he added, "I would have preferred a female . . . " He let the thought uncoil wistfully.

Soko looked to the rubbery entity, back to the spiritual liaison. His throat was dry, and in swallowing to lubricate it his spit caught on the barbs in his throat. He coughed sharply several times. He saw the prisoner's snail-like horns point his way curiously.

"There are women on death row, in other facilities," Friesner said, "but we were concerned that the outcry would be greater. Execution is the will of the majority, or else it wouldn't be practiced. But those who are against it are very vocal, and their disapproval will be unpleasant, so we're hoping to keep this low-key. The warden has already talked to the Colonial Office in Miniosis about this, just to be sure we're on safe ground proceeding. Fortunately for us, in light of your status as a foreign dignitary, we've been given the go-ahead. We'll field the protests as best we can. The warden impressed upon all involved parties that time is of the essence here . . . that you must have your sacrifice within two weeks in order for you to be . . . spiritually reinvigorated, according to your beliefs."

"Excellent," Ambassador Rhh complimented the man. "You have done a fine job in an admittedly difficult situation, Mr. Friesner. I'm sure you will do very well in this new position."

"Thank you." Soko thought Friesner looked genuinely flattered. "So, ah, we'll start to arrange this, then. As quickly as possible, in case difficulties of any sort arise. Before Mr. Kee, um . . . changes his mind, or protests become too . . . troublesome. Hopefully, within the week. The faster we carry this through, the less chance of someone finding a way to bind it up legally. If we're very lucky, it will all be behind us before the public even hears word of it. So . . . I will keep you apprized."

"I thank you," the L'lewed purred.

"Very good, then. Well, I . . . I guess that's it, until later . . . "

"It's been a pleasure, Mr. Friesner," filtered the voice from the container. One of the elastic limbs affixed to the ceiling came away with a sound like tape peeled free, and in lowering, extended in the spiritual liaison's direction. Its end began to flatten into a leaf-like shape somewhat better suited to shaking a human's hand.

Before the appendage had completed its molding, Soko had his pistol out of its holster and pointed not at the being itself but at the speaker grille in its life support device. "Ambassador, do not touch Mr. Friesner."

The limb froze in the air a foot from the liaison. It began to withdraw, the end resuming its less flattened look. "I meant only to express my gratitude in the manner of your kind, Officer Soko, but as you wish. Until next time, Mr. Friesner, and thank you again." The central portion of the L'lewed sank back into the container, seeming to compress itself as it did so, wavering snail horns last. The two willowy limbs went slithering back into their twin nozzles, which then retracted into their cylinders with a grind and a clink. The opening in the middle cylinder whirred shut. The L'lewed was so thoroughly gone it felt as if he had returned to his own dimension, rather than simply hidden himself away like a cobra in its basket.

. . .

Soko absently ran his hand over the back of his neck, feeling the coarse bristles of his glossy black crew cut. His coffee gave off an aromatic steam that countered the chilly scene outside the cafeteria windows. The sky was a blue so bright it hurt the eyes, looked synthetic, the grounds outside the prison glaring with scraps and patches of reflective snow. What hadn't melted away from last week's storm was so frozen now that winter had really descended, it seemed it would never thaw. Soko could see the whole corner of B Wing jutting massively into the scene like the end of a great castle, its featureless white flank adding to the bleakness of the view, though most of it was in blue shadow. Atop every corner of the prison—a massive decoration perhaps meant to make the prison's presence less threatening, less militaristic to those who lived in Punktown—there arose a giant abstracted pine cone. It seemed to Soko a poor trade off, however, for the coniferous forest that had once bordered the outskirts of this Choom town before Earth colonization. Steam from a huge vent billowed up past the window in irregular clouds, turning golden as it cleared the high wall and was suffused with harsh sunlight.

"That was really unnecessary, you know," said Friesner, spreading margarine on an end of croissant. "With the gun . . . "

Soko lifted his coffee, sipped. "Do you know how the L'lewed killed those women?"

"Yes, I do. I called up his file. But he's been very cooperative, and . . . "

"He's going to go home, no matter what he does. He's only here for us to watch until that happens, and to make a show for the public, but he'll go home, even if he claims a fourth victim. Even if that person is his spiritual liaison. He may not wait to see if this . . . sacrifice really takes place."

"Please don't think," Friesner said grimly, lifting a meaningful gaze, "that I approve of this request. But the L'lewed isn't lying . . . these are the religious practices of his kind. And as such, it's our responsibility to respect them, and make it possible for him to pursue his form of worship. He has that right."

Soko dropped his gaze into his coffee cup. "These things his kind sacrifice on their own world. Have you seen pictures of them?"

"Yes," Friesner replied, buttering again.

"And? Are they human?"

"The creatures look . . . fairly humanoid. Somewhat more . . . monkeyish. In a hairless way. They have no civilization, no culture, they use only a few primitive tools. The L'lewed first encountered them on a world in an adjacent system, almost a century ago. They took them home to their world, and as you know, breed them as sacrifices."

"Lovely people," Soko muttered.

"Mr. Soko, all cultures seem strange to one another. You should celebrate that diversity. You're of Japanese ancestry, obviously. Don't you in your home have things that would mystify a L'lewed, a Choom, a Tikkihotto? Perhaps a mounted kabuki mask? A painted byobu screen? A katana and wakizashi in a sword stand?"

"I don't have any of those things," Soko muttered, lifting his cup again.

"You should. Your people have a wonderful ancient culture. A very strange one. Wonderfully strange."

"I'm flattered you feel that way. And I understand you might find it quaint or delightful or wonderful that a man used to stick a dagger in his own guts . . . but this L'lewed murdered three women. Whatever religious practices those women might have followed themselves will never be followed by them again, because this other creature poured himself down their throats and choked them to death . . ."

"Mr. Soko, I know . . . I know . . ."

" . . . and found pleasure in their convulsions, in their death spasms, because this is called 'the Vibration,' when the sacrifice transfers its life force to the L'lewed, who emerges reborn from the victim's . . . lower body. As you say . . . wonderfully strange."

"Look, we all know it was wrong. Yes, it was a crime. A terrible thing. Those women were not animals bred for sacrifice, but unwilling advanced beings. I agree. That's why Mr. Rhh is in custody, that's why he's being extradited . . . "

"Nothing will happen to him back home."

"We don't know that."

"Nothing will happen to him back home. And another will be sent to replace him."

"I heard it said the next ambassador will bring a greater number of the sacrificial animals with him. In fact, with relations going so well between the L'leweds and Earth, their animals are going to be bred in some of our colonies to insure that they're always available."

"How quaint. I guess Rhh just miscalculated his needs."

"He was forced to stay longer than he thought he would have to, before returning home. You have to understand . . . if they go too long without a sacrifice, if they pass a certain point, they consider themselves unclean. Irredeemable for the rest of their lives."

"He ran out of animals. So humans sufficed? Humans are just animals to our new friends?"

"No. But that's why he's here, isn't it? He made a terrible choice. No one denies that, not even him. He says he was desperate."

"Bad enough, what they do to those animals," Soko murmured.

Friesner motioned with his knife at Soko's plate. His untouched food. "Those strips, Mr. Soko? Real meat? From a living creature?"

"I'm not proud of it. I like the taste. But if I saw the same animal being kicked in the street by a couple of punks, I'd crack their skulls open."

"Well, isn't that quaint?" Friesner sighed. "Mr. Soko . . . Ken . . . you've been assigned to accompany me in my meetings with the prisoners while I arrange their spiritual needs for them. I have a very important job, here. Religion gives these people hope, some kind of foundation . . . meaning. It can bring them back from their mistakes, give them a new life. You should feel privileged, too, to be a part of that in any way. Like I say . . . we're going to be together quite a bit. That's why I wanted to have breakfast with you, chat, get to know you a little."

"I appreciate that," Soko said blandly.

Friesner sighed once more. Wagging his head, he cut a piece of melon with a knife and fork. He had no meat on his plate, being a vegetarian. And the most Soko ate from his own plate was a piece of toast, good as that meat smelled.

. . .

In the living room of Soko's small, neat apartment he watched a VT segment about two Choom youths who had beaten to death a woman named Vita Yolk in the course of a robbery. The prosecutor had been after the death penalty, but the youths had been given twenty years each instead. Soko thought that even those sentences combined seemed shamefully insufficient, and switched off the set in disgust.

Against another wall of the room there was a clear, illuminated museum showcase. Inside it, resting on brackets, was a Japanese short sword—a wakizashi—from Earth's eighteenth century.

Soko approached and stared in at it now, the glow from the showcase the only light in the room. He had never dared to remove the sword to handle it, had not touched it in fact since he had been a boy, when his father had handed it to him. It had been in his father's family for generations, originally the weapon of a samurai ancestor, it was said. But how could he have admitted to Friesner how right he had been? He had always found the story of the samurai ancestor a cliche, a stereotype, an embarrassment—not a matter of pride. Now, with Friesner having mentioned the wakizashi, he felt all the more ridiculous for showing it off like this . . . though he had not seen the sword's naked blade in fifteen years.

The exhibit was meant more as a tribute to his father, whose prize possession the sword had been. He had not known that fabled samurai, any of those people, now dust, who had handed the sword down. Only his father. The sword was worth a fortune, he knew. But he had never dreamed of parting with it. Not that he was afraid to awaken one night to find the apparition of an angry samurai, decked out in kabuto helmet and menpo war mask, looming at the foot of his bed. It was respect for the one immediate ancestor who had fathered him.

The scabbard, or saya, of black lacquered wood bore a crayfish design. He didn't know the significance. The hilt was wood covered in pebbled fish skin and then braided. The sword guard, or tsuba, was an intricate work of art all by itself. And in that black scabbard slept a blade of soft iron layered with steel, presumably still bright after these fifteen years since his father had died . . . after these centuries since that samurai had died . . .

Obsessive cultural pride—like religion—kept people apart, he thought, the display's glow under-lighting his grim face, making it mask-like. They both fostered hate, prejudice. Different languages, different prayers. His father had been able to speak Japanese. Soko admired his diligence in learning it, but he would have admired him just as much if he had learned the native language of the Waiai.

It was late. Work in the morning. He reached to a button at the base of the showcase and cast it into darkness.

. . .

"What I do, I do of my own free will," said Oowoh Kee into the camera that had been set up in his cell. "I appreciate the concern of those who will protest against my decision. You should weep not for me, but for my wife, who must live on with the dishonor that has been done her . . . "

The statement was not for the press; they had yet to learn of the arrangement. The statement was being prepared in the event that Kee went through with his unorthodox execution before he was able to be interviewed live . . . as was hoped would happen. It was not so much a prisoner's final record as a kind of protection for the prison, a legal disclaimer.

Soko was off duty. He had inquired ahead about meeting the Waiai. Kee had agreed. Friesner was not present. He had offered to meet the Waiai's spiritual needs. Kee had related that his people had no spiritual beliefs.

Soko waited until the statement was done, the camera removed, before he approached the cell of the condemned man. The field that separated them had a slight violet tint so as to be visible. The cell was Spartan; no pictures, calendars, photos of the wife—of course. The Waiai had turned away, his back to the barrier, but he must have heard Soko come near, for he turned around immediately. The Waiai had remarkable hearing, with channeled orifices ringing their heads all the way around the back from one side of their skulls to the other. And when Kee faced Soko, he revealed his utter sightlessness. What eyes he might have had seemed to have been squashed beneath the weight of his great hairless dome of a forehead, which appropriately enough reminded Soko of the head of a dolphin. The Waiai gave off subsonic waves from an aperture in the center of that bulging dome, which were reflected back in a kind of radar that sculpted images onto some mind canvas. Despite skin yellow as a canary, the absence of eyes and the abundance of ears, the being was one of the more humanoid to have been encountered. His smile was friendly in a reserved way; polite, and completely human.

"Officer Soko. We haven't met before. To what do I owe this pleasure?" The words were not sarcastic.

"I work with Friesner," Soko replied, getting close enough to the barrier to hear its faint hum. "I was . . . curious about you." Intrigued was too strong a word for Soko to admit.

"I imagine that soon enough, others will be curious. They will talk about me. And then they will forget me. And that is fine with me. All that matters is that my wife remember me."

His voice was high and squeaky, as though his throat were made of vinyl, a balloon filled with air pinching out its words. Dolphiny voice.

"You're devoted to your wife," Soko observed.

"She is my life. We were very happy. We were excited to come here . . . to share these many cultures. We harmed no one. We were pacifists."

"You owned a gun," Soko pointed out.

The very human mouth frowned under the crush of skull. "Not at first. We had no idea . . . how things were here. And then we learned. We became afraid. Toward the end, we even talked about returning to our home . . . "

"You should have," Soko said, almost more to himself than to the being.

The Waiai began to pace his cell, lowering his skull as if to sweep the ground before his feet with an invisible cane.

"I know that now. But I do not regret killing those young men, Mr. Soko. If I had told the court that I did, perhaps they might have spared my life. But I am not a liar. I am not ashamed of defending my wife's honor." He stopped, lifted his head. "I am proud of what I did."

"You should have kept trying legal approaches . . . "

"You don't understand us, Officer Soko." The Waiai came so close to the field dividing them that the violet hue glowed dully on his huge cranium. "Our women are sacred to us. They bring life into existence. They nurture that life. When they bleed in childbearing, we call it the Sacrifice. The pain . . . the agony they bear in bringing life. The Sacrifice. The women endure the Sacrifice, and life goes on. And had we had more time . . . my wife . . . my wife and I . . . "

The Waiai turned his head away ever so slightly, as if its weight were becoming too great a burden.

Soko thought of ancient Earth cultures. In many, menstruation was considered a curse, if not blatantly evil. Men made their women take symbolic cleansing baths. Men would not touch their women, or permit their women to prepare their food, for days. The blood feared, not celebrated.

"Those men made my wife bleed," the Waiai squeaked, as much a whisper as he could approximate. "They desecrated her. They stained her." His head came up abruptly. "But don't take that to mean I see her as soiled . . . that I disown her. We do not turn away from those women who are degraded. We avenge their honor. It is the very least we can do for them. Dying for my woman . . . it will be an honor, in a way. Because I am dying for all our women, who bring us our lives."

"Your wife needed you alive."

"She does need my help," Kee admitted. "She needs this money. And with it, I want her to return to our world. I have told her my wish . . . and she swears she will honor it."

"The L'lewed," Soko said, "the way he kills . . . it will be painful."

"No more painful than the Sacrifice," Kee replied.

Soko stared at the being, and nodded slowly, knowing that the Waiai would see this motion in whatever silhouette or hologram he projected inside his skull. It was a gesture of quiet understanding.

"It was . . . my pleasure," Soko told him.

"Come and talk with me again, Officer Soko," the Waiai said, smiling gently.

"Perhaps I will. Good luck to you. And your wife." And then Soko turned away from the prisoner, and walked off down the corridor. Behind one barrier he passed, an obese and apparently naked human lay half covered in bed, a beautiful woman on either side of him. Holograms of a less natural origin; the prisoners were permitted to own various vidgame and holographic systems. The obese man leered at Soko, as if to invite him in to join the party. Soko looked away quickly in disgust . . . not wanting to let some bloated human larva eclipse in his mind the blind grace of the creature he had shared several minutes with.

. . .

Two days later, during the daily hour-long exercise period, a human inmate—also on death row—jammed a homemade dagger deep into the guts of Oowoh Kee.

By the time Soko learned of this, and made it to the infirmary, the Waiai had died. His murderer, who had had nothing to lose in the act, had wildly shouted something about the humanoid being a racist . . . prejudiced against humans . . . for having murdered five of them so remorselessly. Someone told Soko that he felt the attention Kee was receiving from the prison had incited the man's hatred.

Soko wanted to go home sick that day. He had never taken a sick day in his career. Instead, he sought out David-Paul Friesner . . . and found that he was already passing along news of the calamity to Ambassador Rhh.

Friesner barely acknowledged Soko's arrival as he continued to plead with the L'lewed to remain calm. "There's still time, sir . . . we can come up with something . . . another prisoner . . . someone outside the prison, with a fatal physical condition . . . ah, ah . . . someone seeking assisted suicide . . . "

"There won't be time!" the L'lewed's whispery voice hissed from the grille in the middle cylinder of his genie's lamp. His elastic pseudopods, affixed to the ceiling, were taut as steel cable, and the snail-like feelers on his central form writhed like tortured things. "Look how much time was wasted in preparation with the Waiai! You don't understand what will happen to me! My very soul!"

"We have nearly a week before . . . "

"A week! A week! There's no more time!" that seemingly disembodied voice lamented while his ectoplasmic body gave a shuddery spasm. "I will be impure! An outcast to my people!"

And that was how Soko left them, unnoticed as he slipped away. He noted, in leaving the pair, that unlike his last visit to the ambassador, this time the spiritual liaison remained safely on the other side of a violet-tinted barrier field.

. . .

After having checked his voice over the intercom—the same voice that had spoken to her over the vidphone, the vidplate of which was useless to her—Eeaea Kee opened her apartment door to admit her guest Ken Soko.

"Thank you for seeing . . . for having me," Soko told the woman in soft, respectful tones.

She was almost indistinguishable from her husband. Tall, straight, th[e] globe of skull, the bright yellow flesh and small, pleasant smile. "May I mak[e] you some tea?"

"No thank you."

"Come sit down."

He followed her into a living room, cozy despite its blank walls. There were sculptures here and there, however, offering compelling shapes and textures. He found himself reaching out to touch several himself on his way to the worn sofa.

"Did you . . . know my husband well?" Mrs. Kee inquired.

"No. We met briefly. But I was . . . impressed with his love for you. I found myself impressed with your culture."

"I'm flattered," she squeaked shyly.

"I have something I brought with me. A gift I want you to have."

"That's most kind. Something of my husband's?"

"Something of mine." And he leaned forward, extending to her an object wrapped in cloth. She sensed its approach and opened her hands to accept it. "Be careful opening it." he warned her. "It's very sharp."

The Waiai woman folded back the cloth. Felt the smooth lacquered scabbard. Closed one hand on the woven handle. Withdrew several inches of blade, which she could not see flash brightly with the orange of afternoon sun, as if it were still molten in the making.

"A weapon? For my protection?"

Soko smiled. "In a sense. I'm going to take you now to a place that will pay you for that sword. They'll pay you more money than you've ever had, or dreamed of having. And I want you to use that money to respect your husband's wishes. I want you to return to your own world."

Now the being's shy little mouth curved with confusion, dismay. "I can't accept this from you, Mr. Soko! If its value is as you say . . . "

"It is. And you must accept it. If you don't . . . you'll dishonor me."

"But how can I? How can you part with such a thing? So much money . . . "

"If I used that money, I would dishonor my father, Mrs. Kee. I have no son to pass the sword along to. Beyond me, I don't know what fate that sword has. This is the only honorable fate I can think of for it. I want this sword in effect to have been the weapon that killed those men who disgraced you. I want this sword . . . to protect you."

The Waiai lowered her head. She had no eyes from which she could weep, but a strange soft whistling came from her: whether from her mouth or the aperture in her forehead, he couldn't tell.

"You do me great honor, Mr. Kee," she told him. " I accept your gift."

Kee rose and extended his hand to her, so that he might take her now as he'd promised. He could have taken the sword to this dealer in rare artifacts himself, simply brought her the money, but it wouldn't have been the same.

Though she didn't need him to guide her, she gave him her hand as she stood. "Thank you," she said, her smile quivering.

"I thank you, Mrs. Kee," Soko told her, giving a short, sharp bow—as was the custom of his people.

DISSECTING THE SOUL

Madhur Jhabvala couldn't sleep, so she padded barefoot into her kitchenette, made a cup of tea, then sat at her home work station in her comfortable men's pajamas to begin dissection of the brain of the executed prisoner.

The brain currently resided in a tank of violet fluid in the forensics lab of Precinct 2 . . . from Maddie's apartment, a ten minute ride by hovercar through Paxton—an Earth-founded colony called Punktown by its citizens. In order to gain access to the police lab, she had to have her image and voice scanned over her vidphone. This done, she uttered a few passwords to enter her specific point of interest. Now, her primary and several lesser screens were filled with data and a view of the mass murderer's brain in its burbling aquarium. It looked like some mysterious and inscrutable animal dreaming on the bottom, clenching its secrets in swirled convolutions like a nest of tightly coiled tentacles.

Her glossy black hair was still disheveled from bed, her dark eyes heavy-lidded. So was the vertical eye in the center of her forehead. Though she was of Indian descent, however, this Bindi had only cosmetic significance to her and was no more a cultural expression than the bright blue shade she had colored her hair while in college. A female co-worker had teased her that the eye Bindi, being vertical, looked like a vagina in her head. Maddie had joked back that this vagina gave birth to her thoughts.

Having given the date and time, Maddie made further dictations to her computer as she initiated the process of scan dissection. The secondary displays showed the scanner's color-coded three dimensional cross-sections and exploded views with a kind of giddy violence. As she spoke, she used a mouse to guide the insertion of a delicate probe into the reposing creature. Following the probe's progress, the primary screen revealed a greatly enlarged interior view of the organ.

Judging from this man's behavior, it might prove a diseased organ. As a pathologist, she more often examined the other organs of the body to determine cause of death. Only now, she was seeking out what had caused this organ's owner to bring about the death of others. In a case like that of the Waiai who had shot five youths for raping his wife, and whose brain she had examined after he was killed in the prison exercise yard, the reason for murderous behavior was so obvious that her efforts seemed superfluous. Sometimes she found tumors, defects subtle or great . . . and other times the specimen was as perfect as if genetically engineered. But the crimes might be just as horrifying either way . . . and the punishment meted out might be just as harsh whether the cause for the murderer's actions be somatic or psychological. Certainly, no greatly handicapped person would be executed. But this man's acts had been so heinous that Maddie doubted that any tumor or abnormality would have lessened the sentence, had its presence been known in advance. And the man had in fact been offered a brain scan while still alive, in case there was indeed a physical flaw that might make him seem less in control of himself, more sympathetic to a jury. He had emphatically refused a brain scan, however, and the law protected him from having one imposed upon him. While alive. Similarly, he had refused the truth scan which would have made for a quick trial and kept a jury out of the process. But a jury had had to determine the truth, and they had also determined that this blood-soaked creature must not be allowed to live.

"Subject is Peter Maxwell Wegener," Maddie recited blandly, directing the mouse with her right hand, tapping the occasional key with her left. "Executed by lethal injection on seven point twenty point forty-four. The encephalon has been removed, prepped and sustained in amniotic bath." She sipped her tea, then lit up a black-papered herb cigarette. "Thus far, no indications of anomalous features via scan dissection. I am commencing a probe to activate and intercept the subject's memories, so as to record data relevant to his crimes." In a less clinical tone she murmured, "Not to mention I just like sticking a long pointy thing in this sick bastard's brain."

Here, Maddie paused in her work, sat back a bit and blew smoke past the monitor. She wished she had put more lights on in the apartment before she settled down at her work area. On her main screen, she was going to be watching murder take place right before her eyes, or rather right before the eyes of Peter Maxwell Wegener. She had seen such things before, of course. She had also been beaten more than once by her ex-husband. It hadn't become any less unpleasant with repetition.

She had never met Wegener while he was alive. Her introduction to him had involved the opening of his skull. She had thought, however, that he was very good looking for a confessed serial killer, and that he needn't have forced women to have sex with him, and then killed them so as to silence them. It wasn't necessary. But he had wanted it that way. Simple as that. Complex as that.

"Also," Maddie went on, a bit haltingly now, as if struggling to stall for time, "there has been some doubt expressed as to whether Mr. Wegener did in fact kill the fifty-four women he claimed to have murdered. He could only be positively linked to the death of his girlfriend, Lanis Hassan. He confessed to numerous other killings and provided vivid accounts but claimed a poor memory made it difficult to remember dates, names, or exact locations of the bodies. None of the other alleged fifty-three victims has been located or linked to known missing persons . . . "

Had he only wanted attention? To die as a more significant monster? Or had he only been trying to keep himself alive longer by dangling the promise of useful information in other murder cases? He could no longer veil the truth, now. His brain could no longer devise lies, or keep secrets . . . just as it could no longer kill.

A tiny beep indicated that all the memories, experiences, thoughts, feelings and deeds soaked into this fleshly sponge had been fully recorded, filling two whole chips. Maddie consulted her notes for a date upon which Wegener claimed to have murdered one of his alleged victims. She hit SEARCH, and an invisible scout went racing through the doppleganger mind of the killer. The date came up, Maddie hit PLAY, and a scene filled the monitor, a day in the life of the deceased Peter Wegener as seen through his eyes.

Those eyes looked down upon a woman, and Maddie felt an almost nauseous wrench of tension to see that she was naked and he moving atop her. Her head was thrown back, her eyes closed, mouth gaping; dear God, was she dead? But Maddie saw the woman's eyes open and look directly into her own. It was a dreamy look of pleasure. Even of love. Maddie touched a few keys to burrow through further depths of knowledge. She was able to read even the subconscious awareness in Wegener's mind that this was his girlfriend Lanis Hassan, whom he had murdered in a jealous fit of rage only two years later, when she left him to move in with her supervisor from work.

Maddie watched the couple's love-making as if a third party in it, or even half of it (strangely empathizing with both Peter and Lanis), although she wasn't wearing the headset that would enable her to "remember" the physical aspects of the experience, its smells, tastes, tactile sensations. It almost wasn't necessary. Her own memory brought back to her how attractive Peter Wegener had been, his own head thrown back and eyes shut in death as if in pleasure.

Maddie shook herself a bit, as though rousing from a doze. She reached out and banished the scene, partly out of embarrassment, partly out of shame. She fast-forwarded to later in that day, but at this point was inclined to believe Wegener had either been mistaken about the date or had indeed lied about his sins.

When Maddie stopped advancing to play the recording again, she sat back hard in her chair as if struck in the face. Thank God the audio was not engaged. Just seeing the screams without any sound deafened the mind. It was another woman below Wegener now. It was not love in her face, but fear and pain. And blood. Maddie couldn't watch it for more than thirty seconds before she clawed at the keyboard to blot the horrors out.

She got up from her chair, backed away from the work station as if it were Wegener himself, smirking at her, locked inside her apartment with her. She wanted to flee from him, as she had finally fled from her husband. In fear. In pain. But she forced herself to hold her ground.

How could he have done that? Murdered one woman, mere hours after loving another? How could a man be capable of such contradiction? Affection, then unexpected cruelty? It wasn't necessary. Wasn't necessary. She didn't understand it. All this technology to get inside its every cell, and the man's brain was still an utter mystery to her. Was the fault in her own mind, that she couldn't properly read another's? Would another woman have better understood her ex-husband and his latent demons?

So, it hadn't been a lie, about other killings. She was shocked, for some reason. Wegener had claimed a poor memory, but the mind forgets nothing. Everything is saved, preserved. Finding it again is the trick. Maybe he hadn't killed all the women he claimed, but he had killed more than one, so it was likely there would be others. Let someone else catalog them, however. Exhume those graves. She had done her part.

She was weirdly disappointed, she found. She had wanted him to be innocent but for the one crime of passion. He hadn't looked like a monster, to her. Then again, her husband had been a handsome man, as well . . .

A soft whirring sound, and a glance at her keyboard told her that in her haste and awkwardness she had hit REVERSE. She approached her desk to stop it. The read-out revealed that she had regressed Wegener to the age of six. It was two days after Christmas. The proximity of the holiday sparked an odd little curiosity in Maddie. How had this murderer spent Christmas in his sixth year? It was as simple a matter to resolve as a touch or two of her keypads.

Maddie activated AUDIO, settled slowly back into her chair to watch . . .

"Mama, wake up," said a child's voice. It sounded angry, and tearful. "Mama, wake up! Wake up!" A small hand shook a woman's shoulder. She was lying on a sofa, her hair covering her face, closed eyes and a gaping mouth showing through it. Had she died? Maddie wondered, rigid with concern. But the woman grumbled irritably and pushed his hand away. Even without the headset to stimulate her own brain, Maddie could imagine the mother's drunken breath.

The point of view swivelled to look toward a Christmas tree. Its lights weren't turned on, and there were no presents underneath it.

Perhaps they were in a closet somewhere. Maddie didn't believe that his mother had failed to buy any, simply that she had been too drunk on Christmas eve to set them out. But they weren't there. And neither, in effect, was his mother.

"Wake up!" he cried. He sounded closer to sobs, and closer to rage. "Wake up!"

Maddie hit STOP. Randomly, she advanced. Hit PLAY again. And so this continued, for several hours . . . though not once again did she return to a crime scene.

When he was ten years old, Peter's dog was injured by a hovercar that passed over it in the street. His mother (Maddie never saw a father) took him to the veterinarian, and the dog was put to sleep . . . although the vet had informed the mother it could be saved. They hadn't the money, she told him. And so the mother waited out at the desk, leaving Peter and the animal in the stark examination room with its holographic displays of animal anatomy like ghostly carcasses hung up in an abattoir. While the doctor prepped the injection, the small dog—in Peter's arms—watched out the one window eagerly, as if anticipating a return to the outside and a ride in the car after they were done here. Peter buried his face in the fur of its neck. In earlier scenes Maddie had viewed, he had done the same. A half hour ago, Maddie had watched Peter nuzzle the softer fur of its neck when the dog was still a puppy. He had found it while skipping school. A tiny wandering stray that might have died had he not come along and rescued it, given it a home. And now, the dog he had carried home in his arms passed away in his arms, and Peter bucked with hard sobs.

His mother didn't hit him that day, perhaps out of sympathy. But other days she did, and each time she witnessed it, Maddie flinched as if she had been struck herself.

Back and forth in time she flipped, as through the pages of a scrapbook. In high school Peter got in a fight with another boy over a girl they both liked, and Peter pummeled the boy mercilessly. Beat him bloody. Though she didn't access emotions to find out, she felt that Peter enjoyed giving the beating. Sought the blood more than he sought the girl. In any case, it was the last memory that Maddie watched. It was a critical scene, she thought, like the crumbling of a bridge. She didn't want to see more. Not after what she had been watching these past few hours. It was as if she didn't want to remember this person as a killer.

Ten minutes away from here, a brain rested at the bottom of a tank. It would be destroyed in a second execution now that it had been wrung dry. Right now it was still alive, in a way. And it lived on two chips in her computer. An after-life, rather, she supposed. But the seance was over. The night was quiet again; so very still in here. Very lonely in here. A huge cold city lay all around her, outside these walls. It was Punktown. People were dying out there even at this moment. While others loved.

Maddie sat there staring at her series of screens, now all of them blank. The pasted-on vertical eye in her forehead still gazed dispassionately. But tears began to flow from her actual eyes. She felt afraid of the mind she had just stolen inside. She felt hatred for the man who had caused so much suffering and death. And her heart ached for the little boy who had been Peter Maxwell Wegener.

PRECIOUS METAL

The next band to play was DeVeined Shrimp, a Choom quartet. One of the members played an oversized saxophone with thirty finger keys and a ridiculously broad mouthpiece suited to his Choom's ear-to-ear dolphin smile. Their singer wore a slinky black dress, her hair in a glossy black bob, her miles of lips painted a laser red to call further attention to them. Of course, Grey had lived long enough on the world Oasis to take its native Chooms for granted; long enough to find the singer sexy. He watched her through the shifting veil of his cigarette smoke as she cleverly scatted her way through an ancient Choom religious chant, a monotonous dirge that she had turned into a swooping roller coaster ride. They already had his vote.

The previous band had been Idiot Savant, and they milled about the jazz club, chatting it up with friends who had come to offer support and votes in tonight's "battle of the bands" competition. Grey Harlequin shifted his gaze to a few of them knotted in conversation, narrowing his eyes as if the smoke had just stung them. The members of Idiot Savant were robots. Their instruments were cleverly integrated with their bodies, so that these resembled overly baroque chrome and brass saxophones given a vaguely human shape. Only one, the singer, had anything like a human head, an expressionless blind sculpture of brass with black articulated lips like rubber. Their keyboard player was a walking synthesizer and the leader of the band, nicknamed Organ. Grey and his friends called him Dildo instead.

These machines and their ilk were the descendants of a group of robots who had once worked at the nearby Paxton Autoworks, which was all but leveled during the Union War by organic laborers—most of them laid off—rebelling against the use of robots in their place. Most of the automatons had been slaughtered, but a number had lived on after the riots in the ruins of the plant and in other ruins in that war zone of decimated factories. When these were gradually reclaimed and rebuilt (following new battles with a few robot tribes reluctant to give up their squatter's rights), the robots found their way into those abandoned subway tunnels sealed off and forgotten after the great earthquake. Down there, with machinery they took with them from the factories and new machinery they built themselves, they had given birth to successive generations of new robots, who had never known organic masters.

They were arrogant, hateful things, Grey thought, gazing at them through his ragged camouflage of smoke. And they were competitors . . . because even though they had created their own hermetic society within society, they still needed money in order to buy the components and materials for their secret and unlicenced places of manufacture. Their origins being illegal, they could not rent themselves out as legitimate workers . . . nor would they consent to that anyway, out of pride. So instead, they mass produced a product to earn these needed funds. This product was a device called a buzzer, which could be hidden in an organic being's pocket, transmitting signals to an adhesive-backed disk affixed to the wearer's temple (these disks coming in a variety of flesh colors to blend in). The buzzer device would, via this disk, then broadcast pleasure to the brain. There were various settings for intensity, and various species of buzzer—some inspiring wondrous hallucinations, some heightening sexual pleasure, some (often worn by street gangs) triggering an exciting lust for violence. What did these spiteful machines care about the effects they had on organics? In fact, Grey was certain they took great satisfaction in adding to the corruption of the living beings they so despised.

But Idiot Savant did have their human friends and supporters, who were among those chatting with them now. Traitors, thought Grey. A pretty human colonist had her arm slung around the singer's shoulders, even went so far as to plant a drunken kiss on his brass cheek. Must be a buzzer addict, Grey's mind sneered. He didn't doubt that the thing had even slept with her.

Outside the club it was snowing lightly (all that Weather Control would allow—a little atmosphere for the approach of Christmas, not enough to clog the streets). Two men had just entered the club, snow sparkling on the shoulders of their heavy overcoats and on the brims of their hats. One was oriental, the other white. Grey had begun to dismiss them and light up a fresh smoke when peripherally he saw the men cut briskly across the floor, reaching simultaneously under the flaps of their long coats.

Just as his eyes flicked back to them, the dusky club flashed with bursts of light and rang with the loud sharp cracks of gunfire. The white man had one pistol, the oriental a pistol in each fist. The guns had no flash suppressors or silencing features: they must have wanted this to be a dramatic show. People began screaming, diving under tables, glass shattered, the rushing music of DeVeined Shrimp was rudely derailed.

Not recognizing the assassins, Grey at first assumed they belonged to Neptune Teeb, Punktown's top crime lord, and nearly dove for cover himself, but a moment later it became apparent who their true victims were. The members of Idiot Savant.

Organ was slammed back against a wall, flailing and twitching spasmodically like a bug pinned by a sadistic child, the multiple synthesizers in his body whooping and shrilling in a cacophonous performance. One robot bolted for the door but the oriental trained both bucking guns on him. The robot went down, scrambled a bit on what passed for hands and knees, then flopped on his belly and was still. The oriental kept up a few seconds longer, however. Bullets tore holes in some parts of the machine, whined off others. A humanoid Tikki-hotto with nests of clear tendrils for eyes was punched on the jaw by a ricochet and dropped.

The singer opened his black rubbery lips in a wide O and wailed for mercy, but the white man extended his arm and blasted off rounds as fast as his finger could loose them. The brass face was indented only, but slugs that bit into his throat caused arcs of violet electricity to leap free and jump like wind-blown ribbons in the air.

A ricochet shattered Grey's glass beer mug and he threw himself sideways to the floor, hoping the wetness blinding him was beer and not blood from shrapnel-punctured eyes.

The fusillade had ended, the assassins obviously departed. Grey rose from the floor, his sight already restored as he blinked the beer from his eyes. There was still a tumult of noise, however, from persistent screamers. Brushing off his turquoise sports jacket, Grey surveryed the damage, and caught his breath when he settled on the singer, slumped dead by the jukebox. Arcs still danced out of him and connected him to the human woman who had kissed him, via her earrings. She, too, was slumped dead, eyes half-lidded, painted lips slack, a cruel flowing hole punched in the center of the cleavage her dress exposed. People were crouched around her but fearful of touching her with the electricity still linking her to the mechanical cadaver. Grey had taken a few involuntary steps toward the grim tableau, but stopped when several agonized faces turned up at him accusingly.

"Your buddies did this, Harlequin!" a woman screeched at him.

"I'm sure it was an accident," he muttered, sickened at his own excuse even as he said it.

"Mad dog psychopaths!" the woman shrieked. "Gangster!" She rose to her feet, pointing to Grey, yelling at the top of her considerable lungs. "His friends did this! Gangsters! He's a gangster!" She jerked free of a more timid friend's hand when he tried to pull her away.

Grey thought it was a good time to leave, and headed for the door and the snowy street beyond. Eyes followed him, and though every regular in this club must already know that he was this district's captain for the Triad, one of Punktown's strongest organized crime syndicates, he still felt embarrassed and even ashamed as he went.

. . .

Being who he was, Grey was always permitted by the owner of the club to park his vehicle in the scrap of lot around in back. Lighting a fresh cigarette as some measure of warmth against the air's wintry sting, he had nearly reached his hovercar when he heard a strange skittering or scrambling sound, and slowed his pace. His hand pushed his lighter into his jacket, came back out holding a chunky little block of automatic pistol loaded with industrial strength plasma capsules.

Gripping the handgun in both fists, he swung around the front of his car, and saw a giant insect there half propped against the grimy tiles of the club, the creature's armored hide glittering in places with reflected Christmas lights. No—it wasn't an insect, after all, but one of the robots from the club, jagged holes punched in it, a green-yellow fluid flowing from several of these wounds. Its limbs worked as if in agony, claws scraping desperately across the ground and the wall tiles. A moment later and Grey recognized it as one of the members of Idiot Savant; it was the only one composed primarily of a bright blue alloy. During their set, at one point this particular robot had entertained the audience vastly by playing various portions of its own anatomy with a pair of drum sticks, inspiring roars of delight when it drummed its metal crotch.

The distressed machine lifted what loosely served as a head, and eyelessly gazed up at Grey. His machine, the gun, gazed down on it dispassionately with its one empty black eye.

This robot was lucky it had escaped the scene of carnage. Or was it lucky, considering the misery it pantomimed? Was it truly in a kind of pain, or merely suffering nervous reactions? Could it possibly be panicking in fear for its mock life?

It made no sound, staring up at him. It was one of the enemy. Grey thought to finish it off. After all, who would know? Unlike those of the assassins, his gun was discreetly silent.

But he felt no animosity for the wretched thing, seeing it so helpless. If anything, he was more inclined to shoot it just to put it out of its suffering, whatever the nature of that suffering was.

"To hell with it," he muttered more to himself than to the automaton. "It's almost Christmas." He stuffed the pistol back into his jacket, let himself into his car. He was still on guard, wary that the thing might leap upon him now that he was empty-handed, but it merely watched him slip into his car.

It might die of its wounds, or it might crawl away to be repaired by its fellows. At least he had given the pathetic thing a fighting chance. After having been so harshly accused in the club, it made him feel better about himself to show some mercy. A little better, anyway . . .

He left the robot cowering there, drove off into the snow and the night.

. . .

It was still snowing lightly the next afternoon, the windows of the Middle Eastern restaurant ringed in colored bulbs. Grey and the older man opposite him had both ordered taboule and falafel, but Grey had chosen a chicken dish and the older man had ordered lamb. Ng Yueh-sheng, leader of the Triad, had joked to Grey more than once that it was their mutual affection for Middle Eastern cuisine that had inspired him to make Grey a captain. That, and their similar tastes in music.

"You know how I love jazz," said Ng, by way of explanation for the previous night's hit. "It made me sick to think those machines might win a jazz contest over a wonderful group like the Shrimp. Robots stealing this tremendous music that's foreign to them, just taking it over like they try to take everything from us: the jobs of common workers, my own personal business . . . "

"Jazz is foreign to the Chooms, too," Grey offered as politely as he could make it sound. "But they weren't killed." He didn't dare press the point by adding that jazz was not traditionally associated with the Chinese, either.

"Chooms are nearly human. Their feelings aren't a clever sham like the robots' feelings. These things probably really believe in their emotions, which makes things even more sickening. But it wasn't just that I was upset about jazz being played by machines, Grey. They were sent from the Nuts gang. They're the enemy, flaunting themselves in my territory, and making friends they can turn into dealers for them. I've had enough of that. It was time to slap those robots back down into the subway a little. So I brought in a few guns from my brother's clan on Earth, to help keep identification impossible. I wanted it to be public, though, so maybe people around here will begin to think twice about dealing with these toy soldiers, and buying those buzzers."

"But I'm afraid that we might have alienated this neighborhood a bit, sir. They weren't happy about an innocent bystander killed and another one wounded. And the police won't like it, either . . . "

Ng raised a languid hand in a gesture of dismissal. "I'll double their pay-offs for the week of Christmas. That will cleanse their consciences."

"I just feel uneasy, sir, about innocent people . . . "

"You never struck me as so sensitive before, my dear boy." Ng smiled saying this, but many had learned to fear Ng Yueh-sheng's smiles.

"I'm not squeamish. It's just that I never saw innocents go down under our guns before, and I wouldn't think it . . . think it wise to set a precedent."

"My brother's men are a bit crueler than mine, perhaps," Ng allowed. "They have to be, on Earth. You haven't been there since you were a child, correct? Well, it isn't getting any more gentle there, my boy. There are teen-aged killers on every corner that make a Peter Maxwell Wegener look like a choirboy."

Grey sighed, looked down into his small espresso cup, the coffee in it almost a sludge it was so strong.

"Did you know these victims personally, Grey?"

"No."

"Well, try to forget them. I'll have some money sent to their families; anonymously, of course."

Grey nodded, knowing that Ng's gesture was meant as much to placate him as it was to buy the silence of the grieving families. But it was not born of true concern, he knew. Grey Harlequin considered it ironic that his boss's feelings were no less a sham than those of the machines he railed against.

In fact, as much as Grey disliked the Nuts clan himself, he often wondered if—however the robots had originally been synthesized—their emotions were at this point as authentic as his own.

. . .

It wasn't a good sign that Ng would order a hit on Grey's turf without first letting him in on it. Perhaps this indicated a lack of trust on Ng's part; disappointment. And disappointment could be fatal, in this business. Their debate in the restaurant, however understated, might have only aggravated this disappointment. It might be a good idea to get far from Paxton—the "town of peace" its denizens knew better as Punktown—while he was able . . .

While he was still contemplating the need for such a move, Christmas came, and with it an invitation to Ng's yearly extravaganza as if nothing at all were wrong. It would be held at the opulent Paradiso Hotel, and as his date Grey asked a young woman he had only dated for the first time last weekend. He had met Maria at the jazz club, and as she shared his taste for that music they had hit it off quickly. Perhaps she would charm Ng enough to loosen some of the subtle tension between Grey and his boss.

Maria was as lovely as on that first night when she had breezed up beside him at the club's bar. Grey just looked her up and down and wagged his head in awe when he arrived to pick her up. She laughed. Her clingy metallic gown was red like Christmas foil, and with her wide, full lips painted a similar color she seemed a personification of pure sensuality, almost unearthly for her earthy perfection, every man's carnal dream made flesh. Grey felt a deep physical ache, he so hungered for her, but on the night of their first date she had politely resisted his attempt at seduction. He wouldn't press her again; he didn't want to run the risk of chasing this one away. Oh . . . but what a Christmas present it would be to unwrap that foil tonight . . .

On the dance floor, Grey and Maria embraced and swayed dreamily to an ancient Christmas recording. "Who is this?" she cooed, smiling at him from only inches away, making him suffer at her beauty. Her soft chest was flattened somewhat against his. It took him a few moments to think.

"Bing Crosby."

"Bing. Sounds like a Choom."

"No . . . a twentieth century Earth singer."

"Nice. Your boss has eclectic tastes. He seems like a nice enough man. Of course, I've heard stories . . . "

Not from Grey, she hadn't. But he was curious. "Such as?"

"I heard about a band of robots who got all shot up in our favorite club a few weeks ago. They say your boss was behind that."

Grey glanced around, then murmured close to her ear in its fragrant nest of black curls, "I'm not admitting to knowing anything, of course, but I hear that he was offended at the robots playing jazz."

"That's pretty sick, if that's the reason. I thought it had to do with those buzzers the robots sell. I thought your boss suspected Idiot Savant of dealing."

"Buzzers were definitely part of it. But so was the music."

"You sound like you disapprove. Is it because his act was so cruel, or is it just that you think he acted irrationally?"

They passed close to another couple, a Triad captain from another district and his mistress. Grey whispered, "Let's talk about it later, okay?" He drew her a little closer without being lascivious about it. "Maybe we can celebrate Earth New Year together, too, huh?"

Maria hesitated for a second, during which Grey's heart dangled suspended over a well, and then husked, "That would be nice." But she didn't sound as enthusiastic as he would have liked, and his heart didn't feel properly fitted back inside him afterward.

"You don't have to if you have other plans," he said, sounding foolishly like a hurt little boy to himself.

This time Maria's embrace tightened. "I like you, Grey," she whispered, her red lips nearly brushing his ear. "You're nicer than I would have thought, being a gangster."

He chuckled, assuming this was a joke. He thought of the accusations in the club that terrible night . . .

"May I cut in?"

It was Ng, having snuck up on them from behind. As if embarrassed at their closeness, Grey and Maria stepped away from each other. "Sure," Maria said, smiling, before Grey could consent.

Ng took her hand. "You have a lovely girl, here, my dear boy. Maria." He spoke it like music. "What a lovely name."

"My last name isn't so lovely," she laughed. "Rotwang."

"Well," Ng chuckled, "eveyone must have one imperfection at least."

Maria put her arms around the leader of the Triad. "Grey," she said over his shoulder, "can you get me my cigarettes? I left them in my coat pocket."

"Send a waiter to get them, Grey," Ng said. The two were dancing already, a few steps from him.

Maria said, "Oh, Grey's not afraid of a little exercise, I should hope."

Grey's smile was tight. "I'll get them." And he turned from them and began to cross the vast, thronged room.

She was getting rid of him so as to be alone with Ng. It was blatant, and Grey felt like vomiting, he was so angry. So hurt. For all her talk of Ng's cruelty, she was now acting charmed by him. Ng was attractive for his age, but more importantly, a man of great wealth and power. Had she only dated Grey so as to get near him, used Grey to achieve what she really wanted? He felt duped, used. Maybe he was over-reacting. Maybe he should stand in the lobby for a few minutes and gather his thoughts while he smoked a butt of his own. But he was tempted to walk right past the coat room, walk right through the lobby, walk right out into the night and out of this bloody town for good.

When he had reached the wide double doors of the ballroom he hesitated, couldn't help but glance back to see if he could spot the cozy couple.

He could. In fact, Maria had her eyes on him as well. Had she watched him the whole time he had crossed the room? He was about to turn away in disgust when she waved to him. Was it a mocking gesture, or meant to reassure him of her interest in him? With a sigh, Grey lifted a reluctant hand to wave back. Apparently satisfied with this exchange, Maria exploded.

The flash blinded Grey, and in a split-second on its heels came a rolling shock wave of concussion that hurled him backward. He felt strafed with bullets, tearing his skin. His back smashed into the opposite wall of the carpeted hallway

He slumped there, his back half-propped against the wall, blood oozing out of his shrapnel wounds. From where he sat he could see directly across into the ballroom, though it was as hazed as a battle field. There were a few screams, but more moans and whimpers, and mostly there was silence. Grey heard voices from down the hall, from the staircase above, as the hotel guests responded to the cataclysm.

In one stroke, the Triad had been obliterated. Maria had used him, after all . . .

Rotwang. Only now, in view of all this—sitting there with a calm clarity born of shocked numbness—did he realize her joke. He was a lover of old Earth art. He should have caught it before. Metropolis . . .

A man's ragged torso lay in the threshold, its tuxedo and head and limbs stripped from it in the blast. A shallow bowl of skull and scalp lay on the carpet near Grey's feet. And between torso and skull cap, its flesh black and smoking, a woman's arm. The flesh was so deeply burned in spots that the bones inside showed through—glittering bones of metal. A bright blue alloy.

Had she been the same creature he had spared in back of the jazz club? Come for revenge against Ng for his crimes, come to crush the competition? Had she been repaired, and then suited up in a few beautifully crafted layers of cloned human flesh, a terrible Christmas present artfully wrapped? A martyr for her kind, a new martyr for Christmas?

Yes, he decided. And obviously she had sent Grey from the room to spare him. To return his gift of sympathy. But had letting him live to witness the death of the others been a kind of joke meant to taunt him, or a true gesture of mercy?

His eyes settled again on that blue-boned limb. The soft, delicate hand he had been holding only minutes before.

Grey groaned, winced. He didn't know if he would die, or live to be healed and to leave this town. But whatever her ultimate reasons, at least Maria had given him a fighting chance.

SISTERS OF NO MERCY

While waiting for Ayn to come back with the vid of her mission, the other five watched The Evil Men Channel. It was a relatively new VT channel in Punktown, though the sentiments behind it certainly predated interplanetary colonization. The thing to be for today's businessman, the new catch-phrase, the driving ideal, was "evil." There were books entitled *Evil Strategies in Business*, *Get Evil!* and *Live Evil!* It was a term used more by men, though their female counterparts were no less ruthless in their aspirations and techniques. These five young women, once they graduated college, would implement the honed, devastating skills they were learning now . . . and no doubt eventually marry men of the kind they were presently admiring.

The two men in the holograph tank, larger than life—one interviewer, one interviewee—had shaven and branded heads. The interviewee, popular repeat guest N. Ron Hubherd, discussing his business partner's recent ambush-death, was missing his left ear where he'd sliced it off himself at a ritualistic inspirational business meeting, at which he'd also sacrificed a lamb. This had been televised last week.

"That there, ladies, is one testicular evil man," husked Gale, cat mouth curled in a lusty smirk. "Rob Malice thinks he's so bloody because he cut his finger off—I hear he almost passed out afterward. If he ever met this guy he'd be so embarrassed he'd have it cloned back."

"It makes me sick," Shivka agreed, leaning across the bar, wrist flopped lazily with cigarette in hand, "these worms who think they're evil."

"Rob won't have to cut throat—'daddy's' giving him the business on a platter. No testes, that worm."

"Speaking of testes," said Alexandra, "here comes Ayn."

Ayn was all smiles, had the glaze-eyed look some women have fresh from sex. No questions yet—they wanted to see for themselves. Though they could guess the general outcome already, there was a specific detail that generated some suspense.

The Evil Men Channel was replaced by point-of-view footage shot by the special night-vision glasses Ayn had worn tonight. A street of rain-slicked pavement, glistening grimy white wall tiles. The floating camera turned into an alley; they could hear the crunch of broken glass and debris under Ayn's heels. This alley bore no fruit. The camera floated off down another branch, thick with steam hissing from a row of vents. Something small and black, startled, leapt off a malfunctioned garbage zapper. "Shit!" they heard Ayn rasp, and all laughed.

"Scared, Ayn?" Gale smirked.

"Well, I could have been mugged, you know? That isn't exactly the kind of neighborhood I normally frequent."

"I should hope not."

They hushed, more respectful now, as it became obvious that the camera was coming up on a larger black form, this one too numb to be startled, practically unmoving. Watching the holograph tank, seemingly filled with steam, they now felt that they themselves stood over this person slumped against the alley wall. And it could almost have been the vid of any one of them, thus far. Ayn was the most recent applicant. She'd been a good "novice," as they called it . . . but now was her chance to enter the sorority in earnest. At Paxton University, they were the elite, the mysterious, the envied Sisters of No Mercy.

Yes, this one was Ayn's choice. The drooling piece of refuse blubbered and sputtered and ultimately grinned with a disbelieving pleasure that almost cut through his drugged or drunken haze as Ayn opened his soiled pants, worked them down his legs and then bent over him. The camera with her. Tank filled with the vision. Trees of leg hair.

The Sisters whooped and applauded. "Not even a moment's hesitation!" Alexandra cried in delight.

"You've got it," Gale said, nodding. "You are *it*, girl."

"You're beautiful," said the drunk in the alley. "You're beautiful . . . "

And then he screamed.

The camera-view shook from side to side. They heard Ayn grunt. The man kept screaming. Now they heard Ayn gasp, her voice more distinct, her mouth clear.

"He had my hair," she explained.

The camera moved in again, however. Shook viciously from side to side. They saw blood, they heard Ayn moaning

"God," Gale said, "I can't believe you really went ahead and did it like this . . . "

"Really," said Shivka.

They didn't whoop or clap now, merely watched in stunned, almost reverential awe. They had all used knives or scalpels or shears. Ayn had told them she would use her teeth. They had thought she was being unrealistic, and Gale, their leader, had ordered her to bring a knife, knowing that even she herself wouldn't be capable of doing it with her teeth. "You won't be able to go through with it," she had warned Ayn then. "You really have something, kid," she told Ayn now that is was over.

They brought the lights up, and the Sisters finally applauded—though still not wildly. Ayn presented Gale with the bottle containing the prize she had won from her mission. The initiation was over.

The others gathered around as Gale branded Ayn on the left breast with the symbol of the Sisters of No Mercy, and then they celebrated. The awe loosened up a bit; Ayn was hugged and rubbed on the back. Giddy with her triumph, she suggested, "Why not put it in the blendo and mix it in our drinks? That would be a nice ritualistic touch!"

"God, Ayn, you're initiated already—calm down!" Gale told her in laughing amazement.

During the course of the festivities Ayn played the vid back again, froze it on certain images, and after some more drinks played it backwards. Taking Alexandra aside, Shivka commented, "Ayn is going to own a corporation some day, don't you think?"

. . .

He was a mutant on top of being a drunken unemployed piece of living trash. Watery blue eyes the size of balled fists, wisps of white hair. Stinking of shit and urine and drink. Ayn stood over him toweringly while he blinked his unthinking eyes up at her.

She *was* beautiful, as the first derelict had said. Blond hair swept into a pompadour, the flesh around her eyes, of her lips and entire face sexy with a languid puffiness. Fashionably pale, lips a vivid red, green silken suit-dress, and a gun in her purse should she be interrupted in her pursuits down this way.

The mutant certainly wasn't attractive. And he had no job. A man with *no job*. No career. No aspirations. He didn't deserve the little piece of flesh that made it possible for him to be called a man alongside the men Ayn coveted on The Evil Men Channel.

She unfolded the glasses from her purse.

"What are you, some kind of social worker?" asked the garbage at her feet, blended so aptly with the rot and ruin strewn about him, gazing up fish-like.

Stupid freak. What did he know of society, or work? Numbing himself purposely to avoid both. Well, she would cut through that fog soon enough . . .

Blood splashed onto the inside of the holograph tank, now an aquarium of pain.

Gale opened her mouth to say something. It was the weekly meeting of the Sisters, a week since Ayn's initiation ceremony. Ayn had brought a vid for them to watch. Now that it was over, Gale felt the need to say something, to ask something, but before she could, the vid went on into a new episode . . .

This one was an obese black man. Ayn turned to the others to grin. "I put on a nice tight bathing cap this time to protect my hair, after those last two . . . "

"Ayn . . . "

"Watch."

The man fought. Pain made him nearly lucid, and he was strong. The camera-view flew, they heard Ayn curse as she fell, pushed away by the man's foot. She righted herself. A pistol rose into view. Aimed. Puffed silently, twice. Now the man's convulsions were involuntary.

The camera bent low to resume its close footage.

When that was done, Gale almost expected a third episode. There wasn't. "Ayn," she said, throwing up her hands, "what was that dung all about? We initiated you once, didn't we?"

Ayn smiled uncomfortably, glanced from Gale to the other four, and back. "It was for our entertainment, mostly . . . don't you think that was intense? Good solid inspirational entertainment, like The Evil Men, right? What's the matter?"

"Ayn, it's a one-time symbolic ritual, not a hobby, all right? We're the Sisters, the most important sorority P. U.'s ever known, not a club of vampires."

Ayn's mouth gaped slightly open. She held Gale's gaze but couldn't bring herself to look at the other four again. Blood had risen into her sexily puffy white face in rash-like mottled areas. "I'm not a vampire, Gale."

"Well, is this a new pastime for you or what? Did you get a job as a hitman with the Yueh-sheng Triad and forget to tell us?"

"I thought you admired what I did!"

"I did . . . I did, but . . . I was never really comfortable with it. I . . . " Gale straightened up, lifted her chin a little. "I'm not sure we have the same kind of motivations for what we do."

"What are you talking about, Gale? I want what you want—to be evil!"

"Ayn . . . why don't you please go in the other room for a few minutes. Please?"

"Why?"

"So we others can talk."

"Talk? About what?"

"Vote."

"Oh. I see. That's what I thought you meant."

"Please go in the other room, Ayn. All right?"

"Oh. All right. Fine." With calm poise but a still blotchy face, Ayn went to eject her vid disc and pocket it before clicking out of the room on her black high heels.

Shivka was shaking her head the moment the door slid shut behind Ayn. "She's too into the hyper-dramatic, too immature."

"She's just trying to outdo all of us," Alexandra said.

"She's out. I feel bad," Gale said. "She's got enough testes for ten evil men, in some ways . . . but she really needs to get her energy focused. *Very* immature."

"We can always let her try again next year," Alexandra said. "Maybe she won't be so over-zealous after she learns her lesson."

"You've got to have some class and dignity," Gale said, going toward the door to summon Ayn back in. She addressed all four first, however. "Are we all voted, then?"

No one went against the decision. Gale slid open the door. "Ayn. Could you come back in, please?"

Ayn clicked in. Her silken emerald-green jacket and skirt glistened, her pompadour as fixed as a sculpture, restored from hair-pulling and covering by protective head gear. Smudged lipstick cleaned away, lips again as razor-defined as a geisha's. She looked like she was confidently entering a boardroom, head of some new, suitably voracious corporation. *She* the leader, here to address these others, decide *their* fates. After all, hadn't they all turned out to be the slimy little worms they claimed to abhor?

"Ayn," Gale said.

"Yes?" Ayn said, and then shot Gale in the face with the pistol from her purse. The cartridges, depleted from that business with the obese man, ran out before she got to Alexandra so she had to go after her with the knife Gale had given her. That worked out fairly quickly, though she did get her hair pulled again.

Ayn set fire to the room before she left. Worms, she thought, clicking quickly down the street to the subway. The Sisters of No Mercy, they had dared to call themselves . . . and then had tried to reject *her*? Alexandra had blubbered and begged to be spared. That might have been funny had it not been so pathetic.

No, no worms in the Sisters any more; she'd see to that, she thought as she boarded a train that would take her to the affluent, well-policed area of Punktown where she and her family lived.

No, she would see to it that all new initiates *really* proved themselves from now on.

HEART FOR HEART'S SAKE

Nimbus looked out the window into the alley below; at the wall of the facing building, in particular. Some of Teal's handiwork showed there, spray-painted in a variety of bright colors, the shapes so cleanly drawn they appeared stenciled. He had told her once that he had been spreading his graffiti throughout Punktown since he was a child. This work of art was a long strip of Egyptian hieroglyphics. She had never asked him what they said, if he even knew.

She also wondered then how many of his earlier graffiti masterpieces she had seen in her life before she had met him . . . never knowing when she glanced at them, or leaned her back against them to smoke cigarettes, or huddled under them to sleep in alleys on cold nights, that someday their destinies would converge. Never knowing that she would become his partner in a number of senses.

She watched a battered hovercleaner make its way into the alley mouth; as they usually were, the hapless robot was covered entirely in spray graffiti less artistic than Teal's. Its voracious grinding and crashing as it hit the rich filth deposit made Nimbus's jaw tighten. At its approach, a flattened cardboard carton flipped over and two pale youths went scrambling down the alley so as not to be crushed against the floor of trash. White insects under a rock, exposed. A shadow passed over Nimbus's heart.

A hiss of air in an angry pneumatic burst caused her to look around, startled. A hovercleaner up here, too? Her body tensed to run. Old instincts die hard.

Teal sat at his work bench, which ran along the high wall of brick he had painted a glossy pink. A small portable heater blew on him; the loft was large and unevenly heated. A mug of coffee by his elbow. It was as domestic a vision as any Nimbus had ever known. Teal was wrestling with the hissing snake of an air line hooked to a compressor he had salvaged somewhere, his brow knotted with intensity. Nimbus smiled at this sight with a slow fluid spread of warmth throughout her, dispelling the cold shadow like a ray of sun beaming out from behind a cloud.

She padded across to him in her socks, hugged him from behind. He grunted a little irritably and squirmed, still fighting to moderate the flow of air through the line, so she teased him further by bending to nuzzle his ear, her hair falling into his face. He might have snapped at her then, but he had controlled the air level and sighed, sat back from his work, letting his shoulders press against Nimbus's breasts. He reached up behind him to rub her arms. "More coffee?" Nimbus purred, pulling at his ear lobe with her teeth.

"I need to save enough for tomorrow morning. It's all we have left."

"I can buy some. A small package."

"We don't have enough money."

"No?"

"No. Wait until Willie pays me."

"He'd better pay you. He knows you need it."

Willie was an old friend, now with his own modest print shop. Teal did artwork for him, designed logos for the business cards and letterheads of Willie's clients. Right now, this was pretty much the extent of Teal's income. He was fortunate that his uncle was the landlord.

Nimbus came around front to sit on Teal's lap. He smiled wearily, rubbed her thigh through the cottony softness of her much laundered sweat pants. Both had not yet changed out of the warm sweats they wore to bed, or showered for the day. Nimbus found Teal's rough stubble and disheveled short hair as appealing as if he were a small boy fresh from a nap and rubbing his eyes. An almost maternal feeling, she had for him at times. Even after a year, it was all so strange to her, so alien. But so warming . . .

Teal's hand had slipped under the back of her sweat shirt now to slide up and down smooth hard skin. Nimbus could feel him stiffening under her buttocks. She smiled down into his face, got off his legs, took him by the hand.

The bed was close to a glowing orange heater in a corner of the high-ceilinged loft. They could shed their clothing and remain above the blankets in comfort. And they warmed each other in their embrace, in the friction of their bodies, until they were hot and sweating.

Teal curled one of her thighs in each arm as if to carry them on his shoulders, and pressed his lips deeply into the soft white flesh of her belly. He licked inside the squint of her navel. He buried his nose in the musk of her glossy wires. She held his head, his short hair bristling between her spread fingers that arched like her back with her pleasure.

When he looked up at her from down there, his pupils glowed brightly with the heater's orange light. Teal had inherited a mutation which made his pupils a silvery color, like metallic cataracts. His irises were a violet corona around them. He claimed that he saw prefectly well, that his vision was clear and his perception of color normal, but she liked to believe that these were the lenses he focused his imagination through to create his art. She liked having those special lenses focused on her, even though they glowed somewhat eerily now as he crept up along her body, smiling, to stretch out upon her. When his face was above hers, she saw her reflection in those bright discs like twin cameo portraits.

Lodged inside her, he propped himself up on stiff arms to look down between them at where they were locked, and to look at her body in general. As an artist, he was a lover of shape and form. She wondered in what way she might be inspiring him at his very moment, and felt a great fondness for his mysterious mind . . . felt proud that, even with his intensely individual vision, he had allowed her to link her art with his in the way their bodies were merged now.

Those artists of various mediums she had given her body to before meeting Teal had claimed to look upon her as an inspiration. An inspiration for their own desire, she snorted in her mind. Even when they had rhapsodized over her finely sculpted form, in the midst of passion they might as well have been grunting incoherently. Lust for beauty, not Teal's reverent appreciation. All right . . . so there was lust in him, too. But a kind of reverent lust. Teal was no poser as lover or artist.

They had first met in the Café Steam. She had been a performance artist of one kind or another since dropping out of both high and dance school. At the time of her weekly weekend engagement at the Steam, Nimbus had been living on the street for almost six months.

There had been four of them in the troupe at first, three by the time Teal came across them. Nimbus and another young woman wore leotards the departed male member of the troupe had covered with thousands of intricately cut fragments from military model kits and bits of machines and circuitry, enough to layer the surface of the body without building it up, without losing a sense of sinuous form. They had worn headgear—painted the same gray/blue as the rest—fashioned by the same artist, part plastic and part lightweight metal, horned and jagged and delicate and baroque like the headdresses of some ancient race whose pyramids would house clanging, clashing factories. The third remaining member was a nonhuman, an Udotu'ut, whose frenzied limbs wove around the women as they went through manic dances, contrasted by periods of strange couplings as the two women and the flower-like being tightly interlaced themselves into living sculptures that remained motionless for an hour at a time. These stationary periods would be broken only by the occasional croak of, "Oil can . . . oil can," a bit of dialogue from a very old film of The Wizard of Oz.

Teal confessed later he found the visuals of their show, Oil Can, arresting, but lacking any meaning; flash without thought.

But as exotic as Nimbus was in costume, her living conditions were working a darker transformation. She became increasingly ill, lost weight, her lips split with crusted sores. Her human dance partner had a boyfriend now, couldn't let Nimbus use the couch. Sleeping in the subway was dangerous. Cardboard shelters in alleys were not much safer, and winter had arrived. During the weekdays, between the performance gigs, Nimbus took up another line of work, just to be able to eat, and go to a street clinic for medication for a stomach infection she found hard to best. This new work also entailed the use of her body . . .

She had spoken with Teal once before—by then she knew his face from the crowd—and sat in her fluid mosaic of plastic chitin (minus headdress) at his table for a glass of wine he offered. He had offered a film, some night, as well, but she had declined. She had felt too smudged to be going on a date like a high school girl.

But the next occasion she joined him, for coffee this time, and she in her street clothes, they had talked more. He had told her more about his own creative endeavors. Enthused, she had opened up. Confessed the severity of her situation, without telling him of her second—actually, primary—income. Teal offered her a sleeping bag on the floor of his apartment in the building his uncle owned. For some reason she didn't understand, breaking from his unnerving but fascinating chrome gaze, Nimbus had again declined him.

Two nights later, Teal had returned through blowing snow from a trip to a corner market to find Nimbus curled unconscious on his doorstep.

She awoke in his bed. He had removed her clothing, she realized . . . but to bathe her. He had dressed her in his own clean pajamas. At first, she assumed, with a kind of weary resignation, that he had had sex with her unconscious form . . . but he had not. He had only sat in a chair beside the bed, and sketched her. In the days that followed he sketched her nude, but also clothed, and he never touched her thoughout. Her favorite sketch from this early time was an image he had stolen of her sleeping face. This portrait was now framed on the wall. Even with split lips, it had a soft loveliness.

Teal took her to a better clinic. The medications they prescribed at first did little, but with rest and adequate food, Nimbus slowly began to recover. Grow strong. And all throughout, Teal made her his model. Made small smartmetal sculptures of her, and videos of her. She was only too happy to pay him back in this manner. At last, she paid him back for his kindness in another manner. At that point, it was as much for herself as for him.

By then, she had confessed to him how she had been living. He had been concerned, but not repulsed. And in fact, after their first time, he admitted he had wanted this intimacy all along, but had been shy, felt unworthy of her beauty. Nimbus had laughed, but also, she had been impressed. In her prior experience, with both other artists and with her johns, interchangeable in her mind, the rhapsodizing came before or during sex, not after.

And now here they lay in bed together, their juices wrung from them and gleaming on their skin, hot and breathing heavily. It was a bubble of safety and timelessness, this warm bed in a warm corner of a huge cold city in a huge cold space and time.

. . .

The door pounded. "Teal?" called his uncle through it. They had no com-set. Teal and Nimbus sprang from the bed to wriggle back into their sleep clothes, then Teal went to the door.

With his uncle in the hall stood a man in an expensive five-piece suit like those worn by popular VT personality N. Ron Hubherd of the inspirational network for corporate types, The Evil Men Channel . . . this man glancing down at Teal's dress with a sneer of disapproval which he either didn't realize he was showing or didn't care. Teal glanced down at himself and realized he still had enough of an erection left to make a bulge, not to mention the small damp spot at its end.

"Chase Power, Mr. Teal," said the man.

"Sorry, Teal," his uncle began helplessly. "I . . . "

"Mr. Teal, our field agents have tracked down an illegal power hookup to this apartment. You've tapped into the resources of the ceramics manufacturers next door, and they aren't happy that they've been paying for your power these past two years . . . "

Teal found himself staring at the two-jeweled tie clip that indicated the man's rank in his department. "Hey, sir, the hookup was already like this when I moved in . . . "

"Don't lie to me, please, Mr. Teal. You've had this apartment for three years. Our records show that you had a legitimate account with us for the first year but it was terminated for lack of payment."

Teal lifted his eyes, which when he was angry could be quite unsettling. "Well, I paid that up, finally!"

"Finally, yes. But you still owe us for the past two years, Mr. Teal. And that is a sum of twelve hundred munits, with interest . . . which we will have to collect by the end of this month if you wish to avoid legal proceedings."

"Look . . . "

"No, you look, Mr. Teal. If you want to enjoy free power you can do it in prison. But we have a business to run."

"Can't I arrange an installment plan?"

"Not with your record of violation of such agreements. Borrow the money from a friend, Mr. Teal. Maybe your uncle here who professed not to know anything about two years of criminal activity in the building he owns and lives in will lend you the money. But have it to our office by the end of the month, or you'll be a very sorry individual."

"I'm already a sorry individual, to live in a world with gut-eating sharks like you."

"I may very well be a shark, Mr. Teal, but you shouldn't be out in deep waters in somone else's boat, should you? Good day. Miss." The man sent a half-mocking, half-lustful smile past Teal at Nimbus, and gave her a nod. She made green knives of her eyes in return.

When the man had left, Teal's uncle returned alone. "I'm sorry, kids . . . I tried to blow up some smoke, but they've got you. Look . . . I can lend you a couple hundred, but Christmas wiped me out, and I . . . "

Teal sighed, raised a palm to silence the man. "Don't worry. Something will . . . I'll work something out."

Nimbus folded her arms across her chest, gave an involuntary shiver. She had a mental picture of last winter; of building shelters in the alleys, cardboard tents and lean-tos of shipping pallets. But more frightening to her than the thought of returning to that life was a picture of Teal, a sensitive creative soul, being sent to live in a prison filled with murderers and rapists. Her chances of survival in the street seemed better . . .

When his uncle had gone, Nimbus told Teal, "I'm going to go down to the Steam right now and see if they'll take me as a waitress."

"No you aren't! We have work to do. We're artists . . . that's what we're meant to be! You spend your energy pouring coffee like somebody without a microbe of talent can do, and you'll have nothing left for your art."

"We need money, Teal! In a perfect world no artist would have to serve coffee except at their reception, but . . . "

"Wait for this show, at least . . . wait and see what interest I can get in my work. Waitressing. You might as well go back to trawling the streets . . . "

Nimbus turned her eyes away and murmured darkly, "Maybe I should do that."

Teal took an involuntary step toward her, jabbed a finger into the space between them. "Don't even say that!"

"I just want to help you . . . "

"Don't hurt me to help me! I mean it, Nim . . . don't ever even think of doing that again, especially for me!"

"Well, Jesus—you're the one equating honest work like waitressing with prostitution. We can't be dreaming now . . . we can be all wistful and idealistic after we pay our fucking bills! We have to confront some reality, here."

"And it's unrealistic to think I can't sell my work? Is that what you mean? You don't believe that if you only got better notice, you could be a respected performance artist? Jesus to you, Nimbus. I don't know which I'm angrier at . . . your lack of faith in me, or in yourself."

He was always so passionate, so persuasive. If only Teal could have used his clever tongue, clever mind and hands to prevent this from happening, Nimbus thought. But then . . . she had her own mind and hands. They had both of them slept too long in their too-cozy bed. And today, the knock on their door . . . and that hovercleaner, flushing out the dreamers.

. . .

The "Street Art" special exhibition at the Hill Way Galleries two weeks later distracted Teal from the fact that he had only raised a hundred and eighty munits thus far toward his debt. He had slaved months preparing a project in anticipation of this show despite its condescending title, the last two weeks with a noticeable lack of inspired force, but Nimbus was relieved to see his old enthusiasm and drive restored. He was nervous, he was irritable, but that was because he was excited. And she was excited too, because she would not only be a performance artist today, but an actual part of the work of art itself.

Teal was tinkering with his hidden control system right up to the very end, removing panels to reveal a complex nest of cables and hoses, valves and circuit boards. In a bathrobe, Nimbus teased him, "Hey, what's this do?" She closed her hand on a valve and cocked her arm as if to twist.

"Don't touch anything! Everything's under high pressure, you know that! If these hoses let go they'll turn the museum into one big ugly Jackson Pollock painting!"

"Who?"

...

Their ambitious contribution to the week long exhibition was titled Stations of the Cross; or Every Man's a Martyr. Basically it was a huge aquarium made of sheets of lightweight transparent ceramic Teal had found leaning against the trash zapper of the plant next door, rejected for some small blurry marred spots. The aquarium or terrarium was sub-divided into a number of smaller rooms or cells. And Nimbus was inside this tiny clear-walled house, going through her rehearsed motions. A nude painting or sculpture come to life.

Because of the work's size, strangeness and delectable contents, it easily became the focus of the exhibition, and Teal was grinning unabashedly at the amount of people who flocked around the bizarre cage to peer in at its exotic inmate. He felt a bit guilty, yes, for dominating the show but hey, they'd all go check out the other work when they'd had their fill of his. And he wasn't going to let his guilt stop him from enjoying his greatest triumph as an artist. Real critics were here. Owners of small galleries. Art brokers. And collectors . . .

Nimbus wore only a realistic hard mask Teal had cast of her own face, looking like a death mask, with clear lenses to protect her eyes and a filter pack for painting concealed inside. It was very apparent why, this protection. In the first compartment, Nimbus floated as a fetus in red water like a womb filled with her mother's blood. A umbilical cord of sorts pumped air right into the mouth of the mask. She floated as a ball, but then began to kick out at the sides. At last, she moved to the panel leading into the next compartment, and opened it. The blood from the womb exploded into this cell, and concealed hoses blasted Nimbus with mock gore from above and all sides. People stepped back involuntarily. She'd disconnected her umbilical hose. The door had closed behind her to cut off the flood, and now the hoses quit jetting. Soaked in blood, Nimbus was "born."

Now cleansing water sprayed from the hoses, and men smiled to watch Nimbus shower herself clean, a fresh soul ready for the world. The dripping blood was washed from her pubic hair. The water was a bit too cold and her nipples grew hard like erasers. Now warm air blew in, and Nimbus shook out her long hair close to one jet. She positioned herself to let the air reach her pubic hair. Even Teal, who had seen this before, felt an erection growing.

He frowned a bit then. There were no doubt many erections in this room with him now . . . as if he sat in the dark of a porno theater. He saw the slick gills of a nonhuman spectator flutter more quickly. It wasn't so much jealousy he felt; it had been his idea for her to be naked, she who had been uneasy, reluctant, at first. He had wanted the display to be an erotic one as well as thought-provoking. It was guilt he felt. Was he exploiting Nimbus? No more than Renoir had exploited the lush red-haired beauties he had softly painted, he countered himself. But then again, when Teal viewed Renoir's nudes, he felt as inclined to masturbate as to admire their creator's handiwork. Was he selling Nimbus's body . . . as she had once done? Did this make him her pimp? Was this the shelter he had offered her from those days? Was this cell her escape?

Look at her in there, doing this for him, and proudly. But did she secretly feel exploited, humiliated; was she doing this more out of love for him than her own artistic expression? He was so proud of her at this moment, and also felt oddly sick for her. Was this art he had created, or had he subconsciously meant to excite himself by exciting others in his lover? Was this his greatest achievement as an artist, or his nadir as a human being?

He had never been one to verbalize it, but he must tell her it was different with him than it had been with her earlier lovers, as soon as he could. He felt a desperation to let her know that he loved her . . .

The fresh human infant moved into the next compartment. This was the outside world, and it bombarded her with color and stimuli. Winds whipped her. Paint of every color blasted her, mixing into new colors on the palette of her body, her flesh an ever-changing canvas. She swirled, spun, danced in this cell. She tossed a wet mane of blue and yellow. Her pubic hair was green. Now orange. She bent over to let a jet of purple paint explode against her proffered bottom. Men and even women were grinning; was it appreciation, or carnal hunger?

The ceramic sheets had been meant as windows for an apartment building and had been specially treated so as not to let the graffiti of vandals take hold, thus the hurricane of spraying and splashing paint did not obscure the view of the cell's contents. This sheet had been the most marred with blurs, but that was okay; Teal had cut out those areas and affixed long, black rubber gloves which dangled like flaccid penises into the cell. Now people were crowding in, elbowing each other, for a chance to fill those gloves erect, to reach in and touch Nimbus . . . stroke her, caress her. One man in a tailored suit squeezed one of her breasts as if to hold her from fleeing away from him, but she was slick with paint and slid from his grasp, danced to the opposite wall to give the people there a feel. A woman slipped her hand between Nimbus's legs and kneaded her a few moments. Nimbus allowed it, then slid to the floor to roll in the paint, back and forth. The world was exploiting the innocent soul, using it. Dirtying it. The frown in Teal's heart was growing as much as his erection. They had choreographed all this in the loft . . . but it had only been the two of them, then . . .

Look at all the paint in there. Sure, it would be recycled, each color filtered from the other by the computer and restored in its respective tank, but the paint had still been expensive. Rigging up his computer had been very expensive, for his standards. But he hadn't paid for power, and now look at their troubles. He hadn't bought coffee, proper food. He hadn't bought Nimbus much for Christmas. And she hadn't complained. Early on, she had even briefly worked at the ceramic plant before being laid off, but hadn't objected to his use of her money. All this sacrifice for his vision . . . and now he doubted his vision.

Look at these respectable citizens groping at Nimbus, who would tease them by drawing near and pulling away, then come back to let them touch her. Didn't they realize that in interacting this way, becoming part of the art also, they were fulfilling a negative role? Portaying, becoming, those who defile? No, they didn't understand the art, or didn't care to. It was a carnival, a side-show. Strip show. But what had he expected, putting those gloves there? That they would fondle her and simultaneously remark on the significance of the symbolism?

Yes, he had. But he realized he had overestimated his audience.

Was his successfully received artwork, then, a failure?

In the next compartment, a tornado of powder the color of dirt blew out of hoses and stuck to the paint which made carnival glass of Nimbus's body. She was quickly coated. Life dirtying the soul, using it up, withering it, suffocating it. Nimbus danced around in the storm, beat on the walls for release, finally fell and huddled to the floor. She was covered so thickly that at last she resembled a figure from Pompeii.

The wind stopped. The dust settled. The audience grew rapt, and Teal held his breath.

A bright, nearly blinding light burst into the cell, filled it. Dazzled, most people had to look away, shield their eyes. They didn't hear, couldn't see the water spraying into the cell. But when the light dimmed enough, they saw Nimbus standing erect, both arms upraised and the dirt and paint all washed away from her body. Clean and beautiful, the soul not gone in death . . . but restored.

The cell went black. The whole artwork went black. After a few stunned moments, there was an explosion of applause, and tears welled in Teal's eyes. Yes . . . he had done it. It was a complex display. An uncomfortable, and questionable, display. But it was powerful, and beautiful, and he was choked with pride. It almost . . . almost . . . eclipsed all the guilt.

They waited an hour to go through the whole process again, a clock by the display giving a digital countdown. After that, another break. This time Nimbus came out to look at the other art, wrapped in a bathrobe and with slippers on. People congratulated her more so than Teal.

Nimbus, Teal and his uncle were standing about chatting when two men in immaculate suits came to them. One was a human, the other a humanoid from Kali, a blue satin turban covering his black hair, his skin a glossy gray, lips very full and eyes slanted, the eyes themselves entirely black like obsidian. The Kalian shook Teal's hand. "Mr. Teal, my name is Darik Stuul, and I can't tell you how impressed I am with this piece of yours. A brilliant work on the stages of life, the whole life experience . . . and the fact that the display begins anew every hour only makes it more powerful, by demonstrating the on-going cycles of life, death and renewal. Very significant to me as a Kalian, in particular. It echoes my religious beliefs."

"Thank you. It's a universal theme."

"Indeed. I'd like to buy it."

Teal blinked, half chuckled. "Oh . . . ah . . . really?" He felt Nimbus squeeze his arm excitedly.

"It is for sale, isn't it? This is my art broker, David Nussbrown."

"Yeah, hello. Well . . . yeah, sure. Um . . . "

"What are you asking?"

"Well, I'd have to think. I don't really know . . . "

"Ten thousand," said Nimbus.

Teal whirled his head to glare at her, but he looked back when he heard Stuul say, "Sounds very reasonable indeed. Mr. Teal?"

"Sure . . . yeah. Sounds reasonable." He tried to repress his smile.

"David here advised me not to make the purchase, because of the possibility of mechanical failure . . . "

"Well, it is pretty delicate . . . I'm only an amateur at that stuff . . . "

"Such humility! I'll hire an engineer to go over it . . . without tampering with the intent of the piece in any way, naturally. David also says art must not depreciate, and the young woman here will age, obviously, as time goes by, but we'll worry about that as it happens . . . "

"What?" said Nimbus.

"You don't mean . . . you want to buy Nimbus, too . . . "

"Well, you don't buy a person, obviously, but she must come with the piece, absolutely . . . or I'm afraid I must decline. She is so exquisite, so wonderful, that I can't imagine the piece without her."

"Well, sir, she can't live inside that thing!"

"She will live in my house as my servants do, and will be paid five hundred munits a week for her work. She will be free to come and go as she pleases. But from six in the evening, when I come home, to midnight when I retire, she must go through the full routine. Once every hour, resting or whatever in-between. I think that's quite fair. And quite an easy occupation! Of course, on weekends you might be required to perform more often, if I am home . . . "

"You wouldn't consider another performer of your own choice?" Teal said.

"Teal," Nimbus whispered. "Five hundred munits a week! And ten thousand for you! We wouldn't have to worry any more!"

"We wouldn't be together, either."

"I can come see you, every day!"

"Certainly." Stuul smiled magnanimously. In his slate face, his white teeth were startling.

"We need to talk, to think about this," said the artist.

"No we don't," said his partner, his masterpiece. "Teal, if you turn this down you're a fool. And you'll be an imprisoned fool, and then a dead fool. But if you take this you begin becoming an important artist. And a rich artist! This man has friends. His friends will see Stations."

"Absolutely," said Stuul.

"It will just be like me having my own place, and a job."

"For her, it will be just that, Mr. Teal. A job."

Yes, thought Teal. But being a prosty had just been a job, too.

. . .

Nimbus had made a tent for Teal of her knees propped under the blanket. It was a frail tent in the vast cold wilderness of life, but it was all he had and he entered it eagerly, and the shelter of her warm inner slickness as well.

"I don't want you to go," he told her, rocking his hips in a subdued rhythm, rocking himself in her pelvic cradle. "There has to be another way . . . "

"He told you; there isn't. He wants me."

"Yes, he does, doesn't he? He wants you more than he wants my art, I'd reckon."

"Are you being jealous?"

"Of what? That you're going to go live with an exotic rich businessman? What's to be jealous of?"

Nimbus smiled up at him. "You are jealous, aren't you? And insecure. Hey . . . I'm doing this for you . . . " She brought her legs rasping up tighter around him, hooking her feet over the backs of his legs. The orange glow of the heater, now switched to its battery setting with the power shut off, highlighted the gently straining muscles in Teal's neck and upper chest, a hypnotic effect.

"You want to do something for me? Then don't do this. If you do, it isn't for me."

"Yes, it is. Like it or not, it's what's best for you."

"You're not my mother. And I'm not so sure I believe you . . . "

"What do you mean?"

"This is a great opportunity for me, Nim . . . but it's a great one for you, too, isn't it? To live in a mansion in the money sector. Five hundred munits a week. You're doing this for me, Nim, or are you really doing this for you?"

"Get off me." She released him from the jaws of her hungry legs, pushed at his shoulders.

"No, listen."

"Get off me!" She slid out from under him, slickly lubricated with their mixed sweat. Her angry soles slapped the cold floor as she paced. "You don't give me any credit, do you? You think I'm only out for myself . . . "

"You say this is for me but I don't want you to go!"

"I can see you every damn day! So what if I don't live here . . . "

"You won't see me every day. At first, maybe. But you'll like that rich sector, Nim . . . a lot. You won't want to leave it. Not to come into this old neighborhood and be reminded of being homeless. Not to come to this flea bag apartment. Not to spend time with a flea bag like me."

"No credit at all, you give me." Tears glistened hot in Nimbus's eyes. She slipped on a pair of panties. "None. You think I want to live away from you? Fine. Think whatever you want . . . "

Teal watched her dress, lace her heavy black boots, pull on her heavy mock-leather jacket, tinkling with zippers, straps and studs. "Where are you going? To go find Stuul? Stations isn't even at his house, yet, Nim . . . "

"I'm going for a walk."

"He wants you for a freak, Nim. To perform in that thing for a week is not to live in it. He wants you as a pet. And he wants you as a possession."

"So do you."

Teal wanted to protest, to tell her then that he loved her, but he was too angry, too hurt and confused, and Nimbus had already slammed the loft's door behind her.

. . .

They couldn't hear each other through the clear ceramic wall.

It was but the fourth time Nimbus had performed inside her cell for Stuul. The third time, he had had two friends over to watch . . . but he had told her that he would not be permitting any others to view the piece until he gathered his friends and associates for a large, formal unveiling.

This time, they were alone together.

For the first time, he had slipped both arms inside the black rubber gloves, and caressed the paint-bombarded Nimbus when she danced close enough. At one point he caught her by the arm, held her. Not hard, but firmly, and she didn't pull away. His other hand slid between her legs, up between her paint-greased bottom. He slipped a finger inside her, another finger in the other hole. The non-toxic paint lubricated his motions.

Nimbus freed herself more forcefully then, but turned the motion into a whirl of her dance. She nearly fell, but caught herself. She saw Stuul outside as a dark blur. Anger flushed her face inside her mask. Her heartbeat raced. Her mind was so full it went blank. She continued her dance.

She saw his hand extended, waiting to touch her again. Not only waiting, but giving a flicking gesture for her to come back. The gesture was curt, demanding. Impatient. He wasn't happy she had wrenched away.

The gloves were for hands. Those at the gallery had touched her. Stuul expected to do the same. He had paid good money to do the same . . .

Good money that would keep Teal out of prison . . .

Nimbus again spun within his reach. He caught her with both arms. Slipped one around her belly. And his right hand, again, slid between her legs.

Nimbus closed her eyes inside her mask. She wanted to pull away. She really did. Hadn't she suspected it all along, as Teal had? But that ten thousand would get them out of debt, and the weekly paycheck would give them security. She didn't pull away from Stuul. She had no choice, really, but to endure being the toy he had purchased . . .

. . .

Stuul shut off the machine, shut down the artwork, and instructed Nimbus to come out, although she was still drenched in paint. He had spread out a drop cloth so she wouldn't stain his expensive carpeting, which in metallic thread portrayed the nightmarish Kalian god-demon Ugghiutu consuming souls only to defecate them back into existence. Nimbus stepped out reluctantly, full of dread. He had only had the artwork four days and already he was bored with its intended use?

"Lie down, please," he instructed, smiling, caressing her mask's colored cheek.

"This isn't part of the performance," she said in a sleepwalker's voice.

"Miss," Stuul said evenly, smiling, but she saw his chest filling with air through his nostrils as if he were puffing himself up with his determination, and anger. Nimbus thought of a cobra rearing. "Please don't make me dismiss you, and return this artwork. You know you and your partner can not afford that . . . you told me of your lamentable situation. So please . . . lie down."

Several ticking beats. Nimbus again went blank, all her thought reduced to the sensation of the paint drops winding slowly down her arms and legs. And then, without another word, she did as he asked.

The Kalian disrobed, neatly piled his clothing to one side. His penis was shaded much darker than the rest of him, almost black, very long but very thin like a dog's. He had stroked it erect from its protective sheath and it glistened with its natural lubrication. Stuul lowered himself onto her, and then into her. He didn't remove her mask, however. A living statue.

Nimbus watched her expressionless artificial face reflected in his eyes of volcanic glass.

"Yes," he grunted, sloshing down wetly onto her, into her, the paint getting on him. "Yes, yes . . . so beautiful . . . yes . . . uh . . . so . . . uh . . . beautiful . . . "

All around them hung expensive paintings in gilded frames. Sculptures and holograms stood on pedestals. His own private museum . . . and them fucking on its floor.

The next day was worse. He insisted on going through the stages of the art-machine with her. A twin in the womb with her. And he had sex with her on the floor while the paint storm engulfed them, taking her from behind with feverish thrusts, wearing a painter's filter mask to protect his face and crying out inside it when he came, slapping his front against her glossy, many-hued buttocks.

This time was worse because he had defiled Teal's art, she felt, by entering into it where he didn't belong. By invading it, and altering its purpose, its meaning.

While Stuul cried out inside his mask, Nimbus merely cried inside hers.

. . .

Since coming to live with Stuul a week ago, she hadn't gone back to visit Teal once. He would think his prophecies had come true. How could she tell him that the real reason was her shame?

An engineer had come to fine-tune Teal's work. Nimbus watched him wag his head, baffled and amazed. "What a crazy mess! Incredible! How'd he get it to work?"

"Do what you have to," Stuul said, "as long as the results are the same. And I absolutely have to have it working perfectly by this weekend; I'm having a dinner party and I'll be introducing this piece to a lot of important people."

"I'll have to rework almost everything, Mr. Stuul . . . this thing is a disaster and it wasn't built to last."

"I got it at a steal as far as art goes, Mr. Lang." Stuul suddenly appeared to think better of his candor and grinned at Nimbus apologetically. She just stared back at him blank-faced . . . then she gazed again at what the engineer was doing, and thought of the performance she was expected to give that weekend. Rich people watching her like a whore stripping behind glass for a token. Rich people groping her with black rubber gloves. Safe sex. Maybe Stuul would even invite certain special friends to take her, as he had . . .

She watched what the engineer was doing very carefully while she thought these things.

. . .

They wore five-piece suits and evening gowns, tuxedos and glittering sheaths. There was a well-known robot artist which despite its lack of emotions and scarcely anthropomorphic form still managed to convey a tremendous ego. There were Kalians in rich golden robes with rich golden voices, in blue turbans, strutting imperiously. Their women were beautiful in spite of their ritual scarring and smiled politely but were not permitted to speak. Tinkling laughter, tinkling glasses. Nimbus had been instructed to remain out of sight so as not to spoil the impact of her presence inside the artwork, but she peeked out from behind the control center for the artwork, where she crouched.

A familiar face made her freeze. She hadn't recognized him at first, because he was dressed fairly well, but his eyes flashed with reflected light. Teal . . .

Of course, the artist had been invited. Nimbus watched him. In the large room beyond this one, Stuul was shaking Teal's hand and then introducing him to others. Even at this distance, Nimbus could see that Teal wasn't smiling. He looked emptied. She knew him well. She wondered why he had even come. A sense of obligation to his art? Masochism? Or to see her? . . .

She hoped he would understand why she had ruined his masterpiece . . .

"Ladies and gentlemen," Darik Stuul announced, lifting his arms like a side-show barker. "I give you Stations of the Cross; or Every Man's a Martyr!"

Applause . . . and it began. Nimbus was a fetus. She was born to the spilling of blood. She was cleansed to go out into the world. The dinner guests all drew nearer, enraptured, mesmerized. She imagined the erections growing inside tuxedo pants. Even the snotty robot was rapt. She didn't look out at them. Didn't want to see Teal, most of all. He wouldn't be proud of her, this time, watching her.

And now, the child Nimbus portrayed ventured out into the world to be overwhelmed in colors and wind. People moved closer to fill the gloves; Stuul made sure the turban-crowned Kalians, dignitaries perhaps, were the first in line.

The paint storm began, and the top of the compartment blew off like the lid of a jack-in-a-box, hoses thrashing like furious snakes, casting paint of many colors all over the large room, Stuul's private gallery.

"No!" he screamed. "No!"

Tuxedos were spattered. Expensive coiffures were drenched. One of the Kalians sputtered paint out of his mouth, blinked paint out of his eyes, his turban blasted askew. A hologram of Marilyn Monroe smiled, her skirt billowing, as paint streams passed right through her ghostly form. Jets of yellow blew sculptures off pedestals. Jets of red slammed into oils in their gilded frames. The white walls and ceiling became one big ugly painting by Jackson Pollock in mere seconds.

"Teal!" Stuul cried. "Shut it down, will you, shut it down!"

Teal rushed to the controls. He was also saturated. He removed the panels and said, "Jesus . . . you switched it all around!"

"God damn it!" Stuul shoved him aside and yanked at hoses. One snapped free and a jet of red-dyed womb water blasted him right up both nostrils.

Teal began laughing. He looked to find Nimbus, and there she was, having found her way out of the artwork, naked and dripping. She was grinning at him, came to him.

"I'll sue you for damages, Teal!" Stuul raged.

"You tampered with it," Nimbus told him. "You can't hold him responsible. It worked for him."

Stuul clawed at valves, flicked switches. Dust began howling out of the machine to stick to all the paint. "I'll have my money back!" he bellowed.

"Take your money back!" Nimbus shouted over the chaos and screams. "But you can't sue us; this was all your fault. You should have listened to your art broker. And by the way—I quit."

Nimbus took Teal by the hand and in the pandemonium they made their way to a back hallway, where they dripped on the pristine carpeting.

"I'm sorry," Nimbus whispered.

"It's all right."

"It'll be safer for us if we do give him his money back."

"I know."

"We'll need money again."

"We'll think of something. Maybe I can be a waiter. For a while."

A bathroom opened off the hall, and he led her into it by the hand. They stood together under the shower, Nimbus naked and Teal fully clothed, to wash away most of the paint. In a moment they would go and gather her things . . . but right now they kissed under the cleansing stream of water in the bright white light of the bathroom—like two souls reborn.

THE BALLAD OF MOOSECOCK LIP

They were both from Punktown, but it's a big place
Might have passed on a street
Glanced at the other one's face
Sat in one dark room for a film to unreel
Both watched a performance by Nimbus and Teal
Stood a few feet apart on a whispering hovertrain
Both ducked into a book store to hide from the rain
Brine was laid off for six months from the plant
His murmur of unrest now an unbroken chant
Down in Moss Hollow on the outskirts of town
He went to find Dazey
Dressed in leather and frown
Dazey from the old days, trouble on legs
His smile was electric, his eyes powder kegs
Dazey seized Brine, clapped him on the back
Took him to his aeroplane riddled with flak
It lay weed-entangled and grounded for life
He lived there alone (he'd been left by his wife)
Dazey walked Brine through thick misted woods
To the scummed secret pond where he hid all his goods
Shrimp they resembled but with human feet
And when processed to drugs they did well on the street
Dazey plucked one out with a proud father's grin
Brine hesitated, but said, "Count me in."

. . .

Orange Girl
Color swirl
Halloween bright
Orange leotard tight
Black hair jet gloss
But her eyes were the boss
Orange irises too
Orange her hue
Orange Girl's mother was recently dead
Dad longer gone had got shot in the head
Orange's skin of teenage cream
Pocked by the Illness that ended her dream
Took a job as a waitress
To work wore a dress
Couldn't wait to get back in
To her orange-peel skin
Served cold eggs and lived for the tip
At night returned to Moosecock Lip.

· · ·

Brine moved into Dazey's plane that first day
He lay in the dark like a bomb in its bay
Dazey awoke him: "Let's take a little trip
At dawn we meet this mutant
Up on Moosecock Lip."
Brine brought his gun, a Wolff forty-five
He dozed off several times along the long drive
He awakened to hear Dazey loading his clip
"We're here, buddy-boy,
This is Moosecock Lip
The rods are just prudence; the girl is okay
She's a little bit young but I like 'em that way."
To Brine it was a job; he just gave a shrug
Followed Dazey on foot
They carried the drug

"The girl's got the Illness; it killed her mom Sue
It's messed up her system but she can't infect you."
At the crest of the hill they came to her shack
She answered her door
But then turned her back
Alone she would dance with her previous flame
But when people called she shadowed her shame
Dazey showed her the drugs in the dark of the room
While Brine's eyes sought her out through her shelter of gloom.

. . .

Orange Girl
Her life a baton twirl
Eyes black-pearled
Drugs now her world
Dazey excused himself for a pee
Orange Girl made Brine some coffee
Kept her eyes down-cast
Talked nervous-fast
Brine liked her quiet manner
Pictured her mane as a windy banner
He admired her leotard form
Standing close her orange was warm
He meant to ask her for a date
But Dazey chirped it was getting late
Orange Girl, orange gifted
When Brine left her orange eyes lifted
She didn't move to turn on the light
Left herself in punishing night.

. . .

The drugs were all sold, Brine's poverty past
He took his own room
Drove down for breakfast

He chose what looked like a nice little place
Looked up from his menu into a pretty pocked face
(Orange Girl, Orange Girl, no place to hide)
She showed him a smile
Trembled inside
They chatted awhile then he went on his way
"See ya tomorrow"
Ate there the next day
He took her to dinner, her turn to be fed
After some work
He got her to bed
She moved into his room, moved into his light
Left her shack behind on its hill in the night
But the drugs, like her scars, were a part of her still
After two painful months
She moved back to her hill
And Brine, again bitter, dressed in his frown
Packed up his anger
Left Punktown.

. . .

Orange Woman
Orange human
Danced like a flame
In her dark shack, where nobody came
On its roof danced the rain
She smashed her mom's picture
'Cause it mirrored her pain
She lost her job
Was too numb to sob.

. . .

A man in leather passing through
Stopped in a bar to partake of a brew

After more than a couple life had got hazy
A slap on the back
Through the smoke there was Dazey
Dazey was now a big man on the scene
Brine confessed he was back behind a factory machine
Dazey offered him work, Brine turned it down
"How's Orange doing?"
He asked through his frown
"She whores it now, pal; her pimp is Reddream
He's a pretty tough gun, you know what I mean
He has this sawed-off he wears on his hip
He and his boys moved in
Up on Moosecock Lip."
Brine nodded slowly and set down his cup
His eyes sobered clear
"I'm going on up."
Dazey grinned, "I knew you'd come back
Could you use a spare man in your little attack?"
The night's rain had passed, now just a gold drip
From the eaves of the house
Up on Moosecock Lip
A fish-faced mutant answered the door
The first morning blast drove him straight to the floor
Dazey killed as he laughed, "Die, son of a bitch!"
As he unseamed a second with his machine gun stitch
Brine's gun spoke; he had no words to say
As he killed the first thing that got in his way
He'd given up before without a real fight
Let an orange sun fade
Into unending night
Then a shotgun twice-loaded
Came out of a door
And Dazey exploded
Brine heard a girl scream but had no time to think
Bullet mosquitoes flew at him to drink
Reddream the pimp came snarling into view

Brine ducked and fired
Split the pimp's head in two
Brine knelt by his friend but it was too late
Face-down he was drowned in the red pond of fate
He went into the kitchen and found her there
Orange Girl there
Black hair
Hanging in her face
This was her place
Her lair
Hugging herself, eyes wide in the corner
As if some kind of demon had gripped her and torn her
He had to speak softly so she wouldn't take flight
Like a lightning fast deer deeper into her night
"It was easy with our drugs, too easy to run
I want today to be the first battle we've won."

. . .

Orange Girl
Her spirit far-hurled
Once she had danced like the soul of the world
She seemed deaf and dumb
Her scarred pretty face numb
But a smile slowly spread
As she came back from the dead.

. . .

For the first time in years
People far and near
Some happy, some sad
And most in-between
As varied they were as Halloween beings
Saw lights glowing warmly at night on the tip
Of the hill in the distance
Called Moosecock Lip.

"Merry Christmas!" exclaimed five-year-old Ian Declan. It was, however, late summer.

"Happy Halloween, is more like it," remarked a young man to his friend as they passed the Declans going the other way down the mall.

"What did he say?" said Rebecca to her husband.

"Nothing," Declan replied quietly, but he looked back over his shoulder. At the same time the young man glanced back, grinning. The young man was tall, with shoulder-length black hair parted on the side and held with a red barrette, features so attractive he was almost pretty, full lips spread wide to show bright teeth in a bronze face. Declan liked to believe it was something in his own face that made the youth turn quickly forward again.

Between his parents, Ian rode obliviously in his cart, which was more robot than wheelchair and made him something of a half-machine centaur. Tanks under its seat sent tubes snaking into catheters in his flesh. He still had the plastic rings of earlier ports, no longer used, here and there on his body. He'd been linked up to various forms of life support since birth, though it was only recently that he needed the cart to move about, his legs so withered and atrophied it was difficult to believe the child had ever run about their apartment, even for Declan, who had alternately chased and been chased by him.

Vaguely Declan glanced about to see if something in a shop window might have prompted Ian's exclamation, but decided it was just his son's recent attachment to a disc of Christmas songs he had started listening to a few weeks ago, inexplicably. He hadn't been much interested in those songs last winter. Lately, he needed to hear the disc at least once a day, and some days multiple times. Though Ian used only a handful of simple sentences, much-ingrained at his special preschool program so that he would parrot them when needed, he could sing these songs nearly word for word. Declan had loved them as a boy himself, and often sang along with his son. He found Ian's voice lovely, angelic.

The mall tunnels they strolled through had been converted from the subterranean remains of a portion of the city's old sewerage system, damaged in the great earthquake that had also caved in much of Punktown's old subway system. For character, the various tunnels and conduits still bore valves, circuit boxes and smaller pipelines that snaked overhead or along the curved walls between shops, the whole of the walls and pipes and glossy tiled floor painted a ghostly green like a patina of verdigris. Ian loved the place, though in the past he had thrown many a tantrum if not allowed to visit every toy store, to buy everything that struck his fancy. He was generally much better about that now, though it was the Declans' habit to buy him some treat or other on each excursion.

As they came up on one of the mall's several toy- and game-oriented stores, Ian began pointing and making an insistent grunt-like sound. Declan saw a passing couple look over at them. No doubt they had seen mutants even more shocking than Ian in Punktown, but these were usually the product of poverty and ignorance, and not often the offspring of a well-dressed, obviously fairly well-employed couple like the Declans. Even after five years, Declan still felt that apologetic urge to explain to the other couple why this should be so. Why this creature had been allowed to live. That it was against their religious beliefs to abort—though since Ian, they had begun to use birth control. Though since Ian, they had attended their church much less frequently.

Ian reached for the store's garish plastic-colored lights with his thin, glass-like arms. The cart helped support his head as it grew ever weightier, like a boiling storm cloud of milky flesh. Despite its now great size (larger than Declan's own head), the child seemed composed more of spirit than of matter. This was no doubt an effect of his skin, translucent over nets of bright blue vein. But also, his father believed, it was in the purity of his smile, which Declan found beautiful, however tragic those poor eyes.

Their son between them, like an immense fetus in a mechanical womb they both bore heavily, the Declans entered the toy store.

Here, children ran about and chirped in delight. Children with silky hair their parents could stroke. How Declan had bitterly hated such parents, five years ago, when it began. Rather than be grateful that these other children were not afflicted as his son was, grateful that these parents did not suffer as he did, these days Declan found himself merely shutting them out altogether.

Ian surveyed the store's offerings with an intense anxiousness, pulled two soldier figures off the racks and compared them, one in each hand, weighing their merits, then rejected them for a movie tie-in action figure. Able-bodied heroes, all. "Look, honey," his mother prompted him, holding out a cute animal doll that tied in with one of his favorite vids. He barely glanced at it.

"Not enough weapons," his father joked.

"Not expensive enough," Rebecca joked back. She was a beautiful woman, tall, her long, thin blonde hair and pale skin and delicate bones giving her an ethereal aspect. There was a kind of remoteness in the flat blue of her eyes, but a redness about them always made her look as if she had recently been crying.

Both of them sounded tired. Both had anemic smiles.

When they returned their attention to Ian, they found he had settled on a large Randy Atlas action doll. The doll could fire a variety of harmless beams, and project a hologram of Randy's extradimensional sidekick, Ectopup. Ian had Randy Atlas sheets and pajamas at home.

"Oh boy," Declan said, examining the price posted on the shelf. "Thirty munits . . . "

"Honey," Rebecca said, "you already have two or three Randy Atlas dolls . . . "

"Not like that one," Declan said. He held out a monster figure that cost only five munits. "Ian, did you see this? Wow, look at this thing . . . "

"We can't afford this today, honey, I'm sorry," Rebecca told him, prying the box away. Ian began to fuss loudly, cry out in anger. Declan moved his son's cart away from that shelf. "Pick something else," Rebecca went on, replacing the doll. "We just can't afford that today . . . we're short on money, Ian . . . we still have to buy lunch . . . " She went on with her reasoning, though they both knew he would not really comprehend any of it.

After much noise, after many stares, Ian finally, broodingly, accepted a small soldier figure from another aisle. All three of them exhausted, the parents let their son carry his doll to the cashier himself, tears still slick on his face. Behind the counter, the cashier rang up the sale. As the current fad dictated, the young girl wore a black leotard and a sequined Mexican wrestler's mask that hid her face but for her eyes and her mouth. Declan found this fad extremely annoying. The girl was no doubt very pretty under her obscuring mask. Two years ago, youngsters had similarly covered their faces in swirling Maori tattoos (since removed). Their beauty was wasted on them.

. . .

Ian died three weeks before Christmas.

The mall had not been lax in putting up its decorations, so Ian had seen them on one final excursion before he became too frail to leave the hospital. Now, Declan surveyed them again. Red and gold garlands were interwoven with pipes and sheathed cables. Silver globes hung from the concave ceiling like sparkling tumors. Over the intercom, carols were played. Burl Ives sang "A Holly Jolly Christmas."

Declan sat abruptly and heavily on a bench, and set his bag down so quickly that it tipped over. It was one of the songs his son had sung most often.

A young woman leaned down to look into his face. It was not Rebecca; she was at church, where she was more and more often these days, as if to make up for his own total absence. With Christmas coming she had much to help them with, much to focus almost feverishly upon.

"Are you all right?" this other woman asked. She had seen him almost fall to the bench. But Declan wondered if she wasn't as drawn to his appearance as to his obvious anguish. He was an extremely attractive man. Rebecca herself had been immediately attracted to him. The women at work flirted with him shamelessly. Even though he hadn't shaved in two days, and had let his usually neatly cut hair grow out a bit, he was still striking.

"I'm fine," he said, not meeting her eyes. "I'm fine, thanks." He reached down to right his shopping bag.

"You sure?"

"Yes—thanks," he said, not looking up. Peripherally, he saw her reluctantly withdraw. But his gaze remained on the contents of his bag. There was a bright box containing a large Randy Atlas doll in there. On Christmas eve he would put it under the tree. On Christmas morning he would unwrap it and set it on Ian's bed with its Randy Atlas sheets.

Why hadn't he bought it that day? Why hadn't he bought it when his son could have held it in his hands, even if it might be heaped the next day with the many other toys he neglected? They had eaten lunch in the mall that day: twenty munits. Shit it out the next day. Why hadn't he bought the doll sooner? He'd forgotten it after that; he supposed now that it hadn't been in stock again for a while. He should have looked elsewhere for it; ordered it. He might have brought it to Ian in the hospital. They had, in fact, brought him other gifts. But they had forgotten this particular doll, which Declan had only seen again today, when sleep-walking through the toy store.

He got up from the bench, walked again. He seemed to float along without the weight of his wife at his side, and without the weight of his son in his cart. He felt like a ghost that haunted a former home, without knowing why it did so. But he imagined Ian at his side. He even spoke to him in his mind.

"Wow," he muttered softly under his breath, "look at all that, huh?" A miniature Santa's castle had been erected in the center of the main hall, and holographic elves went tirelessly through their film loop labors. Declan watched it for a while. He imagined his hand on the top of his son's hairless and blighted skull. He did not see the other children who gazed raptly at the display; even the elves were more alive to him.

He went to all the places in the mall his child had loved best. He looked through the children's section in the book store. He stared in at dogs in little cells, and tiny fish darting in tanks. He could hear Ian exclaim, "Dog!" Declan had been so proud of him for that. People might have thought it was the dogs he was smiling at, now.

It was a daily seance, and he the medium. But he knew it was all fakery.

In the men's room of a major department store, he splashed cold water in his face and then lifted his eyes to the long, dirty vidplate, which considerately reversed his reflection for him so he saw his appearance just as others did. He saw hatred there, but wondered if others could. It was too profound to show on mere flesh. He hated that flesh, for its handsomeness. Hated his blue-black hair, clear blue eyes . . . resented even the soundness of his mind. He would have preferred his son's vast innocence. He would have liked to obliterate that sound mind in favor of some sort of oblivion.

As he heard Ian's voice in his head, so he heard Rebecca's; she seemed dead to him, too. ("You blame me for all this." Her eyes redder than ever. "Because I wouldn't abort him. Because I made them let him live . . . ")

She didn't believe him that he felt otherwise. That it wasn't her he hated. That it might not even be God—or science—he blamed; might not be so simple to focus his hatred. How could he tell his wife of ten years that he had never loved another person as much as he had loved his beautiful boy?

A sound behind him made him break his lost gaze from his own eyes.

Two men entered the restroom noisily behind him, and self conscious, he dried his hands hurriedly. As he did so, he caught a glimpse in the vidplate of the two men standing spread-legged before the urinals, joking loudly to each other. One jetted a little urine on the other's leg. The other returned fire. They whooped and barked and exchanged a few shoves. Urine spattered the floor. Declan started for the door. A lot of extremely rough kids in Punktown, and unlike many, he had never carried a gun to protect himself and his family.

As he reached for the door, he threw one look back, probably drawn by an extra loud yell. One boy was trying to seal his fly but the other was still pushing. The one who was pushing was in profile, and had long dark hair parted on the side, held with a red barrette, and features so attractive they were almost pretty, full lips spread wide in a bright smile against bronze skin.

For a moment, Declan hesitated at the threshold.

Someone drew the door open from the other side; an elderly Choom man entering the restroom, his huge mouth devoid of teeth so that his head looked half caved in upon itself. Declan flinched, but he quickly slipped past him and back into the store before the two friends had turned and seen him staring.

. . .

He pretended to be studying a display of powered screwdrivers in the hardware section as the youths emerged from the men's room and passed him. Moments later, he trailed in their wake, his shopping bag bouncing against his leg.

He followed them out into the mall proper, down one pipeline and into the next; following the shit through the sewers, he thought. When they entered a music store, however, he paused outside, hovered there vaguely. He watched them through the windows. At last, blankly, he turned away, and a few shops over bought himself a coffee . . . sat on another bench to sip it.

But he could only think how the three of them had sat on this very bench, numerous times. Rebecca also with coffee, and Ian always with a chocolate frosted doughnut . . . the frosting smeared around his lips which were about the only untainted part of him.

Declan stood up, dropped his full coffee into a trash zapper, and retraced his steps to the department store, and its hardware section. There, he looked at screwdrivers and hammers, knives and flammable gases and liquids. At last, he drifted into the camping section. How Ian might have loved to play in that tent they had erected.

Walking briskly now where he had drifted wraith-like only a half hour earlier, Declan returned to the music store. The boys were not there. He was partly relieved, and greatly disappointed. He started toward the food court . . . but hadn't gotten far before he saw the pair through another window, inside a trendy clothing store.

Declan entered it. Though none of what he saw appealed to him, he made a purchase before he shadowed the two young men out into the mall again. But it soon became apparent that they had had their fill of the mall for one day, as they made their way toward one of the exits into the parking levels.

The two friends descended a staircase to their garage level, rather than take an elevator; the stairwell echoed with their tramping footfalls and boomingly enclosed voices. The metal steps ended in a landing before turning and plunging downward again. Below, a wall light fluttered like a bright dying moth against the sickly hospital-green tiles.

Above them, Declan paused on the landing, rummaged in several of his bags. Then, he too plunged below. His own footfalls did not clang or reverberate; he might have been a spirit.

The boys crossed the garage, slipping between closely filed vehicles of every description, reflecting the over-rich blend of Punktown's cultures. Their own vehicle, when reached, was a much dented and scratched black hovercar with Mexican Day of the Dead skulls and figures stenciled all over it, so that it was like some jubilant hearse.

For several moments, from behind a support column, Declan anxiously watched a man in a cloned leather jacket and a woman in an orange leotard duck into their own vehicle and drive off toward the exit ramp. Then he stepped out briskly, and covered the remaining ground between himself and the black hovercar.

"Merry Christmas," said Declan behind the long-haired boy, who had just opened his door but turned toward the voice.

Declan extended his hand as if to offer a gift. He seemed more like some trick or treater at Halloween, however, as his head was covered in a sequined Mexican wrestler's mask.

The bright red flare gun was for campers, to save them if lost. He was lost. It had six chambers in a revolving cylinder. Like Randy Atlas with his helmet and his guns, Randy Atlas the avenger and protector of the innocent, he fired shot after shot directly into the face of the beautiful boy with the long hair.

The murky, low-ceilinged parking garage now danced with flicker and fire. The boy fell back howling against a neighboring vehicle, his hands batting at a pink and molten inferno of a face, like that of an enraged demon. Inside an almost liquid caul of flame, Declan thought he saw its core of flesh half cave in upon itself. He was sorry that the eyes must be melting. Sorry they would not be able to regard that face when at last it cooled. For he would live, Declan trusted. Science could see to that.

The flare gun clicked dry. Declan wheeled and ran. The beautiful boy had fallen, shrieking, between two vehicles, his sputtering glow seen underneath them. The friend, also shrieking, had ducked down out of sight as well, though unscathed.

As he ran—the bag containing the Randy Atlas doll still tucked under one arm, clutched tightly against his chest like a rescued infant—Declan no longer saw fire reflected on the skins of the many vehicles, cold and ranked like coffins in these vaults. Fire no longer glittered on the sequins of the ugly mask he wore over his handsome face, or on the tears in the eyes that shone through it.

For Colin

THE PRESSMAN

Immanuel Glint didn't like the new pressman. It was a robot, of course, and in appearance it put Glint in mind of a mating pair of praying mantises that had been sculpted from steel by Salvador Dali whilst on hallucinogens. At least the many-limbed monstrosity had only one head (which again reminded Glint of romantic praying mantises, since it was the female's habit to chew the head off her lover while in the throes of passion). The new machine was immaculately clean—unnaturally so, as if it were what a robot would look like when it went to heaven. None of the dents, scratches, ink stains on its armored skin that the other pressmen sported. It gave the new pressman a preening, prissy look, in Glint's mind.

Of course, he had to admit his feelings were tainted by the perhaps too-vivid imagination of an artist, since Glint was the art director for Paxton Printing.

He approached the pressman now, a chip of information in his hand. The robot had interfaced with its press by inserting its connectors into the press's control board. Glint saw sheets of paper, letterheads, passing out the other end on a conveyor belt, and alighting into a catcher. The vibrating catcher jogged them into a neat stack.

"Good morning, Manny," the robot said to him in a pleasant male voice (though it had no mouth), sounding to Glint irritatingly like the talking action figure Randy Atlas and swiveling its insect-like head to face him. "You must be bringing that job you need me to run for the new catalog."

"Hi, Buddy," Glint said. If there was one nickname he hated worse than Manny, it was Buddy. The Press Supervisor, Scott, had christened the new worker. "Yes, I have it here." He held up the chip for the huge blank eyes to see.

"Excellent, Manny. You may insert it into my secondary port—don't worry, you won't disturb me."

"Thanks . . . I am in a bit of a hurry for these samples," he said with a twinge of bitterness, feeding the chip into the automaton. "Deadlines, you know," he continued in a murmur. He added, "Unrealistic deadlines."

"I'm sorry to hear you're feeling stressed, Manny. Who is imposing these insensitive deadlines on you?"

"Maya Gendron, from the Corp Head. She's visiting here this week, too . . . breathing down my neck." Glint couldn't believe he was unburdening himself to a machine that was only programmed to banter in the way that the intercom was programmed to play lulling music. But it was like talking to himself, so he vented further by adding, "She's a tyrant. Ugly little troll of a tyrant who could benefit from the company of a man."

"My goodness," said Buddy sympathetically. "She sounds terrible; I'll be sure to stay out of her way. Well, Manny, I'll give you a beep as soon as your samples are ready, and I'll get right on them."

"Great—thanks," he said, turning back toward the offices and his little one-man art department area.

It wasn't even an hour before Buddy beeped, and summoned Glint back to the vast press room. The robot waved a slender bird-like claw at a dozen neat stacks of printed Bar Mitzvah invitations for the latest dealer catalog. "That was quick," Glint had to compliment the sparkling machine, and he examined one of the cards. He frowned at it for a few moments, then motioned Buddy to come closer. "Hey, Buddy, this green is very different from the one in my design. Has your system been color-checked for accuracy?"

Buddy peered over his shoulder at the card. "Oh yes, my system is quite accurate. It's just, to be honest, Manny, I felt the green in this design was a little on the yellowish side. I really admire this artwork, but I found that a bluish green had a more agreeable effect."

Glint looked up at the machine slowly. "Hey . . . now you listen . . . I'm the art director, do you understand that? You can't change my color scheme, here!"

"But, Manny, with all respect . . . "

"No. No. You do not change my designs! This is ridiculous!" Glint reinspected the sample. "Look at this—look! These children! Some of them have brown faces . . . "

"I thought there wasn't enough ethnic diversity before, Manny."

"They're Jewish kids—in Israel!"

"There are black Jewish people, you know, Manny," Buddy seemed to scold him gently.

"*What?* You are just a machine, a *tool!* You do not, do *not* redesign my work, or so help me I'll have you thrown in the trash zapper! Do you comprehend me?"

"Well, if you insist, Manny. I was only trying to help . . . "

"Shut up," Glint growled. "Throw out that dung, run my job again, and don't ever tamper with my color schemes again!" With that, he stormed toward the offices . . . but he stopped long enough to shout back, "And don't call me Manny! To you, I'm Mr. Glint!"

A little over a half hour later, Glint was again beeped by Buddy to come out to the press area. Glint saved the program he was working on, and strode with determination out to the plant—determined not to accept any more insubordination from the new "equipment."

He almost stopped in his tracks when he saw Maya Gendron standing beside Buddy at the end of his press—Maya Gendron, the Chief Art Director at Corporate Headquarters on Earth.

"Hello, Immanuel," said Maya, examining two samples of the Bar Mitzvah invitation. "Buddy was just showing me your card. Nice work." Glint drew nearer to her. She was comparing two different cards, he realized—his version, and Buddy's. Maya went on, "I have to say, though, that I prefer this first color scheme. The blue-green is much prettier, and the mix of different children is a nice touch . . . "

Glint couldn't believe his ears. He glared at the robot, but its face was unreadable. He could feel the blood rising in his own. "Buddy, I ordered you to throw out that first batch, didn't I?"

"What are you talking about, Immanuel?" Maya said. "I just told you, I prefer . . . "

"But, Maya! I gave this . . . this insolent piece of *junk* specific instructions . . . "

"I truly hate to complain, Miss Gendron," Buddy cut in with his soothing voice, "but Mr. Glint has been most unpleasant with me, when all I am trying to do is give our customers the best possible product . . . "

"That's enough!" Glint bellowed at the device. "Shut up, shut up!"

"Mr. Glint!" Maya huffed.

Then suddenly, Glint heard his own voice speaking . . . but it was not coming from his own mouth. It was a recording, he realized, that the robot had somehow made of his words earlier, and now played back. The recording said, "Maya Gendron, from the Corp Head. She's visiting here this week, too . . . breathing down my neck. She's a tyrant. Ugly little troll of a tyrant who could benefit from the company of a man."

When the recording was over, Buddy added, "As you can see, Mr. Glint can be most unpleasant to work with, Maya."

Maya's head cleanly swivelled on her neck as if she were a robot herself, so as to face Glint. "I can see that now, Buddy," she said icily. "I can see that very clearly."

Immanuel Glint could find no further words to say. Buddy had stolen them. And, of course, his job as well.

THE PALACE OF NOTHINGNESS

Titus stopped for lunch at J. J. Redhook's Crab Cabin. Writhing masses of these "crabs"—actually more of a lobster-sized cousin to the silverfish with porcelain-white armor—waited in mesh holding bins in the water outside the cabin, bobbing half-submerged. This body of water was a large cooling tank formerly used by the now closed down Plastech Foundries. These days, the above-mentioned white-crabs called its murky depths home, seeded with the help of Mr. Redhook, who also grew a sort of tendriled weed in the pool, which when cooked had a noodle-like consistency and agreeably salty taste. Titus had had a bowl of this weed plus a single pale ale. Now, he left the Crab Cabin with a large coffee-to-go.

He stood at the fenced perimeter of the former cooling basin, sipping his coffee, which steamed in the chilly air. He loved a good coffee but found that even bad coffee like this had a certain junk-food charm; unacceptable at a nice restaurant but perfectly fine for carnivals, park concession stands, crab cabins and their ilk. The cold, dreamily slurping waters of the large tank steamed as well, in great clouds around the legs of J. J. Redhook, which half-projected out over the pool. The white noodle-like weed mostly grew at the pool's bottom but here and there, tangles of it like the hair of drowned women spread out over the surface. The red paint and glowing windows of the wooden Crab Cabin were a friendly warmth in the misty, towering grayness of the surrounding city of Punktown.

By profession, Titus found the Crab Cabin interesting. He found the looming Plastech Foundries, in whose shadow J. J. Redhook dwelled as a little red parasite feasting off its remains, even more compelling. He was a Properties Investigator for one of Paxton's leading real estate companies. Space was at a premium in Punktown, which could only build up, out and down so much. He scouted out, examined and initiated the purchase of troubled or abandoned property that could be changed into a new housing development where an old one had burned, a new mall where an earlier had failed, a parking garage for a Spartan, icy office block where an outdated factory had once churned with greasy, sweating life.

He took in the cityscape which all but walled up the sky alive, as softly out of focus as a distant mountain range. His reaction to a failing or failed structure was curious, even to him. He loved buildings, architecture. It pained him to see a beautiful Choom theater which predated Earth colonization shut down after a hundred and fifty years. But another part of him perked up in eagerness at the opportunity this presented. A darkened school in which children would no longer swarm energetically, a plant like Paxton Printing now hollowed out and stripped down like a flayed whale while its robot workers were recycled and its live laborers despaired for another place to make their living—these images filled Titus with melancholy. There was nothing quite so lonely as a deserted building . . . unless that was a deserted house.

And yet, these buildings provided his livelihood. And when he encountered them, they made his heart beat faster, and brought out in him something like a fierce possessiveness to stake a claim on them before someone else did. He was a hunter who mourned for his prey, but was very good at tracking it down.

It wasn't the Plastech Foundries—with its many sealed-up windows like myriad blinded eyes—he was here to have a look at today, however (its future was tied up in complex litigation; he had already checked) . . . but another structure, in the same general neighborhood, and he had begun drifting in that direction now.

He had discovered the building while renting an hour on a commercial satellite through his home computer to scour Punktown's secondary industrial sector, mostly given over to office and warehouse space these days. He had laid various templates of the city over his satellite view of the area, trying to ascertain the structure's ownership. One map would seem to indicate that it was within the boundry lines of an old Choom textile mill, but another appeared to show that it was an outer building of an early Earth-owned steelworks complex. One template claimed it was not there at all. This had led Titus to call up earlier satellite photos of the district. There was the building, in every view, dating back decades, and just as enigmatic in each one. Was that its vehicle-filled parking lot in one view, or was that another parking lot for the steelworks? His computer could pin no name, no label to the building, which despite its good size seemed to have reposed in a kind of serene anonymity through many years of growth and decline.

Finally he had pored over the very first survey shots of the Choom city which Punktown had swallowed up, shots taken during the earliest colonization efforts. And the building seemed to be there, but maybe not. It looked familiar, but different. As Titus went back over the various pictures, it seemed to him the building had changed subtly or even drastically in appearance over the years. Different owners, refitting it for their own needs, or a succession of different buildings built on the same spot?

In the earliest shot, the mill or factory had a good half dozen great brick chimneys, and maybe it was thick smoke from these that gave the structure a darkened blurry look, smudged, as if it had been caught in a photograph while moving very quickly.

But now there it was, before him, and even though he had only seen it from on high on his computer, and it had been altered over the decades, he recognized it instantly. It raised itself above outlying sheds and generator buildings of the steelworks, its flank scaled in a mosaic of red brick that looked damp in the misted air. It had few windows, on this face at least, some sealed up but others just nakedly black. He noted none were broken, however; they must be transparent ceramic, because Titus couldn't imagine the neighbors would let them go unshattered. It still possessed several chimneys, if less grand than the castle towers of its past, and a rust-streaked metal dome or cupola atop one section that might once have stored gas or some liquid, or only been cosmetic. Might it still store something; might the place still be vital, in operation? Why had he assumed upon his discovery of the building that it was abandoned? Well, certainly, most of the factories in this sector had been abandoned over the past twenty years. But as he neared it, he didn't find anything that would counter his first impression. It resembled nothing so much as a ghost ship—however well preserved—that had spontaneously and unaccountably resurfaced from the bottom of the sea. A sunken ship with its name long erased.

Wandering around it at a respectful orbit, he searched for a way inside, if this were possible today. One side door of metal was firmly shut. A pair of dented and paint-chipped loading dock doors were locked as well. On these, he noted, there was a symbol stenciled in white, either a company logo or a character in a language he wasn't familiar with. On the opposite side of the building he found another door, and he put his hand on its latch with no real optimism. It clicked casually. It was unlocked.

He hesitated. In the dirty glass, he saw his own face reflected back at him. The handsome features of a black man of forty-one, with his still-smooth skin the lustrous deep brown of a chestnut. Behind the lenses of his glasses, the whites of his eyes were a mellow ivory like old piano keys. He thought he had a sad face. It watched him expectantly, as if another man stood on the other side of that door waiting for him to open it and let him out.

He didn't know if he would be trespassing, but he could claim sincerely to ignorance if caught. He was here to explore, wasn't he? He had let himself into many a deserted edifice before. He pulled the door open, and it didn't even squeal.

But again, he hesitated on the threshold. It was gloomy beyond, though gray light came in through those windows that were uncovered. He produced his flashlight from his trouser pocket . . . and he was mindful of the licensed handgun he carried in a shoulder holster hidden by his overcoat. Punktown was a rough city even in its less derelict regions. Abandoned buildings were an attractive shelter for much of the city's considerable homeless population, especially when winter was nearing.

Back at J. J. Redhook, he had asked the counter man who served him what he knew of the building.

"Used to be a ceramics plant, I thought I heard somebody say once. If it's the one I'm thinking of, it's out of service now. One of our kids who harvest the weed went in there one afternoon with his buddies, he told me, and they ran into this mutant that was living in there. A mutant or some offworlder—who knows? They said the thing looked like a devil crossed with a nightmare, and it chased them the hell out of there."

"I heard about that place," another counter man had spoken up. "They made chemicals there, I think . . . for, uh, photography. And there's an old guy who lives in there, just one old man. He must've put on a mask or used a holograph projector or something to run those punks out of there. If it was that moron Brandon and his boys, I'd have run them out myself."

So as he stood in the open doorway, Titus didn't know whether to be on the lookout for an elderly homeless man, or some dangerous mutant or alien. Maybe, he thought, trying to joke with himself, it was some elderly alien mutant. More than likely—and as logic would dictate—the building was host to numerous lost souls. Well, he'd encountered them before; had even had to play rough before. He thumbed on his beam and stepped inside.

It was an open lobby or courtyard of sorts which tunneled upwards through the center of the structure. The high ceiling of it, though nearly lost in murk, was the interior of that dome he had seen outside. The lobby's walls were also of brick, and arched interior windows looked down from them. Metal footbridges with meshed safety railings ran across the vertical tunnel, connecting one side to the other on four levels, but no stairs or elevator were in view. Titus crossed the bottom floor to a door of metal. His dark reflection in its narrow window again looked like someone on the other side peeking through at him, until he shone his light on the glass and banished his own ghost.

As he had hoped there was a stairwell beyond it, and he began to ascend. It would have been pitch black in this enclosed space if not for his torch, and he was grateful when he came to the first landing that it opened out into the lobby again, with its dim patches of sunlight. He stepped out onto the first of the metal footbridges, stopped half way across to finish his coffee. Rather than carry the empty cup with him, he politely set it down on the edge of the walkway, then continued across. Another door opened to him. He entered a long hallway of brick with an arched ceiling, and an elevator door close at hand. Though it might still have a long-lasting emergency power cell, he didn't take the chance of using it and strolled further down the tunnel-like corridor, letting his beam and his whim guide him.

One of the hall's doors he peered in through let him into a large room filled with great dark hulks of complex machinery. Even stepping close to one of these imposing entities—cautiously, as if he feared it would suddenly spring into gnashing, clanging life— he wouldn't venture an interpretation as to their original function. A pass of his beam along brick walls revealed a few charts, schematics or diagrams of some sort, though he saw no evidence of written language that might indicate the origins of the building's last owners.

As he proceeded along the second level, and then the third, Titus was struck by the relative cleanness of the plant. There had been no fires that had gutted it, no chemical spills that had necessitated its evacuation (though physical calamity seldom was the reason for a factory's demise, economic calamity being more wrathful than acts of God). But more than that, there were no signs of habitation by the homeless and disenfranchised. None of the usual graffiti coating the walls, scattered beer and wine bottles, paraphernalia of drug use. No stink of urine, no garbage, indeed no rodents or bugs that would be drawn to the refuse of such invasion. A place this big should be swarming with various tribes of the homeless, competing nations of the homeless in a kind of microcosm.

What was keeping them away? Granted, the place had an eerie, unsettling stillness. But the people who dwelt in Punktown were not distinguished for their meekness. It was tooth and claw in Punktown, whether one wore soiled rags or a five-piece suit. What about this place could so disturb a gang who might desire a spacious hang out, or a band of angry mutants, that they would leave it pristine, uninhabited? Had there in fact been some dangerous spill that Titus was blissfully and perhaps lethally unaware of? Or was the building just so skillfully anonymous that these people were simply unaware of its existence?

He had now reached the fourth level, paused on the footbridge that spanned the lobby to gaze down into it, from this height a brick abyss. He could tell by the soft pattering against those windows that looked outside and the further graying of the light that a rain had started to fall.

Wait. He leaned against the railing, craned his neck out into space to study the walkways below this uppermost one. He had left his empty coffee cup on the first footbridge. It was no longer there.

So he wasn't alone. Again he became conscious of the heaviness of his gun nestled to his ribs. What was it, then? Some withered little troll of a man? Some demon with a face of fiery rage?

He continued across the bridge, continued with his exploration, determined to briefly take in this last floor before he departed to make an initial report. His pushed his glasses up the bridge of his nose. They were recording everything he saw and heard, so that he would have a record of his investigation to present with his report.

He entered at last into another spacious, if rather low-ceilinged room filled with Cyclopean machinery. Bundles of cables snaked up walls, across the ceiling like living roots or vines run wild, trailing off into gloom. Everything was sepulchrally still. And yet, there was in fact a faint ticking sound that Titus, holding his breath upon discerning it, thought might be the rain against a window. But he saw no window. An insect, scrabbling across the floor? As he turned his head, seeking its source, his gaze fell on one of the machines. He made his way to it, pointing his light. When he reached it, he shut the light off. Because there was a subtle light coming from a tight little cranny of the machine, a pale glow deep inside it. Stealthily, he pressed his eye to the opening.

A single glass vacuum tube of some type, emitting a firefly's soft green luminesence. And also, one tiny piston working up and down, creating the cricket-like ticking sound he had heard. That was all. It was like finding one last ember glowing in a burned building . . . the last dying beats of a dinosaur's heart.

Something else caught his attention as he straightened up. His beam was reflected back at him from the rear wall. As he wound through the machinery to reach it, he determined it was made of glass colored a dark yellow, like a wall of amber.

It seemed very thick and it was dusty; he rubbed it with his coat's sleeve, then pressed both his light and glasses to its surface, wishing he had brought his bulkier recording glasses that permitted him to see in the absence of light. Was that another room on the opposite side of the murky glass wall?

Abruptly, he shut his flashlight off, and jolted back from the wall. Just as the beam had begun to pass across the legs of a narrow cot like a prisoner might sleep in, pushed against the back of the small room beyond, a dim light had begun to grow inside the chamber. It continued to grow, casting a yellow illumination from the glass across Titus and the surrounding machinery. He took several more steps backward.

And now, a figure that must have been in the cell all along came forward from the bed to the glass. It was silhouetted by the diffused light behind it. He could tell only that it was a woman, naked, too dark to see the face of but her outline attractive. The figure pressed the palms of its outstretched arms to the glass. Again, Titus jolted back. It seemed to be putting its face, now, to the wall . . . to be peering out at him . . .

Inexplicably, he turned and fled. His coat snagged on a machine and he tore the fabric in wrenching free of its bite.

His footfalls clanged across one metal footbridge. Another. The stairwells were too dark; he nearly lost his footing in one and plunged to his death . . .

Outside at last, he lifted his face to the mounting rain, which seemed to fall from the glistening brick skin of the building looming above him.

. . .

In his living room, Titus found a woman reclining on her side on the sofa, her legs drawn up, dressed in a cozy over-large sweatshirt, black sweat pants that clung to shapely legs, socks warming her feet. A mug of coffee rested on the floor within her reach, her head turned toward the vidtank. She didn't appear to have heard him come in, or was too absorbed in the program she was watching to acknowledge his presence. And yet, the VT was not on; the screen she stared at was blank. It was not his VT Titus had forgotten to turn off when he left, but his holograph projector. He touched a keypad and the attractive black woman vanished . . . just as she had nearly two years ago now. Even her cup of coffee disappeared.

He poked his head into one of the two bedrooms, but no, it was empty; there was no apparition of his son in there. That boy was now back on Earth. Titus had left his son's posters on the walls, and the small bed still reposed in the corner.

Tossing his torn and sodden coat over the back of a chair, he sat at his desk and inserted the tiny pellet from his recording glasses into his computer system. His screen saver showed an old-fashioned wrecker's ball swinging into an anthropomorphic, cartoon-faced cathedral that winced and yelped and was diminished with each goofy-sounding blow. Now, his recording came on, and he fast-forwarded through much of it.

He paused several times while viewing the part in which he had peeked into the machine with its soft inner phosphoresence. Maybe it was the poor light, which he tried to make corrections for in the image, but the miniature piston did not show up clearly. It was a dark smudge or blur, as if it had been moving much too quickly for the eye to follow, though this had not been the case as he recalled it.

At last he viewed the portion of the recording where he had approached— and gazed into—the glass wall.

He wanted to pause on the dark face of that imprisoned phantasm. Zoom in on it. Lighten the image. He dreaded what might be revealed to him there; what eyes had gazed upon him.

But he never saw it. Where he had before been able to see into the glass, the recording remembered a different view. The wall was still aglow, as if its very material gave off light. But there appeared to be no room beyond it. All he saw, like cracks running throughout its surface, was a silhouetted latticework of dark veins. The thickest branches of these could even, when he zoomed in, be seen to subtly pulsate.

He thought of a praying mantis that pretends it is a flower. But that was perhaps too violent an image. Maybe, then, a moth whose wings imitate the color and texture of bark.

But he thought also of dead things. And what they might leave behind.

The next morning, he was not quick in preparing for work. His supervisor called him, but was amicable enough about it. Seeing that Titus was still in his pajamas and robe, he told him to take the day off if he wasn't feeling well.

"Oh—what was up with that place you were going to go have a peek at?" his supervisor asked him, before signing off. "Did you ever make it over there, yesterday?"

"It's nothing," Titus said quietly, gazing into the screen, wondering what it was he was protecting or preserving. "There is no building there."

THE RUSTED GATES OF HEAVEN

Ahead of them as they made their way into the wooded grounds ran the Bellakees' twin pets Hapi and Gbekre, hamadryas baboons whose fluffy capes—and indeed, entire bodies—had been dyed a brilliant blue, and their eyes a metallic silver. Interesting hieroglyphics had been shaved into their fur and branded on their long dog-like faces.

Mendeni was familiar with Hapi, a baboon-headed god of ancient Egypt, but Mr. Bellakee had to explain that Gbekre was a baboon-headed god of the Baule tribe of old Earth's Ivory Coast, whose job it was to judge the dead. Effigies in his likeness, Bellakee had gone on—knowing that as an archeologist Mendeni would be interested—had often been found to be stained in the blood of sacrifices.

Mendeni thought the baboons would have been impressive enough without their embellishments, but he wasn't about to give voice to his opinion when the Earth-born couple were being so gracious.

The great monkeys galloped off, crashing through and disappearing into the thick underbrush of the dense forest. The Bellakees had no fear that they would lose their pets, as their entire sprawling estate was surrounded by a high invisible wall of energy. Following a worn path with his hosts, Mendeni was nostalgically moved to recall picnics in the woods with his parents and brothers in his youth. It was hard for him to believe, even though he was a young man, that those forested areas had ever been as extensive as they were. Of course, everything from a playground to a summer's day seemed so much larger and longer to a child, but he knew it had more to do with the accelerated growth of the colony city of Paxton over the last two decades. But Paxton, or Punktown as it had come to be called, had existed before his birth, so that even though he was himself a Choom, native to this world Oasis, he had never dwelled in anything but a city of the Earth people. The Choom town that had preceded it was merely the grain of sand that the black pearl of Punktown had formed around.

The ground was spongy with a bed of orange-brown needles, the path dappled blue and gold with rustling shadow. The house where they had lunched was lost behind them. After the house, which had struck Mendeni as some eccentric but fascinating art museum, he was not surprised to find that the grounds beyond it had been much landscaped and coiffed into equally ostentatious gardens . . . but now they had entered into a more natural section of the dark woods.

He was already acquainted with his surroundings in a way, however, as he had looked at satellite pictures of the property previously. That was what had started it all, in fact. Paxton University's history department had been granted limited use of the satellite in order to search for the ruins or traces of historical sites in what little forest remained in this region. He had been discouraged from viewing corporate-owned properties at anything but a discreet distance, so he had reluctantly turned away from his puzzled examination of an oddly unfocused factory his wandering scans had chanced upon in Punktown's second largest industrial sector, and he had been flat-out forbidden to scan private property . . . but when he saw what was on the Bellakees' land he couldn't restrain himself from approaching them. Luckily for him, they had welcomed his interest . . . made him their guest today for the first time.

"Here we are, my boy," announced Mr. Bellakee proudly, as if he had installed the relic on the grounds himself. He turned to grin at Mendeni, his smile white as paper in his tanned face. Mrs. Bellakee was smiling more subtly, as befitted her aura of reserve. She was a strikingly beautiful woman in her early thirties, younger than her husband by two decades. Lipstick as red as her glasses were dark, the two seeming to define her face. Mendeni had found his eyes constantly returning to that face and her fit, graceful body despite all the art in the house and flowers outside it. But his eyes were now drawn to the object his host indicated, as the trees seemed to part like curtains to reveal it.

It was an idol built by his own people, a century before the arrival of Earth colonists; a temple of the Raloom faith, of which Mendeni's own paternal grandfather had been a member. The idol/temple was in the form of a huge head and shoulders, rising up from the ground as if the rest of its titan's body might be buried below. The great bust was entirely fashioned out of iron, once a majestic black but now corroded to a rusty red. The Chooms were outwardly identical to the Earth people except for their mouths, which spread back nearly to their ears. This feature was reflected in the iron face, the mouth held in a huge solemn frown. It would be difficult to tell if the eyes depicted were meant to be open or closed through the rough-textured coat of corrosion, had Mendeni not already known that the eyes of Raloom were eternally gazing into the soul of each and every one of his worshipers.

"What do you think?" asked Mrs. Bellakee in a respectful whisper, as if they stood in a great cathedral. She stood so close beside him that their shoulders touched. He found himself deeply inhaling her perfume. "He's quite handsome, isn't he? I think he looks rather like you, actually."

"It's magnificent," he managed, his attention torn between the two works of art. "I've never seen one whole before except in a museum. Again . . . I really have to thank you two. This is a true thrill for me . . . "

"Come inside it," invited Mr. Bellakee, leading the way. Grinning, waving beckoningly. The others followed him as if he were a priest conducting them within. There were metal steps behind the iron sphinx, ascending into the back of its head. The metal doors opened smoothly—and Mendeni realized that they were newly fashioned doors on clean new hinges.

How could they alter the relic like that? How could they tamper with it so? But before he could verbalize his concerns in some polite way, the three of them were inside the temple.

"Oh my God," Mendeni muttered under his breath.

It was to Mendeni as if they had scooped out the brain of one man to implant an alien brain in its place. Gone was the circular altar that should be in here. Instead, there was a circular bed. Jars of aromatic oil burned sultrily, and there was a vidcamera mounted on a tripod.

Mendeni turned to his hosts in horror, uncomprehending, and saw that Mrs. Bellakee was pulling her thin summer dress up over her head. Her sunglasses were gone but the lipstick smile remained. Now she was as naked as a goddess or a sacrifice in the wavering light from the oil jars, so that their glow and aroma seemed to be generated by her body.

"I've seen you looking at me," she said, again in a whisper, as if in mocking awe of the place.

Mendeni glanced at Mr. Bellakee, who rested a reassuring hand on his arm. "Don't worry, my boy, I'm not asking to join in. I'll watch from the house."

He gestured at the camera. "My wife liked your look when she saw you on the vidphone . . . and I'm sure you liked hers."

"But . . ." Mendeni began. His eyes darted back to that glorious flesh against the rough rusted walls. Oddly, the decaying metal seemed more transitory, the soft flesh more lasting.

Bellakee patted his arm again and kissed his wife's cheek on the way out. Then Mrs. Bellakee lay back on the bed, propping up one leg. Smiling at him, both horizontally and vertically. Waiting for him, an offering to the new goddess.

At last, after staring at her a while longer, Mendeni was almost surprised to find his fingers working at his shirt's seal strip. Outside, he heard one of the two frolicking baboons grunt loudly, wildly at the other.

As he lay atop her, he found he couldn't look at her beautiful face any longer. Instead, he lifted his gaze to the curved walls. The inner skull of the great Raloom . . . who, though he had been lobotomized, though his eyes were on the outside of the temple and crusted in decay, seemed to be gazing sternly and despairingly straight into Mendeni's soul.

1: KEEPING UP WITH THE JONESES

They had made it snow again this weekend, as they would every weekend until Christmas. Not on the weekdays, hampering the traffic of workers, or so much today as to inconvenience the shoppers; rather, enough to inspire consumers to further holiday spirit, and further purchases.

High atop the Vat, a machine that to some might resemble an oil tanker of old standing on its prow, Magnesium Jones crouched back amongst the conduits and exhaust ports like an infant gargoyle on the verge of crowning. His womb was a steamy one; the heat from the blowers would have cooked a birther like a lobster. Jones was naked, his shoulder pressed against the hood of a whirring fan. When he had instant coffee or soup to make he would boil water by resting a pot atop the fan's cap. He was not wearing clothes lest they catch fire.

Not all the cultures were designed to be so impervious to heat; some, rather, were unperturbed by extreme cold. On the sixth terrace of the plant proper, which faced the Vat, a group of cultures took break in the open air, a few of them naked and turning their faces up to the powdery blizzard invitingly. It had been an alarming development for many, the Plant's management allowing cultures to take break. It suggested they needed consideration, even concern.

Jones squinted through the blowing veils of snow. He recognized a number of the laborers. Though all were bald, and all cloned from a mere half dozen masters, their heads were tattooed in individual designs so as to distinguish them from each other. Numbers and letters usually figured into these designs—codes. Some had their names tattooed on their foreheads, and all tattoos were colored according to department: violet for Shipping, gray for the Vat, blue for Cryogenics, red for the Ovens, and so on. Magnesium Jones's tattoo was of the last color. But there was also some artistry employed in the tattoo designs. They might portray familiar landmarks from Punktown, or from Earth where most of Punktown's colonists originated, at least in ancestry. Animals, celebrities, sports stars. Magnesium Jones's tattoo was a ring of flame around his head like a corona, with a few black letters and a bar code in the flames like the charred skeleton of a burnt house.

Some artistry, some fun and flourish, was also employed in the naming of the cultures. On the terrace he recognized Sherlock Jones, Imitation Jones and Basketball Jones. He thought he caught a glimpse of Subliminal Jones heading back inside. Waxlips Jones sat on the edge of the railing, dangling his legs over the street far below. Jones Jones held a steaming coffee. Huckleberry Jones was in subdued conversation with Digital Jones. Copyright Jones and M.I. Jones emerged from the building to join the rest.

Watching them, Magnesium Jones missed his own conversations with some of them, missed the single break that he looked forward to through the first ten hours of the work day. But did he miss the creatures themselves, he wondered? He felt a kinship with other cultures, an empathy for their lives, their situations, in a general sense . . . but that might merely be because he saw himself in them, felt for his own life, his own situation. Sometimes the kinship felt like brotherhood. But affection? Friendship? Love? He wasn't sure if his feelings could be defined in that way. Or was it just that the birthers felt no more strongly, merely glossed and romanticized their own pale feelings?

But Jones did not share the plight of the robot, the android . . . the question of whether they could consider themselves alive, of whether they could aspire to actual emotion. He felt very much alive. He felt some very strong emotions. Anger. Hatred. These feelings, unlike love, were not at all ambiguous.

He turned away from the snowy vista of Plant and city beyond, shivering, glad to slip again into his nest of thrumming heat. From an insulated box he had stolen and dragged up here he took some clothing. Some of it was fireproof, some not. The long black coat, with its broad lapels turned up to protect his neck from the snow, had a heated mesh in the lining. Worn gloves, and he pulled a black ski hat over his bald head, as much to conceal his tattoo as to shield his naked scalp from snow. He stared at his wrist, willing numbers to appear there. They told him the time. A feature all the cultures at the Plant possessed, to help them time their work efficiently. He had an appointment, a meeting, but he had plenty of time yet to get there.

As much as he scorned his former life in the Plant, there were some behaviors too ingrained to shake. Magnesium Jones was ever punctual.

. . .

Walking the street, Jones slipped on a pair of dark glasses. In the vicinity of the Plant it would be easy to recognize him as a culture. The six masters had all been birther males, criminals condemned to death (they had been paid for the rights to clone them for industrial labor). Under current law it was illegal to clone living human beings. Clones of living beings might equate themselves with their originals. Clones of living beings might thus believe they had certain rights.

Wealthy people stored clones of themselves in case of mishap, cloned families and friends, illegally. Everyone knew that. For all Jones knew, the president of the Plant might be a clone himself. But still, somehow, the cultures were cultures. Still a breed of their own.

Behind the safe shields of his dark lenses, Jones studied the faces of people he passed on the street. Birthers, Christmas shopping, but their faces closed off in hard privacy. The closer birthers were grouped together, the more cut off they became from each other in that desperate animal need for their own territory, even if it extended no further than their scowls and stern, downcast eyes.

Distant shouted chants made him turn his head, though he already knew their source. There was always a group of strikers camped just outside the barrier of the Plant. Tents, smoke from barrel fires, banners rippling in the snowy gusts. There was one group on a hunger strike, emaciated as concentration camp prisoners. A few weeks ago, one woman had self-immolated. Jones had heard screams, and come to the edge of his high hideout to watch. He had marveled at the woman's calm as she sat cross-legged, a black silhouette with her head already charred bald at the center of a small inferno . . . had marveled at how she did not run or cry out, panic or lose her resolve. He admired her strength, her commitment. It was a sacrifice for her fellow human beings, an act which would suggest that the birthers felt a greater brotherhood than the cultures did, after all. But then, their society encouraged such feelings, whereas the cultures were discouraged from friendship, companionship, affection.

Then again, maybe the woman had just been insane.

. . .

To reach the basement pub Jones edged through a narrow tunnel of dripping ceramic brick, the floor a metal mesh . . . below which he heard dark liquid rushing. A section of wall on the right opened up, blocked by chicken wire, and in a dark room like a cage a group of mutants or aliens or mutated aliens gazed out at him as placid as animals waiting to eat or be eaten (and maybe that was so, too); they were so tall their heads scraped the ceiling, thinner than skeletons, with cracked faces that looked shattered and glued back together. Their hair was cobwebs blowing, though to Jones the clotted humid air down here seemed to pool around his legs.

A throb of music grew until he opened a metal door and it exploded in his face like a boobytrap. Slouched heavy backs at a bar, a paunchy naked woman doing a slow grinding dance atop a billiard table. Jones did not so much as glance at her immense breasts, aswirl in smoky colored light like planets; the Plant's cultures had no sexual cravings, none of them even female.

At a corner table sat a young man with red hair, something seldom seen naturally. He smiled and made a small gesture. Jones headed toward him, slipping off his shades. He watched the man's hands atop the table; was there a gun resting under the newspaper?

The man's hair was long and greasy, his beard scruffy and inadequate, but he was good-looking and his voice was friendly. "Glad you decided to come. I'm Nevin Parr." They shook hands. "Sit down. Drink?"

"Coffee."

The man motioned to a waitress, who brought them both a coffee. The birther wasn't dulling his senses with alcohol, either, Jones noted.

"So how did you meet my pal Moodring?" asked the birther, lifting his chipped mug for a cautious sip.

"On the street. He gave me money for food in turn for a small favor."

"So now you move a little drug for him sometimes. Hold hot weapons for him sometimes."

Jones frowned at his gloved hands, knotted like mating tarantulas. "I'm disappointed. I thought Moodring was more discreet than that."

"Please don't be angry at him; I told you, we're old pals. So, anyway . . . should I call you Mr. Jones?" Parr smiled broadly. "Magnesium? Or is it Mag?"

"It's all equally meaningless."

"I've never really talked with a culture before."

"We prefer 'shadow'."

"All right. Mr. Shadow. So how old are you?"

"Five."

"Pretty bright for a five year old."

"Memory-encoded long-chain molecules in a brain drip. I knew my job before I even got out of the tank."

"Of course. Five, huh? So that's about the age when they start replacing you guys, right? They say that's when you start getting uppity . . . losing control. That's why you escaped from the Plant, isn't it? You knew your time was pretty much up."

"Yes. I knew what was coming. Nine cultures in my crew were removed in two days. They were all about my age. My supervisor told me not to worry, but I knew . . ."

"Cleaning house. Bringing in the fresh meat. They kill them, don't they? The old cultures. They incinerate them."

"Yes."

"I heard you killed two men in escaping. Two real men."

"Moodring is very talkative."

"It isn't just him. You killed two men. I heard they were looking for you. Call you 'hothead,' because of your tattoo. Can I see it?"

"That wouldn't be wise in public, would it?"

"You're not the only escaped clone around here, but you're right, we have work that demands discretion. Just that I like tattoos; I have some myself. See?" He rolled up a sleeve, exposing a dark mass that Jones only gave a half glance. "I hear they get pretty wild with your tattoos. Someone must enjoy himself."

"Robots do the tattooing. They're just accessing clip art files. Most times it has nothing to do with our function or the name that was chosen for us. It's done to identify us, and probably for the amusement of our human coworkers. Decorative for them, I suppose."

"You haven't been caught, but you're still living in this area, close to the Plant. You must be stealthy. That's a useful quality. So where are you staying?"

"That's none of your concern. When you need me you leave a message with Moodring. When he sees me around he'll tell me. Moodring doesn't need to know where I live, either."

"He your friend, Moodring, or is it just business?"

"I have no friends."

"That's too bad. I think you and I could be friends."

"You don't know how much that means to me. So, why did you want me? Because I'm a culture? And if so, why?"

"Again . . . because you killed two men escaping the Plant. I know you can kill again, given the right incentive."

"I'm glad we've got to that. So what's my incentive?"

"Five thousand munits."

"For killing a man? That's pretty cheap."

"Not for a culture who never made a coin in his life. Not for a culture who lives in the street somewhere."

"So who am I to kill?"

"More incentive for you," said Nevin Parr, who smiled far too much for Jones's taste. Jones seldom smiled. He had heard that smiling was a trait left over from the animal ancestry of the birthers; it was a threatening baring of the fangs, in origin. The idea amused him, made him feel more evolved for so seldom contorting his own face in that way. After his smiling heavy pause, Parr continued, "The man we have in mind is Ephraim Mayda."

Jones raised his hairless eyebrows, grunted, and stirred his coffee. "He's a union captain. Well guarded. Martyr material."

"Never mind the repercussions; he's trouble for the people I'm working for, and worth the lesser trouble of his death."

Jones lifted his eyes in sudden realization. He almost plunged his hand into his coat for the pistol he had bought from Moodring. "You work for the Plant!" he hissed.

Parr grinned. "I work for myself. But never mind who hired me."

Jones composed himself outwardly, but his heart pulsed as deeply as the music. "The union is cozy with the syndy."

"The people I work for can handle the syndy. Mag, those strikers out there hate you . . . shadows. They've lynched a dozen of your kind in a row outside the Plant barrier. If they had their way, every one of your kind would go into the incinerator tomorrow. You yourself got roughed up by a group that got inside the Plant, I hear." Parr paused knowingly. His spoon clinked in his mug, making a vortex. "They broke in. Trashed machines. Killed a few of your kind. I heard from our mutual friend that they found you naked by the showers, and cut you . . . badly."

"It didn't affect my job," Jones muttered, not looking the human in the eyes. "And it's not like I ever used the thing but to piss. So now I piss like a birther woman."

"Didn't bother you at all, then? Doesn't bother you that Mayda works these thugs up like that?"

They were angry. Jones could understand that. If there was anything that made him feel a kinship with the birthers, it was anger. Still, the weight of their resentment . . . of their loathing . . . their outright furious hatred . . . was a labor to bear. They had hurt him. He had never intentionally harmed a birther. It was the Plant's decision to utilize cultures for half their workforce (more than that would constitute a labor violation, but the conservative candidate for Prime Minister was fighting to make it so that companies did not have to guarantee any ratio of nonclones; freedom of enterprise must be upheld, he cried). Let the strikers mutilate the president of the Plant, instead. Let them hang him and his underlings in the shadow of the Vat. But didn't they see—even though Jones worked in their place while their unemployment ran out and their families starved like the protestors—that he was as much a victim as they?

This man was under the employ of his enemies. Of course, he himself had once been under their employ. Still, could he trust this man as his partner in crime? No. But he could do business with men he didn't trust. He wouldn't turn his back to Moodring, either, but in the end he needed to eat. Five thousand munits. He had never earned a coin until he had escaped the Plant, and never a legal one since.

He could go away. Somewhere hot. Have his tattoo removed. Maybe even his useless vestige of "manhood" restored.

Parr went on, "A third bit of incentive. You're no fool, so I'll admit it. The people who hired me . . . you once worked for them, too. If you decline, well . . . like I say, they'd like to get a hold of you after what you did to those two men."

Slowly and deliberately Jones's eyes lifted, staring from under bony brows. He smiled. It was like a baring of fangs.

"You were doing well, Nevin. Don't spoil it with unnecessary incentives. I'll help you kill your man."

"Sorry." Ever the smile. "Just that they want this to happen soon, and I don't want to have to look for a partner from scratch."

"Why do you need a partner?"

"Well let me tell you . . . "

. . .

2: THE PIMP OF THE INVERSE

From his perch atop the Vat, with its stained streaked sides and its deep liquid burbling, Jones watched night fall in Punktown. The snow was a mere whisking about of loose flakes. Colored lights glowed in the city beyond the Plant, and flashed here and there on the Plant itself, but for less gay purposes. Once in a while there was a bright violet-hued flash in the translucent dome of the shipping department, as another batch of products was teleported elsewhere on this planet, or to another. Perhaps a crew destined to work on an asteroid mine, or to build an orbital space station or a new colony, a new Punktown, on some world not yet raped, merely groped.

He watched a hovertruck with a covered bed like a military troop carrier pull out of the shipping docks, and head for the east gate. A shipment with a more localized destination. Jones imagined its contents, the manufactured goods, seated in two rows blankly facing each other. Cultures not yet tattooed, not yet named. Perhaps the companies they were destined for did not utilize tattoos and decorative names—mocking names, Jones mused—to identify the clone workers. Jones wondered what, if anything, went on in their heads along the drive. They had not yet been programmed for their duties, not yet had their brain drips. He, whose job it had been to bake these golems, had been born already employed, unlike them. They were innocent in their staring mindlessness, better off for their mindlessness, Jones thought, watching the truck vanish into the night. He himself was still a child, but a tainted innocent; the months since his escape had been like a compacted lifetime. Had he been better off in his first days, not yet discontented? Disgruntled? There were those times, he in his newfound pride would hate to admit, that he felt like a human boy who longed to be a wooden puppet again.

He listened to the Vat gurgle with its amniotic solutions, pictured in his mind the many mindless fetuses sleeping without dream in the great silo of a womb beneath him. Yes, Christmas was coming. Jones thought of its origins, of the birther woman Mary's immaculate conception, and gave an ugly smirk.

He lifted his wrist, gazed at it until luminous numbers like another tattoo materialized. Time to go; he didn't like being late.

. . .

So that Parr would not guess just how close Jones lived to the Plant, he had told Parr to pick him up over at Pewter Square. To reach it, Jones had to cross the Obsidian Street Overpass. It was a slightly arched bridge of a Ramon design, built of incredibly tough Ramon wood lacquered what once had been a glossy black. It was now smeared and spray-painted, dusty and chipped. Vehicles whooshed across in either direction, filling the covered bridge with roaring noise. The pedestrian walkway was protected from the traffic by a rickety railing, missing sections now patched with chicken wire. Furthermore, homeless people had nested in amongst the recesses of the bridge's wooden skeleton, most having built elaborate parasite structures of scrap wood, sheets of metal, plastic or ceramic. One elderly and malnourished Choom, a former monk of the dwindling Raloom faith, lived inside a large cardboard box on the front of which, as if it were a temple, he had drawn the stern features of Raloom. The pedestrian walkway was bordered on one side by the railing, on the other by this tiny shanty town. Some of its denizens sold coffee to the passers-by, or newspaper hard copies, or coaxed them behind their crinkly plastic curtains or soggy cardboard partitions for the sale of drugs and sex.

Jones knew one of these shadowy creatures, and as if it had been awaiting him, it half emerged from its shelter as he approached. Its small house was one of the most elaborate; as if to pretend that it belonged to the bridge, in case of an infrequent mass eviction, it had constructed its dwelling of wood and painted it glossy black. The shack even had mock windows, though these were actually dusty mirrors. Jones saw his own solemn face multiply reflected as he approached, his black ski hat covering his tattoo.

The tiny figure moved spidery limbs as if in slow motion, but its head constantly twitched and gave sudden jolts from side to side, so fast its features blurred. When still, they were puny black holes in a huge hairless head—twice the size of Jones's—almost perfectly round and with the texture of pumice. No one but Jones would know that this was no ordinary mutant, but a culture defect from the Plant, an immaculate misconception, who had somehow escaped incineration and to freedom. Who would suspect that they had been cloned from the same master? The defect had once stopped Jones and struck up a conversation. Jones's hairless eyebrows had given him away. When not wearing dark glasses, Jones now wore his ski hat pulled down to his eyes.

"Where are we going at this hour?" crackled the misshapen being, who had named itself Edgar Allan Jones. Magnesium Jones could not understand why a shadow would willingly give itself such a foolish name, but then sometimes he wondered why he hadn't come up with a new name for himself.

"Restless," he grunted, stopping in front of the lacquered dollhouse. He heard a tea kettle whistling in there, and muffled radio music that sounded like a child's toy piano played at an inhuman speed.

"Christmas is in three days, now," said the flawed clone, cracking a toothless smile. "Will you come see me? We can listen to the radio together. Play cards. I'll make you tea."

Jones glanced past Edgar into the miniature house. Could the two of them both fit in there? It seemed claustrophobic. And too intimate a scene for his taste. Still, he felt flattered, and couldn't bring himself to flat-out refuse. Instead, he said, "I may not be around here that day . . . but if I am . . . we'll see."

"You have never been inside . . . why not come in now? I can . . . "

"I can't now, I'm sorry; I have . . . some business."

The globe of a head blurred, halted abruptly, the smile shaken into a frown. "That Moodring friend of yours will lead you to your death."

"He isn't my friend," Jones said, and started away.

"Don't forget Christmas!" the creature croaked.

Jones nodded over his shoulder but kept on walking, feeling strangely guilty for not just stepping inside for one cup of tea. After all, he was quite early for his appointment.

. . .

"Ever been in a car before?" Parr asked, smiling, as he pulled from the curb into the glittering dark current of night traffic.

"Taxi," Jones murmured, stiff as a mannequin.

"Mayda lives at Hanging Gardens; it's a few blocks short of Beaumonde Square. He's not starving like the folks he works up; he has a nice apartment to go home to. It's that syndy money."

"Mm."

"Hey," Parr looked over at him, "don't be nervous. Just keep thinking about your lines. You're going to be a vid star, my man . . . a celebrity."

. . .

3: THE CARVEN WARRIOR

Parr let Jones off, and the hovercar disappeared around the corner. Jones cut across a snow-caked courtyard as instructed, his boots squeaking as if he tramped across styrofoam. He slipped between apartment units, climbed a set of stairs to another, and found a door propped open for him. Parr motioned him inside, then let the door fall back in place. Jones heard it lock. He didn't ask Parr how he had got inside the vestibule.

Together they padded down a gloomy corridor across a carpet of peach and purple diamonds. The walls and doors that flanked the men were pristine white. This place reminded Jones of the cleaner regions of the Plant; primarily, the seldom seen administration levels. He listened to the moving creak of Parr's faux leather jacket. Both of them wore gloves, and Jones still had on his ski hat and a scarf wound around his neck against the hellish cold he could never get used to.

A lift took them to the sixth floor. Then, side by side, they made their way down the hall to the door at its very end. Quite easily, Parr knocked, and then beamed at his companion.

Jones pulled off his ski hat at last, and pushed it into his pocket. In the dim light, his hairless pate gleamed softly, the fiery halo pricked into his skin burning darkly. He hid both hands behind his back.

"Who is it?" asked a voice over an intercom. Above the door, a tiny camera eye, small as an ant's feeler, must now be watching them.

"Enforcer, sir," said Parr, his voice uncharacteristically serious. And he did look the part in his black uniform; leather jacket, beetle-like helmet, holstered weapons. He had cut his hair to a butch and shaved to a neat goatee. He held one of Jones's elbows. "May I have a word?"

"What's going on?"

"Your neighbor down the hall reported a suspicious person, and we found this culture lurking around. He claims he's not an escapee, but was purchased by an Ephraim Mayda."

"Mr. Mayda doesn't own any cultures."

"May I please speak with Mr. Mayda himself?" Parr sighed irritably.

A new voice came on. "I know that scab!" it rumbled. "He escaped from the Plant, murdered two human beings!"

"What? Are you sure of this?"

"Yes! He was from the Ovens department. It was on the news!"

"May I speak with you in person, Mr. Mayda?"

"I don't want that killer freak in my house!"

"I have him manacled, sir. Look, I need to take down a report on this . . . your recognizing him is valuable."

"Whatever. But you'd better have him under control . . . "

The two men heard the lock clack off. The knob was turned from the other side, and as the door opened Jones pushed through first, reaching his right hand inside his coat as he went. He saw two faces inside, both half-identical in that both wore expressions of shock, horror, as he ripped his small silvery block of a pistol from its holster to thrust at their wide stares. But one man was bleached blond and one man was dark-haired and Jones shot the blond in the face. A neat, third nostril breathed open beside one of the other two, but the back of the blond's head was kicked open like saloon doors. The darker man batted his eyes at the blood that spattered him. The report had been as soft as a child's cough, the blond crumpled almost delicately to the floor, Jones and then Parr stepped onto the lush white carpet and Parr locked the door after them.

"Who are you?" Mayda cried, raising his hands, backing against the wall.

"Into the living room," Jones snarled, flicking the gun. Mayda glanced behind him, slid his shoulders along the wall and backed through a threshold into an expanse of plush parlor with a window overlooking the snowy courtyard of Hanging Gardens. Parr went to tint the window full black.

"I'll give you money, listen . . . " Mayda began.

"You do remember me, don't you?" Jones hissed, leveling the gun at the paunchy birther's groin. "You emasculated me, remember that?"

"I didn't! That was those crazy strikers that got in the Plant that time . . . that was out of my hands!"

"So how do you know about it? They told you. It was a big joke, wasn't it?"

"What do you want? You can have anything!" The union captain's eyes fearfully latched onto Parr as he slipped something odd from his jacket. What looked like three gun barrels were unfolded and spread into a tripod. Atop it, Parr screwed a tiny vidcam. A green light came on, indicating that it had begun filming. Parr remained behind the camera, and Mayda flashed his eyes back to Jones to see what he had to say.

Jones hesitated. What he had to say was rehearsed, but the lines were a jumble in his head, words exploded to fragments by the silent shot that had killed the blond. He had killed a man . . . for the third time. It came naturally to him, like a brain-dripped skill; it was a primal animal instinct, survival. So why, in its aftermath, should he feel this . . . disconcertion?

His eyes darted about the room. He had never been in such a place. Tables fashioned from some green glassy stone. Sofas and chairs of white with a silvery lace of embroidery. A bar, a holotank. On the walls, a modest art collection. Atop several tables, shelves and pedestals, various small Ramon sculptures, all carved from an iridescent white crystal. Animals, and a Ramon warrior rendered in amazing detail considering the medium, from his lion-like head to the lance or halberd he brought to bear in anticipation of attack. Each piece must be worth a fortune. And yet there were men and women camped outside the Plant who were on a hunger strike, emaciated. And those who were emaciated but not by choice. And Jones recalled that woman sitting in her shroud of flame.

His disconcertion cleared. Jones returned a molten gaze to the terrified birther. The anger in his voice was not some actor's fakery, even if the words were not his own.

"I'm here to make a record, Mr. Mayda . . . of the beginning of a rebellion, and the first blow in a war that won't stop until we clones are given the same rights as you natural born."

It was clever, he had mused earlier; the Plant would be rid of the thorn in their lion's paw, and yet the law and the syndy would not hold the Plant responsible. No, it would be a dangerous escaped culture who killed Ephraim Mayda; a fanatic with grand delusions. Still, Jones had considered, wouldn't this make birther workers at the Plant, unemployed workers outside and a vast majority of the public in general all the more distrusting of cultures, opposed to their widespread use? Wouldn't this hurt the Plant's very existence? And yet, they surely knew what they were doing better than he. After all, he was just a culture . . . educated by brain drip, by listening to human workers talk and to the radio programs the human workers listened to. Educated on the street since that time. But these men sat at vast glossy tables, making vast decisions. It was beyond his scope. The most he could wrap his thoughts around was payment of five thousand munits . . . and Parr had given him half of that when he climbed into his hovercar tonight.

"Hey," Mayda blubbered, "what are you saying . . . look . . . please! Listen . . ."

"We want to live as you do," Jones went on, improvising now as the rest of the words slipped through the fingers of his mind. He thought of his own hellish nest, and of Edgar's tiny black shed of a home. "We want . . ."

"Hey! Freeze!" he heard Parr yell.

Jones snapped his head around. What was happening? Had another bodyguard emerged from one of the other rooms? They should have checked all of the rooms first, they should have . . .

Parr was pointing the police issue pistol at him, not at some new player, and before Jones could bring his own gun around Parr snapped off five shots in rapid succession. Gas clouds flashed from the muzzle, heat lightning with no thunder, but the lightning struck Jones down. He felt a fireball streak across the side of his throat, deadened somewhat by the scarf wound there. He was kicked by a horse in the collarbone, and three projectiles in a cluster entered the upper left side of his chest. He spun down onto his belly on the white carpet, and saw his blood flecked there like beads of dew, in striking close up. Beautiful red beads like tiny rubies clinging to the white fibers of the carpet. Even violence was glamorous in this place.

Mayda scampered closer, kicked his small silvery gun out of his hand. Jones's guts spasmed, but his outer body didn't so much as flinch. He cracked his lids a fraction, through crossed lashes saw Parr moving closer as well. For a moment, he had thought it was another man. Since firing the shots from behind the camera, out of its view, Parr had shed the bogus forcer uniform and changed into street clothes.

"I thought I heard a strange voice in here, Mr. Mayda!" Parr gushed, out of breath. "I dozed off in the other room . . . I'm so sorry! Are you all right?"

"Yes, thank God. He killed Brett!"

"How'd he get in here?"

"I don't know . . . Brett went to answer the door, and the next thing I knew . . ."

Parr didn't work for the Plant, Jones realized now, poor dumb culture that he was. He cursed himself. He wasn't street smart. He was a child. He was five years old . . .

Parr worked for Ephraim Mayda, captain of a union, friend of the syndicate. Mayda, whose trusting followers killed others and themselves to fight for a job, to fight for their bread and shelter, while his job was to exploit their hunger, their anger and fear.

And the vid. The vid of a murderous clone attacking a hero of the people, stopped just in time by a loyal bodyguard (while another loyal bodyguard, poor Brett, had been sacrificed). One murderous forerunner of a much larger threat, as he had proclaimed. The vid that would unite the public against the cultures, lead to an outcry for the abolition of cloned workers . . . to their mass incineration . . .

He had almost seen this before. He'd let the money dazzle him. The bullets had slapped him fully awake.

"Call the forcers!" Mayda said for the benefit of the camera, sounding shaken, though he had known all along he was safe.

Through his lashes, Jones saw Parr stoop to retrieve his silvery handgun.

Jones's left arm was folded under him. He reached into his coat, and rolling onto his side, tore free a second gun, this one glossy black, a gun Parr hadn't known about, and as Parr lifted his startled head, Jones let loose a volley of shots as fast as he could depress the trigger. Parr sat down hard on his rump comically, and as each shot struck him he bounced like a child on his father's knee. When at last Jones stopped shooting him, his face almost black with blood and holes, Parr slumped forward into his own lap.

Jones sat up with a nova of agony in his chest, and a nova of hot gas exploded before his eyes as he saw Mayda bolting for the door. The shot hit the birther in the right buttock, and he sprawled onto his face shrieking like an hysterical child frightened by a nightmare.

As Jones struggled to his feet, staggered and regained his footing, Mayda pulled himself toward the door on his belly. Almost casually, Jones walked to him, stood over him, and pointed the small black gun. Mayda rolled over to scream up at him and bullets drove the scream back into his throat. Jones shot out both eyes, and bullets punched in his nose and smashed his teeth, so that the face remaining looked to Jones like Edgar's with its simple black holes for features.

The gun had clicked empty. He let it drop, stepped over Mayda's body, over Brett's body further on, and then stopped before the door, snuffing his ski hat over the flames of his skull. But before he opened the door, he changed his mind and returned to the plush, vast parlor just for a moment . . .

. . .

It was an hour to dawn when Magnesium Jones reached the house of Edgar Allan Jones on the Obsidian Street Overpass.

Edgar croaked in delight to see him, until the withered being saw the look on the taller culture's face. It took Jones's arm, and helped him as he stooped to enter the tiny black-painted shack.

"You're hurt!" Edgar cried, supporting Jones as he lowered himself into a small rickety chair at a table in the center of the room. Aside from shelves, there was little else. No bed. A radio played music like the cries of whales in reverse, and a kettle was steaming on a battery-pack hot plate.

"I have something for you," Jones said, his voice a wheeze, one of his lungs deflated in the cradle of his ribs. "A Christmas present . . . "

"I have to get help. I'll go out . . . stop a car in the street," Edgar went on.

Jones caught its arm before Edgar could reach the door. He smiled at the creature. "I'd like a cup of tea," he said.

For several moments Edgar stared at the man, gouged features unreadable. Then, in slow motion, head blurring, it turned and went to the hot plate and steaming kettle.

While Edgar's back was turned, Jones reached into his long black coat, now soaked heavy with his blood, and from a pouch in its lining withdrew a sculpture carved from opalescent crystal. It was a fierce Ramon warrior, bringing his lance to bear. He placed it on the table quietly, so that the stunted clone would be surprised when it turned back around.

And while he waited for Edgar to turn around with his tea, Jones stripped off his ski hat and lowered his fiery brow onto one arm on the table. Closed his eyes to rest.

Yes, he would just rest a little while . . . until his friend finally turned around.

The eye altering, alters all.
—*William Blake*

Anoushka didn't care for virtual bookstores. Well, she spent time in them if she couldn't locate a particular book elsewhere, and admitted that they had their value ... but because so many favored them, rhapsodized over their convenience, she felt inclined to disparage them in her defense of Paxton's innumerable tangible bookstores. A frequent argument in favor of the virtual shop was that one didn't have to leave the comfort (and safety; this was Paxton, better known as Punktown, after all) of one's home. But that was just it. Anoushka wanted to venture out into the city ... to occupy a physical space other than that of her apartment. To sip a coffee in those shops that incorporated a café, to listen to living breathing musicians rather than the recorded jazz, folk and ethnic musicians inserted into many of the VR shops. Some VR stores even had cafés, and if you had the right interface equipment you could smell the aroma of brewing coffee, and imagine you were tasting it. Anoushka found this offensive. One might as well pickle one's brain in a jar, wire it up to a state-of-the-art computer, and draw in all of one's life experiences that way. Pseudo life. Bogus life. A why-be-alive life.

For the same reason, she favored the solid article, the artifact, of a physical book over a net book, a disk book. Something she could hold in her hands, that she could smell (she loved to press her nose into the open cleft of a book, and inhale its bright new ink or its musty age). Anoushka would no sooner favor a virtual book over a tangible book than she would choose a robot child over a flesh and blood infant. A VR lover over a man formed from living cells.

On the net it was even possible to tour most of this vast, Earth-established colony city on the planet Oasis without having to brave its much-publicized and well-founded dangers. (There were some sections that were so unsafe as to be, in a sense, uncharted, unmapped; terror incognita.) Anoushka was willing to take those chances, so as to shop in a Vietnamese market. To buy some fried dilkies, a root favored by the native Choom people, from a street vendor. To feel the sun on her face in those streets that weren't lost in the shadows of skyscrapers (some of which might more readily be called skypiercers). And it was one of her greatest pleasures to explore a bookstore for the first time. At least the net came in handy in listing Punktown's many bookstores, large and small. But sometimes she stumbled upon an unlisted one, quite by accident. That was an especial delight.

It was summer; the air so thick that one might think the sewers had overflowed and their rancid waters risen to drown the city. Or Anoushka imagined this sea upon whose bottom she walked to be the juices wrung from millions of sweating bodies. Her round shoulders, bared by her sleeveless white blouse, were filmed in a sticky membrane of her own perspiration. Her skirt, clinging to full hips, was a silvery satin. Her garments made her pale, brown-yellow skin appear darker. She wore sandals. Men looked at her as she passed them. With her thick black hair, falling in lush snarls to the small of her back, huge dark eyes and full lips, she was very attractive. At the pharmacy where she worked, however, men were usually too irritable or old or both to flirt with her as she filled their prescriptions. Sometimes she wore a bindi, but not today, though there was a tiny gem in her left nostril.

At the end of her block, Anoushka descended into the subway to catch a tube to Ratchet Ave. Station. The neighborhood where she emerged was much like her own; not the best nor the worst Punktown had to offer. She had discovered a nice Indian restaurant here the last time she'd been through, on an errand . . . and it being the weekend, she had decided to have a bit of an excursion, a bite of lunch.

This street was lined in buildings left over from the Choom town that predated colonization, most of them of red or brown brick. A number of modern buildings had been made to resemble them, to preserve some sense of tradition, but elsewhere Anoushka saw newer buildings that had been built directly above the ancient structures on thick legs containing elevators, dwarfing the brick buildings in their less weathered shadows, and looking nothing like the native edifices whatsoever. Several of the old buildings had sealed windows and doors, were abandoned, crumbling, covered in graffiti, with ivy-like tendrils covering the sides that might catch a measure of sustaining sunlight during the day between the tides of city shadow.

She found her restaurant, read a book from her shoulder bag while she ate. She had been lucky to be seated by the front window, and would glance up from her food and book to watch pedestrians and vehicles, equally diverse in character, pass by outside. A man who darted across the street in the direction of the restaurant caught her attention . . . at first only because she was afraid he'd be struck by a hovercar, then because of his appearance.

Trying not to be blatant about it, she watched as he entered the restaurant and approached the reception counter. He seemed to be picking up an order he'd called in. He was not an Indian himself, though of course only half the patrons were, this afternoon. Tall, dressed in a black T-shirt several sizes too large for his slender frame, hanging loose over tight black jeans. Bulky black boots. His hair was shoulder length, parted in the center, black and more snarled than her own. Against all this black, his skin looked like blank paper. His nose was long, his lips very full and almost feminine. Anoushka found him terribly attractive.

Also black were the goggles he wore, their thick cup-like eyepieces snug to his face so as to let no light around them, so as to reveal not even a glimpse of the eyes beneath them. He looked like he'd taken a break from welding to grab a bite to eat. Maybe they were just his way of dealing with the summer sun and looking enigmatic besides.

Bagged food and some bills were exchanged, and the man left. Anoushka watched him dodge back across the street, and when he was out of sight returned to her reading. A brief distraction, a bit of candy for the eyes.

. . .

As Anoushka exited the Indian restaurant a small misshapen being, no doubt a mutant, walked directly across her path, its oversized head shaking from side to side uncontrollably. Given a start, she veered to avoid it, and another man hurrying along the sidewalk bumped her left shoulder. For a moment she felt a jolt of alarm; two years ago, a Coleopteroid had stolen her pocketbook and when she'd tried to hold onto it had slashed her across the wrist with one of its chitinous forelimbs, cutting her to the bone. The man who'd jostled her stopped to apologize, and looking up into his face she saw he was a Tikkihotto. Sometimes Anoushka thought that the human-like races such as the Tikkihotto and Choom were more unnerving than the beetle-like Coleopteroids and other nonhuman beings. They were almost entirely human in appearance, so the features that distinguished them (such as the Chooms' ear-to-ear grin) seemed incongruous, more like deformities. Another human-like race, the gray-skinned Kalians, said that their god Ugghiutu had seeded the universe with humans, who had then adapted to their various worlds.

"Sorry," the tall man said. Even his voice was entirely human.

"No problem," Anoushka said, her teeth bright against her dusky skin. For a moment she stared up at the alien's face. From the deep sockets of his skull, translucent filaments writhed in the air, like delicate sea plants stirring under-water. Like the rippling cilia on a microscopic organism. These tendrils were what the Tikkihotto had for eyes.

The man continued on his way. Anoushka wandered in the other direction. She wanted to explore this street a little farther before she turned back toward home. Prior to today, the Indian restaurant was as far as she'd ventured.

She saw a Tikkihotto woman with her infant child riding in a backpack. Its eye filaments squirmed as merrily as its stubby fingers. An older Tikkihotto man walked by her, his tendrils wavering more slowly, and looking whitish and opaque, less transparent with age. At the same time, Anoushka began to see shop signs that were written both in English and in the complex hieroglyphs of the Tikkihotto. So . . . this was a bit of a Tikkihotto neighborhood, then. She hadn't known it existed here. But it didn't surprise her, as she'd grown up in a largish Indian neighborhood on the suburban fringe, even gone to school with mostly her own kind. In that sense, she felt that her parents had sheltered her a bit. They had no doubt been as much concerned with protecting her sense of cultural identity as with protecting her from Punktown's rampant crime. Still, Anoushka felt that up until her teens, she had been isolated from all but that little microcosmic community like an enclave within Punktown. She felt that if she hadn't been so segregated, a race like the Tikkihotto or the native Chooms would not cause her the slightest unease.

Well, this area was by no means exclusively Tikkihotto, and Anoushka did not feel like an intruder—or in danger for being different, as she would in other, more homogeneous neighborhoods. She was even intrigued. Was that fast, twangy, bleating music she heard from an open window above her Tikkihotto in origin? What was advertised by the occasional sign that had no English translation whatsoever? Though the Tikkihotto written language might best be described as hieroglyphics, it also seemed to incorporate geometric designs, and the figures in the pictographs—while sometimes suggesting people, animals, physical articles—were more often than not unidentifiable. They either portrayed people and animals in a very abstract form, or they actually illustrated nothing except the abstraction of thought and concept. Whatever these symbols expressed, it was in a language suitably complex for the complex visual organs of these offworlders.

As she walked along the noisy street, Anoushka spied one sign that was written only in English. It was a vertical strip affixed to the brick face of an old Choom building, at the second floor level:

B

O

O

K

S

As simple, as generic, as that. But it was enough for Anoushka. Without hesitation, she headed directly for the structure's recessed, paint-blistered door.

. . .

The ground floor of the building was gutted, dark, though Anoushka thought she heard a rustle of movement from an open doorway in the hall. Ceiling plaster swollen and cracked, or broken to reveal bare slats. Graffiti on the water-stained walls. It was, in fact, Tikkihotto graffiti. Blurry, multicolored gibberish that almost made her eyes ache. Trying to interpret it was like looking for Whistler's mother in a Pollock painting. She hastened to the stairs, not bothering to try the unreliable-looking lift at the gloomy hallway's end.

On the second floor landing, she found herself before a closed door painted a bright glossy red that looked almost stickily fresh, a contrast to what she'd seen thus far. A sign fixed to the door read: **RETKU'S BOOKS.**

When she opened the door, a discreet beep alerted the counter man to her entrance. He sat at a low long table on which rested his register and the remnants of his lunch. He looked up at her over the rim of a mug of coffee. She couldn't see his eyes, though, through the black lenses of the goggles he wore.

Anoushka almost froze on the threshold. One moment ticked by. "Hi," she said.

The man she'd seen in the restaurant nodded, swallowed his mouthful of coffee. "Hi."

The table was several paces from the door. She looked beyond it now, into the bookstore itself. It was smallish. Shelves lined the walls, formed a few aisles, and books were also heaped on more long tables and even overflowed boxes under these tables. Classical music played softly. She saw only two other people, both women, in the store, lost in their browsing . . . a young Earther and an elderly Tikkihotto.

"First time here?" asked the man behind the counter.

Anoushka took a couple of steps into the store at last, pulling the door shut behind her. She noted how nicely restored the hardwood floor was, glossy as amber. "Yeah. I was just out exploring. I've never heard of this shop before."

"I've been here three years now."

"Really?" She glanced around again, taking another step closer to the counter as if stealing up nonchalantly on the seated man. As if stealing up on herself, hoping the rest of her wouldn't notice what she was doing. "So, you're the owner, then?"

"I am."

"That's great. I've always thought it must be nice owning a bookstore."

"Well, like anything, it has its headaches."

"Oh yeah, sure."

"What do you do?"

"I work at the pharmacy counter for the *Superdrugs* on Polymer Street."

"Ahh. Well, you must have gone to school for that."

"Mm-hm." She was near enough now to a book rack display to pluck up a paperback at random. "But books have always been my favorite drug," she joked awkwardly.

"I can relate to that." He smiled.

This close, she was no less impressed with his looks and figured him to be a few years older than herself. And now she'd noticed that on one side of his goggles there was a small knob and several keys, and on the other side a tiny glowing red light. So they weren't sunglasses, then, or a stylish affectation . . . she guessed that they were a recording or enhancement device. Maybe he used them to scan and store his inventory, or perhaps even to read books, projected onto miniature screens.

"I saw you in the restaurant down the street a little while ago," she admitted. Then she regretted it. It made it seem as though she'd followed him here. Sounding to her own ears as though she were babbling, she hurried on as if to put her first comment in context. "Are you interested in Indian culture?"

"Oh sure," he said. Then: "Not that I . . . you know . . . really know much about it . . . "

"Have you ever read Indian authors?"

"No, I haven't, sorry to say."

"Aww, really?" She took on a faintly teasing tone, found herself even a closer step to the low counter, still absently handling the paperback which she hadn't even glanced at. "You aren't familiar with classical stories like *Ramayana*? *Shakuntala*?"

"Afraid not." An apologetic shrug.

"Writers like Kalidasa? Tagore?"

"Sorry and sorry. But I'll seek out their work, on your recommendation."

"Not that I only read ancient Indian authors, or modern ones . . . "

"Well, I don't just read Tikkihotto authors, either."

"Ahh," Anoushka said, nodding. It was not so much a response to his comment, but a realization. Tikkihotto. He wasn't a human. At least, not her kind of human. Now she understood what lay behind those impenetrable lenses. She had imagined lustrous eyes as dark as his hair. The idea that Medusa-like coils were bunched inside those cups repelled her. Repelled her because she had been so attracted to this man. Irrationally, it felt almost as if he'd deceived her . . . like stories she'd read about a trick finding out that a prosty he'd rented was really a man in drag.

"Do you read Tikkihotto?" He gestured at the book in her hands.

At last, she flipped the book open. She supposed the pretty purple cover with gold embossed lettering had peripherally caught her eye. Now, her fingertips resting on that embossed cover as though it were braille, she realized those foil letters had been in hieroglyphics. So was the entire text of the book. The characters and symbols were brightly and variously colored. She glanced at a few pages only . . . then, embarrassed, returned the book to its rack.

"No," she admitted, "I don't."

"Don't feel badly. Actually it can't be read by Earth humans without special translating specs . . . sort of like these." He tapped his goggles. "It's the way we see. You know how the colored symbols intertwine, and make new colors where they overlap? That expresses various layers of meaning. Some characters must be read left to right as others are read right to left. The length of serifs, the space between symbols, the thickness and thinness and angles of symbols. All layers of meaning. And it all has to be taken in simultaneously."

"Wow," was all Anoushka could think to say.

"Your writing . . . well, I mean English . . . is so different, I had a hard time learning it," he laughed. "I ended up using a direct brain feed to get most of it." He tapped his temple.

"That's how most people learn it. But it must be a very simple language for you, comparatively." There was less enthusiasm in her manner now. She found she wanted to go.

"So do you speak . . . Indian?"

"I can speak Bengali, yes."

He nodded. There was a long empty moment. Was he sensing that she had withdrawn something from the air between them? He said, "Um, don't be afraid to look through my store, though. It isn't all Tikkihotto books. About half, really."

"Thanks." She'd do that. Why not? It was still a nice little bookstore. And this man was pleasant enough. Just not as enticing as the illusion she herself had created. She felt guilty suddenly for resenting him. She was acclimating to his revelation.

"I'm Kress," he introduced himself, extending his hand. "Kress Retku."

"Anoushka Roy." She let him squeeze her warm, damp palm. "Well . . . I guess I will have a look around your store, then. Thanks, Mr. Retku."

"My pleasure, Anoushka."

. . .

Half out of a sense of obligation, since she had engaged the store owner in conversation, Anoushka had purchased a single book the afternoon she discovered *Retku's Books*. It had been two weeks ago. In the interim, she had tended the usual succession of surly, impatient customers queued up to her counter at *Superdrugs*. She had gone home to her small flat, alone now that her roommate had moved in with her boyfriend. Last weekend she had visited her parents in their miniature Indian colony in the suburbs. During the evenings she had lain in her bed reading from the novel she had bought two weekends before. And through it all, a figure would appear as if half glimpsed through the thick blinding fogs of dull routine. A figure in black with skin very white, and the feature that set him apart from her most hidden as if behind a mask.

Anoushka pretended to herself that her return to the Indian restaurant for lunch (she looked for him to reappear there, in vain) was a spur-of-the-moment decision, and the return stroll to *Retku's Books* even more so . . . though on a submerged level she had known before, had planned it during the grindingly slow hours of her work week.

When she entered the store, grateful to leave that murky vacant ground floor behind her, a slight relief but a greater disappointment awaited her. Behind the long table that served as a counter near the door sat a middle-aged Tikkihotto woman, whose serpentine eye tendrils raised as if to sniff her out.

"May I help you?" the woman asked, sensing Anoushka's hovering conflict.

"No," she replied, "thank you. Just browsing." And like a cat that pretends it meant to miss its ambitious jump, she headed straight into the narrow aisles of books.

She was grazing through a home guide to pharmaceuticals and subliminally aware of another person in the aisle when she heard a familiar, unaccented voice. "Do you prefer nonfiction or fiction, then, Anoushka?"

Lifting her eyes from the book, she saw Kress Retku standing a few paces away. She hadn't recognized him peripherally because he had on a white T-shirt and green combat pants today. The shirt bore the cartoony logo for a band popular a few years ago, Tikkihottos playing their exaggeratedly long eye tendrils like guitar strings. He was, however, wearing those black goggles again.

She smiled. "Hi. Um . . . I prefer fiction."

"Me, too. Sorry I haven't looked into any of those authors you mentioned last time you were here . . . maybe you'd write their names down before you leave?"

"Certainly. And . . . maybe you could write down the names of some Tikkihotto authors, whose works have been translated into English."

"Of course. Though naturally they lose a lot of their sense of layering."

She teased, "You're a bit of a snob about the Tikkihotto language. How lacking English is by comparison."

"No, I don't mean to be. Something very complex and multi-leveled in English like Nabokov's *Pale Fire* very much appeals to me . . . then you have some popular Tikkihotto authors like Jekee K'lenz who uses our layered language simply to fill her books with too many cardboard characters, too many garish soap opera plots interweaving."

"Is the Tikkihotto spoken language as complex as the written one?"

"No . . . oddly, they're quite different. We have multiple eyes, not multiple tongues."

Anoushka had heard a rumor whispered about the Tikkihotto, and the sensual possibilities of multiple tongues brought it back to her. She wondered if it might simply be like the myth of oriental women having horizontal vaginas. But word had it that a Tikkihotto man was inclined to insert his optical fibers into various orifices of his lover's body . . . so as both to stimulate her and to stimulate himself by viewing her in an exceptionally intimate manner. The concept mostly horrified Anoushka. Mostly.

"Have you had lunch yet?" he asked her, pushing his long hair behind one ear in a nervous gesture.

"Yes, actually . . . "

"Oh. I was, ah . . . do you think you might want to go for a coffee? If not today . . . some other time?"

If he had asked her on the first day she came here, she would have made some excuse. Today, she averted her eyes shyly and shrugged, but showed her bright teeth and said, "Sure. That would be nice."

"Great. A little book talk, huh? And I have Oneek over there to mind the store for me. But look around first, Anoushka . . . I don't mean to rush you."

"All right," she told him. "I'll come looking for you when I'm ready to go."

"Excellent," he said. And grinned. "Thank you."

. . .

They sat in a small greenhouse-like atrium structure that had been added onto the front of an old brick building whose ground floor had been converted to a café, sipping their coffee and barely noticing the variegated pedestrians beyond . . . darting about like colorful fish in a vast aquarium. They had moved onto the subject of mysticism, comparing the Earthly concept of the seven chakras to the Tikkihotto five inner wheels of life force. Kress enthused over a first edition he had once possessed of the Tikkihotto author Skretuu's mystical and controversial *The Veins of the Old Ones*. But he had sold it to the proprietor of *Dove Books*, another book store Anoushka had not previously encountered, for five thousand munits in order to help finance *Retku's Books*.

"I worked so hard to open that store," Kress said, turning his head at last to watch passing vehicles out the bubble-like enclosure around them. Anoushka saw the street activity reflected in the obsidian of his lenses, and wanted to ask him why he hadn't taken them off . . . though she also didn't want to ask. Didn't want to see the ocular filaments that would prove him to be of an alien race. Kress went on, "I hate to imagine I may lose it . . . "

"Why would you lose it? Is it hard to meet the rent? Are you not getting enough customers?" Her concern was genuine.

"Soon I may not be able to manage it anymore. I have two employees to help me, but I'm not sure that would help me enough . . . "

"You need more employees, but can't afford it?"

"No." Kress faced her. Now she saw herself doubly reflected in the lenses. "I'm going blind."

"You're . . . ?" Anoushka sat back from the table a little, absorbing Kress in a new light. "I'm so sorry. I hadn't known."

"That's all right." He smiled, shrugged as if it were a trivial topic, glanced around now at other patrons. Anywhere but at her. It was as though he were ashamed, had admitted impotence to her.

"How well can you see now?" she asked. Was it vain to wonder how well he could see *her*?

"I can see at least as well as you can. With the help of these." He tapped the rim of one lens, near the knobs and keys of its adjustment controls. "I can still get most of the meaning of my written language. But not all of it. And it's a degenerative disease . . . "

"But someone must be able to do something! There has to be an operation . . . organic transplants . . . inorganic implants . . . localized cloning restoration . . . "

"There are treatments for everything, pretty much. The issue is only whether you can pay for it. Any major treatments would be very involved and extremely costly, Anoushka. A lot of insurance companies would discourage it. And, in fact, I don't even have health insurance."

"Oh God, Kress, I'm so sorry . . . it's terrible . . . "

"Such is fate." Another shrug. She could see it was a bitter subject, and

Kress' good nature had been speedily eclipsed.

"But it isn't hopeless, right? If you can get the money together someday . . . or get the right insurance . . . "

"I'll never be wealthy, Anoushka. I manage to get by doing something I love. It's the most a person can reasonably expect. To expect more is to torment yourself. I'm trying to make peace with my life, and with this condition."

"There's a difference between making your peace and being fatalistic. Giving up."

"I didn't work so hard to open that store to give up," he fairly snapped. "I didn't say I was giving up."

"I thought you had implied that," Anoushka murmured.

Kress sighed, wagged his head. "I'm sorry, Anoushka. I'm sorry I'm acting like this."

"I understand. I don't blame you. It isn't fair."

"I'm reading as much as I can now, while I can. In case I may never be able to change this."

"There are audio books," Anoushka offered feebly, feeling stupid for saying it. Knowing how inadequate it sounded, she made a joke of it: "Though your written language being so *wonderfully* complex, I imagine they must need five narrators reading simultaneously to capture all those layers that English lacks."

He snorted a little laugh.

"I'd read for you," she said next, in a more serious tone.

Kress lifted his head, the goggles looking like empty skull sockets in his head. "You would?"

"Yes." She swallowed bashfully, but held his gaze as best she could without seeing his eyes, which she had originally imagined to be lustrously black like her own.

"Then I'll read for you, too," he said. "I'd like to read some Tikkihotto work for you. While I still can."

"That would be nice."

"I'm glad I met you now, Anoushka," Kress said very softly. "While I can still see how beautiful you are."

She didn't know what to say to that, so she only smiled gently.

. . .

Alone in her small flat, after a day in which a man at the pharmacy had called her a "stupid cow" because his prescription still wasn't ready, Anoushka had a dream. She had ventured into the little Tikkihotto neighborhood to meet with Kress . . . but the bookstore was on the first floor in the dream, instead of the second. The door was still red and glossy, but when she opened it the room beyond was empty; gutted, stripped and lightless.

She returned to the street, as if hoping to catch sight of Kress walking away in this direction or that, before he disappeared from sight altogether. Someone took her arm, and she whirled, startled. It was her tiny mother, looking grave, her father with a disapproving scowl just behind her.

"Come home," her mother said.

. . .

"I want to apply for a job," said Anoushka, standing at the counter.

"You'll have to fill out an application," chuckled Kress, not looking up from the book spread open in front of him.

"Seriously, Kress."

His head lifted. "Noush . . . you can't afford to leave your pharmacy job. I can't afford to pay you what you make . . . "

"I want to work part time. On the weekends. I can use a little extra money. And I can help you . . . "

"When I can't manage things myself?"

"You said you needed more help, to keep things running . . . "

He stared at her for several suspended seconds. "I appreciate what you're doing, but . . . "

"It isn't charity."

"But you feel sorry for me."

"I don't pity you, Kress. But is it all right to be concerned about you?"

"Anoushka . . . "

"I don't want to see your store have to shut down, and I don't want to see you have to give up something so important to you."

Kress glanced across the room. There were only a few scattered patrons. She knew it was never very busy in here; he made just enough sales to squeak by. When he looked back to Anoushka his voice was a whisper. "I want to be involved with you."

Her nod was a nervous jiggle. "I want that, too."

"But you know your parents won't want it."

"True."

"My parents won't be too thrilled about it either, frankly."

"I guess they'll just have to get used to it."

"And you haven't seen me without my specs."

She didn't have a ready reply for that.

He hadn't intentionally kept his being a Tikkihotto secret from her, but he had kept his encroaching blindness a secret. Still, Anoushka realized that she was having an easier time accepting the blindness than his being of an alien race. She had been dreading seeing him without his goggles. But she knew it couldn't be postponed any longer.

"Take them off," she said. "I want to see you."

"It will be ugly for you."

"Are my eyes ugly for you?"

"No. I find your eyes lovely."

"Then maybe I'll find your eyes lovely."

"You say that, but I see fear in your face. I can read the layers in it, like I can read my language."

"Take off the specs, Kress."

"It's inevitable, I suppose," he muttered, reaching both hands up to them. He depressed a key, and the tiny red light on the opposite side went dark. The goggles came away in his hands.

Involuntarily, Anoushka drew in a sharp breath.

"They're diseased," he reminded her. Then he said, "I'm sorry."

His ocular tendrils were as many as a normal Tikkihotto's, and swarmed like the arms of a sea anemone . . . were stubby at first, retracted to better fit inside his eye gear, but extended into long filaments. Rather than being translucent, however, each strand was opaque; a gray deepening toward black.

Tears began to film Anoushka's own eyes. She had to look away. Now it was her turn to say, "I'm sorry."

"I don't blame you if you don't want to see me anymore," he told her. "In any way." He began to replace his goggles.

"Don't," she said. She forced herself to look at him again.

"It isn't just that they're diseased," he noted. "Even if they weren't, they'd repulse you."

"I guess I'll just have to get used to them."

She came around the edge of the counter. There was a second chair in case two cashiers needed to sit there, though that was seldom. She pulled it close to him.

"I can't see you as well without my glasses," he said, as if in an excuse to hide behind them.

"Leave them off for now." She held up a volume that she had brought along with her this afternoon. "I want to read to you."

Kress smiled, and nodded his assent. "All right." He closed his own book; she saw how he had to feel for it.

"These are poems by Rabindranath Tagore. He was an Indian."

"So I would gather."

"Shh."

While she read, several customers approached the counter. Anoushka made the transactions for Kress; he talked her through it, still not replacing his goggles. Finally they were alone, the lowering evening sun extended long dimming bands across the honey-colored floorboards, and Anoushka read to him:

"Once you gave me
  as a loan to my eyes
  unlimited daylight."

THE LIBRARY OF SORROWS

Nothing a murderer could tell MacDiaz in interview revealed as much as the decor of their apartment, he had found. Some proved dull, conventional, with nothing more unusual in their apartment than a pair or two of souvenir panties; their method of killing might be as blunt and to the point as a single bullet through the skull. Others proved far more imaginative, even whimsical, in their aesthetic tastes and in the dispatch of their prey. These people were both more fascinating to MacDiaz, and more frightening. They made the former seem merely like sharks, unthinkingly driven to glut a hunger. These others were like artists, surgeons, very black comedians all in one, and MacDiaz knew as soon as he entered the crime scene that this killer was one of the artistic types.

The walls of the living room abounded with the mounted skulls of humans, animals and aliens (the animals and aliens somewhat difficult to differentiate from one-another, at times; more species intermingled in the colony city of Punktown than one might encounter in a lifetime as a citizen). The walls had then been entirely covered with black glossy sheets of plastic that had been snugly vacuum-formed over the skulls, giving them all the aspect of fossils in obsidian. Knickers, the uniform in charge when MacDiaz arrived, told him, "I didn't think he could possibly be responsible for all the skulls . . . figured he got most of them from medical catalogs or the black market . . . until I went in his bedroom . . . "

Well, MacDiaz took that as his cue to examine the bedroom. He need not dwell on the museum-like displays any longer, in any case; the images were recorded indelibly in his mind to be replayed at his leisure, later. His memory was photographic; indeed, it was a museum of photographs, in itself . . . and contained more skulls even than this collector had amassed.

As Knickers led MacDiaz down the hall, he informed him how the killer had been taken into custody without a struggle, and that he was a thirty-three year old librarian at the Paxton Conservatory of Music and that he had the goddess Kali tattooed on his chest; the yellow ink used for her eyes glowed so brightly that he wore strips of dark tape over them, apparently so they wouldn't show through his clothing at work. MacDiaz thought the tattoo sounded tacky after the austere beauty of the parlor, but maybe the killer had gotten the tattoo as a younger man. In any case, they had reached the bedroom.

Here, the decor and the prey were one and the same. MacDiaz was put in mind of a dark cave with a ceiling dense with stalactites. He counted thirteen naked male bodies, all with their backs to him, hanging from the ceiling. At first he thought they were hanging in the conventional sense, their heads lost in shadow, until he saw that the ceiling was composed of some heavy dark fluid which gently rippled and lapped, perhaps because of the subtle swaying of the pensile bodies . . . or vice versa. The heads and necks of the bodies had been inserted into this ceiling of fluid, and thus suspended. Either the fluid or some other property of the room preserved the bodies, so that none looked to be in advanced decay; the most MacDiaz noted was some bloating, and discoloration in the lower portions where blood had settled, but the flesh and limbs appeared supple. He didn't touch any of this strange crop, however.

MacDiaz walked amongst them, slipped between them, ducking his head and doing his best not even to brush the pendulous cadavers. He observed them from the fronts, took in tattoos and rings, trendy ritual scars and brands that told him some of the victims were college kids, maybe from the conservatory. His eyes photographed it all, and when he was satisfied, he instructed Knickers and his men to take down one of the bodies.

There was some difficulty; in fact, when the body came suddenly free at last the officers tumbled to the floor with it splayed across them. It was headless, and for an irrational moment MaDiaz thought they might have tugged too hard at the body, dislodging the head and leaving it in the weird ceiling. But the bodies were all found to be headless, just their necks holding them securely in the inky liquid. MacDiaz would learn later that many of the skulls in the living room were indeed those of the victims.

Several hours later, when the last of the young men had been removed, MacDiaz again stood in the parlor. He noticed a violin case on the coffee table. Was the killer a frustrated musician, who played before the skulls of his captured audience, perhaps naked, tears running down his face at the beauty of his music, at the appreciative locked gaze of his fossilized admirers? The detective went abruptly to a window, drew aside the heavy black drapes. The light of day was refreshing, and he opened the window to let in the cool air and let out some of the poison in him. The city stretched before him in layers of paling gray, dense stalagmites to the stalactites of the bedroom, a tainted coral reef teeming with life, hovercars floating like swarms of fish. Like swarms of flies above the great misty carcass of Punktown.

He forced himself to submerge the image of the killer playing his violin, but he couldn't drown it; not only did he remember everything he saw via the sliver of a chip wired into his brain, but everything he thought or imagined. He could file the image away and leave it there. In theory, leave it there, and never have to see it again unless he sent fingers paging through his mental files for that folder. But in reality, the images seemed to swim up of their own volition. When he lay in bed, they were projected on his inner eyelids, and when he opened his eyes, they were projected on his dark bedroom ceiling. It was the imp of the perverse. His subconscious mind drew them out when his conscious mind wanted to turn away. It was like biting a nail until it bled; not something one consciously chose to do. When he had been a boy, he had picked at his scabs, and eaten the dead skin that came off, and been dismayed at the sudden welling of blood and had sucked at that, too, as if to drink it away. Summoning the pictures was like the need to kill a person. It was a call that one was compelled to obey, almost without hope of disobeying.

. . .

The Columbarium was the name of the full-care housing center where MacDiaz went once a week to see his mother. He called her, additionally, once or twice a week. On birthdays or holidays he took his wife and two young children to see her. Once his youngest daughter had awakened screaming in the night, and explained tearfully that she had dreamed she was trapped inside Nana's bed with her, and Nana was dead and she couldn't get out. She had asked to sleep with her parents, and MacDiaz had held her, staring at the dark ceiling while watching the pictures that came unbidden. His mother, younger, smiling, so pretty . . . her thick red hair which he had almost obsessively played with as a small boy, twirling the strands around and around his fingers in rings . . .

One of the attendants at the counter asked if he wanted her to accompany him. He told her he was all set, but she offered to buzz Mrs. MacDiaz just to let her know her son was here to see her. That done, MacDiaz grunted his thanks and walked the familiar halls hung with bland artworks, his shoes squeaking against the too bright floor. His mother's number was 3-33, easy enough to remember but he knew the way by heart. His implant had recorded every minute stain on the floor or wall, every interchangeable mock-Impressionistic landscape framed on the walls, the scuffs or chipped paint on every one of the drawers set into the walls in rows of three. He came to the drawer stenciled 3-33, and stood staring at it, hesitating. It was in the uppermost row. He didn't bother selecting a folding chair from one of the receptacles spaced along the walls between each group of drawers, as he could seldom bring himself to remain long. He needn't worry that others would be impatient for him to move out of the way of the drawer they sought, however, since he was the only person in this lonely stretch of hallway.

At last he pushed a keypad, and said, "Hi, Mama, it's me." Then he lifted a latch, and pulled the drawer smoothly out of its niche in the wall, swinging it down on its arms to about the level of his waist.

He smiled down at her, and she smiled weakly through her bubble up at him. Her headset, on which she spoke with him when he called and on which she and the other tenants of this nursing home spent their days watching movies, soaps, talk and game shows, lifted out of her way so that she could see him with her naked eyes. She had to squint them to adjust. She was a skeleton which he doubt could have taken two steps, were it freed from its glass sarcophagus. Her face was a skull's, barely sheathed in skin. He thought of the skulls in the apartment he had just left. Her white hair was a few mere wisps like the smoky tendrils of her spirit, struggling to be free of her but trapped inside this bubble.

"What were you watching?" he asked, knowing her love of movies, a passion they had always shared.

"A gardening show," she told him, her voice creaky over the speaker.

"Don't you ever go on-net any more, Mama? It would be good for you. Talk to people . . . "

"Lie to some young man that I'm a sexy curvy redhead?" she joked. "I'm too tired to talk. I'd rather watch my movies . . . watch those people talk. I tried some of the VR channels, but I'm too tired even as a ghost in the machine. I just want to watch, not do. I'm just so tired . . . forever tired . . . "

MacDiaz would often imagine how it was for his mother when she was slid back into the wall, alone in her life-support cylinder, her womb, lost in her video dreams. Unable to escape. He thought he understood her prison. But in a way, she had inflicted his upon him. She and his father had wanted him to have that chip implanted in his boyhood. It would give him a better chance in life, a better job, give him more capabilities in a competitive world where such technology was equally accessible to every single person . . . who could afford it. He had had no choice; a parental decison, like circumcision of old. But he did not leave her alive in her prison as a vengeance. Her present condition was imposed upon them both by the laws he served; if he could, he would open her bubble right now and cut her snaking support cables so that she might pass at last into true rest.

"How are the girls?" she asked him, her favorite topic, and he told her. Sometimes he brought vid chips of them at play or on vacation for her to watch. Luckily, she did not ask him how his work was. His parents hadn't really approved of his becoming a policeman, and he didn't want to tell her now the pain it brought him. Tell her that he wasn't sure how much longer he could do it . . . how it wasn't getting better with time, but worse, as he saw more and more horror, until his mind seemed ready to burst with its burden, those images that never dissipated, only jockeyed for position. That the interior of his skull was one crime scene, limitless, stretching in all directions to a bloody infinity.

. . .

He sat at the kitchen table, glass of orange juice before him. His wife had come scuffing out from the bedroom a few minutes ago to see if he was all right; he had gently sent her back to bed. They had made love tonight. How could he ever tell her that more often than not these days while they were making love, he was dredging up the memory of another night of love-making, ten years ago, when she had been more slender, prettier, more in her bloom? It was as though he were cheating on her with an earlier version of herself. And then there were those times when he recollected a night spent with his old college girlfriend. Or recalled—as if she stood before him then and there—some nameless teenage girl who had stood in line in front of him when he was thirteen years old . . . waiting to get on a carnival ride . . . and he staring at her long legs, smooth as those of a plastic doll, and the tight shorts that gripped her buttocks.

It was a sweet memory, not just carnal—he remembered the sparkle of sun on her long, rare blond hair as much as he remembered the flesh of her legs and the sparkle of gold down on them—but it seemed too real, too immediate, so that it competed with the reality he was living now, the time he was living now, and made him feel displaced. Lost within himself. He should be accustomed to his memories; he had worn his chip for over thirty years. But as a boy, his mind had been spacious. He had had the room to move in it, to hold memories at arm's length and regard them properly. But the house was now full, a storage room, a warehouse, the windows obscured with piled debris and the pictures far more horrifying than any he had imagined as a child, or even as a novice policeman. The more time went on, and the more his life experiences accumulated to become immediately accessible to him, the more his life-long condition felt alien to him.

Even now, that picture of the golden girl rose up in him, simply because of the train of thought he was in. Angrily, he clubbed the image back down, and to replace it sent his mind scanning through his case files. He plucked one out, threw it open on the desk of his forward mind.

He thought it sad that he had to chase away the ghost of a blond, smooth-skinned girl with this ghost of a gang member whose eyes had been ritually shot out, but he sat there nevertheless sipping his orange juice and slowly taking in every detail of the scene in which the boy lay. He even saw again his own face, darkly reflected in the pool of blood widening and widening out from the kid's exploded head.

. . .

MacDiaz arrived at this crime scene only moments after the uniforms, and consequently all the bodies had not yet been discovered. He caught just a glimpse of one denuded, sprawled skeleton on the living room carpet before pressing deeper into the old apartment with its large rooms and high ceilings, his drawn handgun like a dog to lead him. He took note that all the shades were down and curtains drawn so that the place had a sepulchral feel and stink. While a uniform plunged into one bedroom, MacDiaz turned the knob of another.

The door budged but a few inches. Was someone leaning their weight against it, or barricading it shut? He ducked to one side, lest he be shot through the panel, trying to dart a glance through the crack. Only gloom beyond. Well . . . what was he to do? He had enough protective mesh woven into his coat and vest to stop half of the projectiles and rays one might encounter, so he backed up a bit to gather momentum and then was hurtling shoulder-first against the door. It gave half-way with a loud crackling and splintering sound before jamming again, and MacDiaz made himself a moving target, barreling through the opening with gun thrust blindly.

His feet crunched on an uneven surface and he nearly lost his balance. There was a body on the floor just in front of the door, nearly as skeletal as the one in the other room but still with the dregs of skin to it. He found no one else in the room, under the bed or in the closet. Putting on a light, he turned his attention back to the corpse, now anxious to find out if its head was really as large as it seemed in the murk . . . for it was this that he had shattered with the door and under his shoes.

The burst of light sent a swarm of insects scurrying. Startled and revolted, MacDiaz felt an irrational urge to point his pistol at them. But at the same time he saw that it wasn't the corpse's head he had shattered, he realized the scattering creatures weren't insects. "Oh great," he hissed, seeing that he had inadvertently squashed a good number of the tiny beings to death.

They were a race called the Mee'hi, and they knew better than to kill other intelligent species so as to feed off them and build their nests . . . they had been warned several times, and threatened with total expulsion from this world. The head of the wasted human had been turned into a nest like a sand castle made of some black extruded matter, a miniature city like a microcosm of Punktown, its rough but delicate spires and minarets now mostly crushed and toppled. The face of the cadaver was engulfed but for the mouth, its lips curled back to expose a terrible yellow grin.

"Damn you," MacDiaz growled at the darting creatures. No doubt they would raise a fuss about those he had trampled, claiming he had done it on purpose in retribution. Well, his eyes had recorded all, and if need be his memories could be extracted to show a jury that the killings had been accidental. Still, he knew he had just killed more beings in one step than had his last several murderers combined.

"Hey, guys," he called out the door to the uniforms, "get in here!" He was afraid the Mee'hi might all escape through chinks or cracks in the walls, and glanced around him for something to start catching them in.

A voice startled him, and his eyes jolted back to the figure on the floor. Whether man or woman he couldn't tell, but he saw the fingers curl ever-so-slightly, and a deep slurred sound came from between the clenched teeth, like a recording played at a very slow speed. The poor being was still barely alive, the last of its juices not yet wrung from it. Maybe it had even thought itself dead, its eyes covered in that black resin, until MacDiaz had burst in to awaken it.

Pitiful monstrosity. For another irrational moment, MacDiaz wanted to press his weapon to its caked skull and put it out of its suffering, but the uniformed officers had suddenly joined him. All he could do now was pray that once the thing was freed of the nest, which was both killing it and keeping it alive, it would pass at last into true death.

. . .

She had been failing. Part of him welcomed this, though not as large a part as he might have imagined, and where once he would have felt guilty secretly hoping she would soon die, now he felt guilty secretly hoping she would remain alive.

This time when he came to see her, she stared up at him through her bubble with suspicion and perhaps even fear, as if he had come to her bedside to murder her. She covered herself with her blanket to her chin and demanded, "Who are you? What do you want?"

"It's Roger—your son," MacDiaz told her, and glanced around him for assistance. Couldn't they increase her medications? Inject something into one of the tiny ports along the wall to enter her artificial and then actual circulation to temporarily bring her back around, coax out from the dimming maze of her brain the frail soul that was lost there?

But at last, as her mind cleared a bit on its own—maybe she had just awakened from a doze, or his face had cut through the fog—she remembered him. But her voice was tiny like a child's and she kept asking every few minutes who was taking care of her dog, Lady . . . which had died five years ago.

MacDiaz was exhausted when he left her; she had fallen back into a doze and he had lingered a while, just staring at her face. As he threaded his way back through the halls, an elderly man shuffled up to him and lightly touched his arm. The man had tears in his eyes, and for a moment MacDiaz wondered if he might have escaped from one of the drawers in the walls.

"Excuse me, sir," the old man moaned, "I can't find my wife. She's in one of these things . . . but I can't find her. I can't remember her number . . . "

MacDiaz took the man back to the desk, and left him with a tech who would find his wife's number in her file. But as he left him in her care, MacDiaz was foolishly concerned that instead of finding the wife's drawer they would lock her husband in another one.

. . .

In his dream, MacDiaz was alive, but had been drugged or entranced, perhaps dazed by a blow, and he was dragged naked through a dark apartment, into a room where the ceiling was a gently rippling pool, too murky to see into. From this overhead pond, other nude figures hung by their necks, dangling as casually as coats tucked away in a closet . . . or more like carcasses hooked in a meat locker. With a grunt, the vague, shadowy person who had been dragging him along hoisted him up in his arms and then, straining, pressed MacDiaz's head into the chilly rippling pool.

Then he was left suspended there, and staring sightlessly into a black void. But his vision began to adjust; indeed, his eyes began to cast two yellow beams—like Kali's eyes, he thought in the dream. Images came indistinctly at first: pale fluttering shapes, gray staggering forms . . . at a distance his beams of light couldn't reach. But these shades drew closer, moved in and out of his rays, which followed the weaving path of this one only to switch to illuminate another. The figures shambled ever closer, and in so doing, revealed the catastrophic condition of their apparitional forms. A shotgun suicide with his face blown open from the inside. A woman with her washed bare chest like a white sheet covered in a calligraphy of stab wounds . . . a profusion of small black dashes so clustered that they resembled a horde of insects feeding on her. He was seeing into the land of the dead, he realized, though he was still alive, though the other bodies with whom he dangled lacked their heads, and thus saw nothing. He was alone, and terrified, helpless to free himself . . . and worst of all, there were no mysteries revealed, there came no enlightenment from his privileged vision. There was only what he'd seen all along, but immortalized in a limbo where it never faded, where the dead could never find rest from their haunting.

A sharp pain just below his left eye awakened him, and instinctively he slapped at the spot. Sitting up in bed, he reached out to the lamp beside him; his wife groaned irritably at the sudden glare and rolled away from him.

On the blanket across his lap, MacDiaz spotted a grayish-translucent insect, wriggling on its back, injured by his swat. It was a Mee'hi, and he realized it had bitten him in his sleep.

From the bathroom he brought a plastic cup, and scooped it in there, and he took it back into the bathroom with him and closed the door. He contemplated the squirming creature. Had it stowed away in his shoe or clothing from that crime scene he had investigated several weeks ago; but why wait until now to attack him? Perhaps it was the first scout of an entire horde that was seeking him out in revenge. His temper rising, MacDiaz kicked open the lid of the toilet and began to tip the cup so as to dump the tiny alien into it. But he hesitated. It would be murder, and conscious this time. Though the evidence would be flushed away, the crime would be recorded in his mind, and his memories were routinely extracted and utilized for court cases. Whether out of a sense of morality or self preservation or both, he closed the toilet lid and transferred the wounded being into a capped pill bottle.

The next morning, he saw that the flesh around his eye had become pink and swollen; light made the eye burn so painfully and water so profusely that he could only find comfort in squinting it shut to block out light entirely. Even then, his right eye watered a bit, too—either in sympathy or because the poison of the bite was spreading.

He slipped the vial with the still scrabbling being into his jacket pocket, and on his way to work stopped at the hospital to have the bite looked at . . . after first leaving his prisoner to be cared for as well. The physician who saw him (he was seen quickly when he revealed he was a policeman) informed him that male Mee'hi did indeed inject poison, though it was generally only dangerous when the bites were numerous. Further, this was a bite from an immature male, whose poison was not yet fully effective. "Maybe he escaped that crime scene," the doctor guessed, "and has spent these past few weeks hunting you down out of vengeance." He seemed to find the notion amusing. Somehow, though, this idea made MacDiaz pity the thing a bit. Immature . . . a child, perhaps. Filled with grief, maybe over the death of siblings, parents. Angrily lashing out, hopelessly seeking to defeat a far larger and stronger enemy.

After asking MacDiaz which pharmacy he preferred, the physician sent a prescription for an antibiotic over to the *Superdrugs* on Polymer Street, where MacDiaz knew a pretty Indian woman usually worked the counter. Her face flashed before him now. Once she'd told him she worked part-time for a book store. If he so much as glanced at every page of every book in that store, he thought, he would essentially become that store. The thought made his skull want to droop forward.

"Doctor," MacDiaz said, slipping back on his jacket and then the dark glasses he had donned to soothe his tortured eyes, "I have a Mnemosyne-755 memory chip that I received at the age of ten, and I was thinking of . . . having it removed . . . "

"Yes, they have better chips than that available now, certainly . . . "

"I don't want it replaced . . . I just want it removed."

The doctor smiled, cocked his head a little, again as if amused. MacDiaz didn't like him. "Why?"

"I just don't want it any more," the detective replied somewhat testily.

"Well, I have a chip and I'm quite happy with it . . . I don't see how a doctor dealing with as many races as I do could do without one."

"I'm sure it's useful to you. But I'd like mine out, and I was wondering how involved and expensive such a procedure would be. Whether most insurances would cover it, or . . . "

"Well, see, you don't have to have it removed. It can be simply shut off, which is a very easy procedure, and doesn't require surgery."

"I would want it out."

"It wouldn't just suddenly turn itself back on, you know . . . unless you changed your mind later and wanted it switched back on. It's not going to reactivate if you bump your head," the doctor chuckled.

MacDiaz rose to leave. "Thank you," he said, more testily than before, and strode from the office.

. . .

"I'm sorry, Mr. MacDiaz," the tech said, hurrying out from behind her desk as if to intercept him, "we haven't had a chance yet to move her . . . are you sure you don't want to wait?"

He wasn't sure, but he started along the familiar path, the tech scurrying to keep up. There was no one outside the drawer to indicate anything was out of the ordinary, and he was glad he hadn't come here to make this discovery on his own accidentally. Of course, that wasn't possible; the life support system had alerted the desk that there was a problem, so no one would have made any surprising discoveries. Still, the mental picture of opening the drawer to that discovery was unavoidable.

The tech moved around him to activate the drawer, and the bubble flowed out of its niche in the wall, lowered on its arms to proffer its solemn burden.

"Oh my God," MacDiaz whispered, as if there was still some surprise, after all. In the moments it took for the drawer to open and bubble to lower, he had imagined what his mother would look like dead. Her face twisted in a grimace, her eyes bulging from their sockets, her flesh purple and black. But there was calm . . . her mouth in that strange little smile of the dead. Her lids weren't entirely closed, however; a subtle thing, but subtly disturbing.

As he had on that visit when she hadn't remembered him, he took in her unmoving face for a long time, the tech waiting expectantly. Her hair—once red and thick and which he had twined small fingers in—just gray wisps; her cheeks—once smooth and soft under boyhood kisses—withered and concave. Her eyes—which had taken in her movies—half open and half shut. That small detail seemed to mock him. It was an undecided detail. An incomplete detail. They should be shut. She should be at peace, entirely.

"Close the door, please," he husked to the attendant, turning away, tears beginning to course down his own cheeks. He had seen enough. He had owed her one last visit. But he did not want to take in any more . . . he did not want to remember her this way.

. . .

"You know," this other doctor informed him, after she had finished her scan of the chip in his brain, "there are chips now that allow the user the option of singling out and erasing any memory you want to be rid of. You have complete control, and can even shut the chip off entirely during those times when you don't want it to be in use . . . just with a simple thought."

"I don't want a new chip," he reiterated. "Just this one out."

She sighed. "Well, of course that's your choice. I just wanted to make you aware of all your options . . . especially where it might have some impact on the kind of work you do."

"I'm very much aware of that," MacDiaz told her.

And so it was done that afternoon. As he lay resting, waiting for his wife to come pick him up, he thought that if his mother had had a memory chip, she would never have forgotten who her son was. In her small prison she could have spent happy hours reliving all the best parts of her life, liberated by and lost in those recollections . . . even their tastes and smells, the feel of a cool evening breeze against her face. In her delirium, she might even have come to believe they were her present. But then, it might have made her imprisonment all the more profound . . . knowing that despite sensation those were merely memories, however beautiful . . . times past and gone, not present experience. Further, there would be the bad memories trapped inside that small bubble with her . . . the disappointments and anxieties and fears of a long life, inescapable. The death of a pet dog sharply relived, perhaps over and over, each time like the first . . .

Lying there recovering, at first he wondered if the chip were indeed gone. Staring at the gloomy ceiling, he could still project his mother's face there . . . the half-lidded eyes. But when he pushed further back, searching for the scene of that room of hanging headless corpses, he found it was a softer image, more abstracted than precise. He closed his eyes and let out a shaky little breath. A kind of peace came over him, as if he had been exorcized. He didn't dare look for the face of his mother in her youth. He knew it wouldn't be there, not clearly. But he had photographs, and vids, to be briefly visited. It was a sacrifice he could live with. Anyway, he would find that feelings persisted when pictures did not.

His wife came to drive him home. And days passed, weeks, months, and the faces of the dead—burst by bullets, grinning mysteriously at their own fates, bloated like the faces of pudgy plastic dolls and shriveled to crusted skulls—began to fade to smoke and shadow. Gray and difficult to see. As elusive and vague as ghosts—and memories—should often remain.

In the bar's subaqueous illumination, the eight men at the two pushed-together tables all glowed the same misty blue-green. It was a trick of the light, an external gloss: they were anything but alike. Aside from the fact that they were all killers, of course.

The most obvious difference was that half of the party wasn't human. The four Vlessi sat at one of the two small tables, their hulking bodies pressed tightly shoulder to shoulder, which might have proved a problem had they been drinking. They didn't drink, and that made Jasper Conch more wary of them than their intimidating appearance. At least the things had been cordial enough, respectful enough to meet his team here . . . but it made him feel less inclined to drink his own beer, as if he feared that once he was sufficiently intoxicated, the Vlessi would simply kill him and his friends here and have it done with.

Back to their intimidating appearance: each of the aliens was taller than the tallest of the human assassins, and the only clothing they wore was a gauzy orange scarf (except for the leader, who wore lime green). Conch had once heard of another human in another bar who had playfully tugged at a Vlessi's scarf. The Vlessi had playfully tugged the man's adam's apple out.

Each Vlessi had a sleek white coat like a dog's belly after it's shaved for an operation. Their chests were long and narrow, shallow and bony, their arms and legs as thin as a deer's, and in fact their feet were more or less hooves (which had led to their nickname: the White Devils). Their hands were large and humanoid, however, the nails the same black as their hooves. Their heads were large atop the popsicle stick bodies, and hung forward as if with their weight. These heads resembled nothing so much as a human pelvis, shot through with open hollows and covered in that thin, short-furred skin. No visible mouth, no place even where a brain could be imagined to be housed. Set into the various cavities of this skull-pelvis were six tiny eyes, lidlessly staring like those of a doll. And these doll eyes seemed haphazardly glued on, to the extent that they varied in placement from one Vlessi to the other, and were not situated on any given creature with a sense of symmetry. Nature abhors the asymmetrical, Conch knew, but maybe the Vlessi had their own brand of nature.

No clothing: no place to hide a gun. They didn't use guns, then? Though Conch should find that encouraging, he didn't. It bothered him even more than their sobriety. Come to think of it, he had heard the White Devils drank blood, but he dismissed that as urban legend (especially since no mouth was even apparent, despite their translated speech). Then again, maybe they did drink blood . . . just to maintain their reputation.

Brass, one of Conch's boys, leaned his creaky cloned-leather coat against his own to murmur grinningly in his ear: "I think the one on the right is a female. Her nipples stick out more. See that? Look, man, look. See? Either that or the wanker's caught a chill. You see that? I'm getting excited looking at that thing. Six perky pink nipples, man. One in my teeth, one in each hand . . . between my toes . . . "

Conch smiled and ground out his herb cigarette. "Shut up, man," he murmured back. He was half-listening to one of his other friends, Hans, describe the warrior code of the feline Ramons to the Vlessi, and how their swords compared favorably to those of Earth's ancient samurai. Conch hoped Hans didn't get started on samurai; such a cliche, he thought. Enough with ronins and bushido, and Hans' misogynistic manga and anime. The wanker even had a garish dragon embroidered on the back of his leather jacket, as if all his Yakuza tattoos weren't enough. Sometimes he wore a Chinese kung-fu suit, though, just for a little variety Conch supposed. But for all his affection for ancient warriors, Conch had never known Hans to shy away from carrying a good gun.

Conch's third man was Indigo, who just sipped a shot a molecule at a time and smiled faintly at the chatter of the men and the watery, garbled translation of the Devils' voices, never joining in himself. Indigo was crew-cut and goateed, lean as a greyhound, with eyes both bright and dark under low brows. If the Devils couldn't tell from his vibe that he was the deadliest of the crew, then they were more bone-headed than they looked. Indigo was thirty, a few years younger than Conch, who was the oldest of the lot.

No seasoned, graying and paunchy syndy killers, they. No syndy affiliation at all, though they had had some peripheral dealings and errands in their early teen years, before they carved their own little niche as freelancers. Porko's boys had once tried to put them down, but they had skinned one of his hitmen alive in a basement and the greasy wanker had left them alone after that. They didn't conflict with syndy operations much, anyway. For a good five years now they had taken nothing but corporate contracts, like this one.

"Oh, yeah," Brass was saying, as one of the establishment's nude dancers came crawling in their direction along a branch of the caged catwalks that crisscrossed the entire room. She stretched out on her belly so that Brass, standing, could pinch her nipples through the mesh of the catwalk floor. He ran his fingers over the webs of metal indenting her soft belly and thighs, sectioning it off into so many succulent little squares. Then, he lifted his face to her, so that she—a Tikkihotto—could stroke his cheeks and throat with the dozens of translucent ocular tendrils that swam from her eye sockets. "Oh, yeah," he repeated. "Touch me, baby, lick me." Her nests of writhing eyes caressed the broad black stripe of trendy war-paint makeup that he wore down the center of his forehead, ending half-way down his nose. She seemed to like seeing/feeling his high, defined cheekbones—though Conch felt they were too defined, his lips too puckered in a sexy-kissy plastic Cupid's bow, since Brass' lower face had been shot off and then rebuilt according to his glamorous specifications.

Conch tuned back in on the conversation . . .

"How long have you four been together?" the leader of the Vlessi asked.

"Oh, since we were kids, about," Hans babbled on. "There was nine of us in all in those days . . . but we lost one guy four years ago, another guy three years ago, and last year we lost two guys to one assassin alone. He was a Ramon, in fact—meanest fucker we ever went up against. He was a one man team. Didn't seem too sporting, at first, until he took out our two boys. He got one of them with a sword, in fact. Cut him almost in half. Scariest fucker I've gone to head with. All business. He wore a conservative suit—not the traditional Ramon robes—but he was a Ramon warrior through and through."

"But you beat him, ultimately, one would surmise."

"Oh, yeah—Indigo brought him down."

Conch saw the leader of the Devils turn his six tiny eyes in the quiet man's direction appraisingly. Indigo didn't even look up from tracing his finger in a water ring on the table.

"You said there were nine. Four are alive, and four are dead. What about the ninth?"

"Oh—we lost one guy early on to a fate worse than death—marriage!" Hans laughed. "That was Blink. He didn't want to play anymore."

Conch noticed that Hans was conversing, while the Vlessi was assessing. Assessing their past successes, and losses. The Devils were definitely not the most fun opponents they had met with prior to a duel.

"So how many of your crew did there used to be?"

"Four," the Vlessi replied in its drowning voice. "We have lost none, since we began."

Hans seemed to grow a little less gregarious. He tossed Conch a look, but Conch ignored him, taking his cue from Indigo. He motioned to the waitress to come over, so that he could order some food—something to soak up the alcohol already in his belly.

. . .

"So what did you think of the vampires?" asked Conch, as the four made their way down the broad sidewalk, strolling in a line. All four wore cloned-leather jackets of varying shades and lengths, against the chill of night in the city of Punktown.

"Hey," Brass said earnestly to the others, "I hope you blokes know I was only kidding about getting excited by that one with all the nipples."

"Now if it had had multiple clams, that would've been a different story, huh?" Hans teased.

"I didn't see a clam on any of them," Brass replied earnestly. "Or a cue, either."

"They might not have cues but they've got balls," Indigo said quietly.

"Yeah," said Conch. "They're sharp, and we'd better not take them for granted."

"Where were their guns?" asked Hans. "Or do you think they use swords?"

"Fuck you with your swords," Brass groaned.

"They don't use guns," Indigo answered with calm certainty.

"What, then?" asked Hans.

"I don't know yet."

As they strolled, a gang of tough-looking youths coming from the other direction parted to go around them. The youths hadn't heard rumors about these men, but they had the street instincts to know they weren't to be mocked or challenged. The four friends stopped at a corner under a street lamp, its sickly greenish light making them look like they were submerged in a tank of vile fluid such as dissected organs or deformed infants might be preserved. A helicar hummed high over their heads as it took the corner, and a shuttle whooshed through a transparent tunnel that connected one vast office block to another across the intersection. From atop one glass tower down the street, a flock of luminous green holographic birds emerged, wheeled in the sky, came together to form the word **FLOCK CORP.**, then scattered and returned to the lens atop the tower. Hovering above another structure was a bluish holographic hand large enough for a god, which continuously spelled out, in sign language, the name of that company: **AUDIOPLANTS**. The four men were on the fringes of Industrial Square, not far from the offices of Ziggurat Pharmaceuticals, the company that had given them their current contract.

"Anyone up for going to *Snakeskins*?" Brass asked. It was an exclusive strip club in the vicinity, where local businessmen liked to lunch with clients whose favor they sought. There, beautiful women first discarded their clothing, then peeled off their cloned flesh exteriors to reveal their robotic selves beneath. "Now that we dumped our boring friends?"

"Not me," Conch sighed. "We're on a job now."

"We don't start until next week!"

"Doesn't matter. You go ahead. After meeting the vampires, I want to keep my knife honed."

"Now you sound like Hans," Brass groused.

"I'll go with you," Hans told Brass, unmindful of the insult.

"Then we'll see you boys. Just keep your ears pricked. We don't know if the Devils follow the same rules of etiquette and fair play we do. Their table manners could be entirely alien to us."

"We're always on guard." Brass patted a hard lump against his side, slightly bulging his knee-length leather coat. "You know us."

"Right," Conch said, a sudden roar of cold wind ruffling his spiky, short dirty-blond hair. "We'll all meet up again tomorrow afternoon, then. The basement."

They wished each other goodnight. Brass and Hans disappeared around the corner, and Conch and Indigo accompanied each other to the end of the

next block, where they parted ways. Before they did, Conch said, "In the morning I'm meeting with the suits at Ziggurat. I'll keep a feed open so you can
listen . . . as long as they don't have filter guards to block it. I'll tell them we had
a courtesy meeting with our opposing team so they'll know what good sports
we are, and I'll pick up the front money."

Indigo nodded. Conch said goodnight. Indigo nodded again. Like duelists
putting distance between each other, they turned and walked in opposite directions.

. . .

The corporate headquarters and local production operations for Ziggurat
Pharmaceuticals were, not surprisingly, housed within a looming multi-tiered
pyramid of greenish ceramic blocks made to look old, cracked, on the verge of
ruin. Jasper Conch supposed the greenish hue was meant to represent the slime
or moss of a jungle in which such a temple might be found, or the light shining
through a leafy emerald canopy. Or perhaps it had been artfully stained in the
juices of pulped money.

In the lobby, he watched a great central vidtank which showed a looping holographic film touting the company's products and successes, showing gowned
workers and robots cheerfully waving from inside sterile cores, and happy office drones glancing up from their computers to smile at the camera. Conch
looked around for a magazine in vain, sighed, ached for a cigarette, rose when
he saw a man walking energetically toward him across a veldt of forest green
carpet with his hand already extended.

"Mr. Conch, good to see you again. Come to my office, please."

Conch shook the man's hand before following him. "Mr. Abbas."

Hamid Abbas was slight, darkly handsome, impeccably dressed, and Conch
had no idea what his title or exact function was within Ziggurat Pharmaceuticals. Previously, they had met outside the company. As it was Sunday morning
(by the Earthly calendar), the building appeared empty except for the guard
who had met Conch at the security stop, where he had been scanned for weapons. With a little smile, Conch had handed over a snub-nosed Decimator .220
from his shoulder holster and a little palm automatic loaded with plasma capsules from an ankle holster.

They settled into Abbas's office, the walls of which seemed to be padded in
a thick black foam. Conch seriously doubted now that Indigo would be able

to eavesdrop on their conversation in here, but at least the enforcers wouldn't, either. These little corporate contests were illegal . . . though of course, because no one but the hired mercenaries or hitmen were directly endangered, the authorities tended to look the other way, especially since a great deal of money was always concerned, and money oiled the gears of society to a silent smoothness. On one occasion a homicide dick named MacDiaz had become a real nuisance, but that was because an innocent bystander got popped, and it was the contenders who had done the sloppy shooting; Conch prided his team on never having harmed a noncombatant.

"So." Abbas smiled and knotted his hands atop a desk fashioned entirely of synthetic—or perhaps authentic—jade. "You met the dreaded Vlessi."

"We're trying to find out more about them."

"Well, I can tell you a little. They come from the same planet the Anul do. When shady things happen, and the Anul are involved, chances are the Vlessi are in the shadows with them. They fear the Vlessi . . . but they aren't against using them."

The competitor that Ziggurat had challenged to this duel was called Rescue Pharmaceuticals. It was a company owned and run by a group of powerful immigrant businessmen from the world of the Anul . . . and their best-selling product was the pink pill used to combat the disease called "orb weaver," to check the advancement of that increasingly prevalent threat in its victims. Ziggurat had sought to create its own drugs to slow the development of the disease, and Rescue had contested their rights to do so, claiming exclusivity to the medical solutions involved. Ziggurat had countered with ugly accusations such as that the Rescue drugs were nothing but placebos, in any case. Rescue had protested indignantly, offering samples for analysis by a third party. The battle had raged in court, become a blinding blizzard of paperwork, a jungle of red tape that lawyers lost their way in. Thus, Ziggurat had met with Rescue with the proposition that they settle the matter out of court, so the production of both their products would no longer be held up in limbo, with the prize being that if Rescue won, Ziggurat would refrain from manufacturing the pills to battle orb weaver . . . while Ziggurat's prize would be to continue production unchallenged.

"Naturally, Rescue accepted our invitation," Abbas explained. "They don't want the court involved any further . . . because despite their protestations, most of what they produce is in fact placebos. Even drugs that make the disease advance *more* quickly. They see orb weaver as their friend. As a source of endless profit. We don't. We aim to truly help its victims. Rescue produces enough of the authentic, beneficial drug to put out there and to offer for analysis if probed too deeply . . . but they can fend off most probes by filling palms where needed."

Conch smiled grimly, lounging far back in his chair and swiveling. He hadn't taken off his leather coat and he had put his sunglasses up on his head, making his hair stand up jaggedly. "If Rescue is so unorthodox, what makes you think they'll respect this agreement if you win?"

"Well, a duel like this is a matter of honor, Mr. Conch. Like the honor between your group and the Vlessi team. Besides," and Abbas gave a smile that a man other than Conch would have found chilling, "if Rescue goes back on its word, we will pay you a handsome fee to eliminate the heads of their corporation."

"I see. And I imagine that Rescue has told their soldiers to do the same to your chiefs, if you should break your agreement?"

"I'm sure they have been so instructed. You must have heard about similar arrangements in such matters . . . "

"Yeah. It's not the first time. It's a smart bit of insurance."

Abbas leaned forward with exaggerated concern. "I'm terribly sorry, Mr. Conch . . . I've been rude. Can I offer you an espresso? Some water?"

"Mind if I smoke?" Conch peeled aside his jacket to show the pack sitting in the pocket of his black silk shirt, right next to his empty shoulder holster.

Abbas made another exaggerated expression, this time of apology. "I'm sorry, Mr. Conch . . . this is a pharmaceutical company, remember?" He smiled gently. "Smoking is harmful to one's health."

Before he left the building, Conch stopped in a rather claustrophobic, closet-sized single person men's room off the lobby. After relieving himself and washing his hands, he splashed a little cold water in his face, since a dull headache was coming on. As he straightened, he confronted himself in the mirror. Maybe it was that the unkind starkness of the lighting, which called into sharp relief each pore, each subtle wrinkle, each imperfection, made his own countenance ugly and alien to him . . . or maybe he had a flash of memory about the time he shot another good-looking young man, a contract hit, in the face in a public rest room. Whatever the reason, his own reflected face disturbed him. He forced his eyes from it, left the room and shut off the light behind him.

Sitting in his parked hovercar, his window down so he could smoke his herb butt, Conch got Indigo on his console vidphone. As he had suspected, Indigo had not been able to listen to the conversation in Abbas's office, so Conch filled him in. Then he asked Indigo: "What did you find out about the vampires on the net?"

"Not much. It looks like they seriously don't want anything known about them. They definitely come from the planet Anul . . . but the Anul people aren't helpful about it. They pretty much shun the Vlessi, have myths about them. They tend to call them demons and vampires and dung like that, too. One pretty persistent myth is that the Vlessi aren't really native to Anul . . . they supposedly came there through a hole in space."

"Then . . . they're probably extradimensionals. And their rift or portal just happened to open up on Anul."

"Maybe. If there's any truth to the myths. But the myths get weirder."

"How so?"

"Another nickname the Anul have for them would translate as something like "double," or "spirit." I think an equivalent in Earth folklore would be doppelganger."

"Meaning what?"

"Apparently some Anul people feel that the Vlessi are their own doubles. They believe there's one Vlessi for every Anul. I guess what they mean is the Vlessi are the Anul themselves . . . from a parallel dimension."

Conch blew raspberries, not to scoff at the stories but just out of a lack of something to say. "So . . . what do you think?"

"I'm open to the extradimensional beings idea. But doppelgangers . . . "

"It's all just dung the Vlessi have put out there to scare the Anul, and anyone else who might cross them. Good publicity, that's all. War cries and painted faces and bagpipe music. We aren't afraid of that stuff, are we, Indigo?"

"Bagpipes, maybe," Indigo said.

. . .

When Jasper Conch was a young boy, who did not at that time call himself Jasper Conch—because at that time he didn't have to be concerned about vengeful people tracking down his family—he performed a strange mental ritual before he went to sleep at night. It was a ritual of self torment, an imp of the perverse.

Jasper would imagine that he must clamber into his bed quickly, and once there, he must not let his hands or feet protrude beyond the edges of his narrow mattress . . . lest they be severed by his force field when he activated it. He would then reach behind him, touch an imaginary button on one of the posts of his headboard, and an invisible shield would enclose his bed from all sides and above, like a mosquito net made of pure energy.

Only moments after he was safely enclosed in this unseen sarcophagus, the first of the zombies would stagger through his bedroom door . . . followed by many others. The undead would crowd into his room, fill it until they could barely even move. With their skeletal faces of an almost luminous shade of corrupted green, their eyes flashing green like those of hyenas filmed in infrared, they would press close around his bed, mash their faces and their hands right up against the force field, gazing in at him hungrily, grinding their teeth like Jasper's brother sleeping innocently in the next room, but unable to get at him.

His terrors, his walking fears, had emerged from the dark. But he had found a way to keep them at bay. And even though he knew they would remain there until morning, longing to get a hold of him, he could now turn on his side, burrow into his pillow with one arm over his face, and sleep safely.

As a man, as Jasper Conch, he had used the combination of money, imagination and technology to make this childhood fancy come true.

The bed in his apartment, though its mattress was much wider than in those days because sometimes he had company though usually not for very long, had four high posts at its ends. Spaced along each post and each leg of the bed were small green crystal balls that looked purely decorative. But once he was in his bed, he could slide aside a panel camouflaged into the intricate carvings of his headboard, touch a control key, and activate an invisible repulsor screen which would radiate from the crystal lenses and entirely surround his bed . . . all four sides, top and even bottom, an improvement over his childhood design, in case some hungry fiend might slither beneath the bed to attack him through the mattress.

Conch did not fear zombies, or even ghosts. He was not superstitious. But sometimes, fancifully, because he had imagination, he half-wondered if those zombies he had seen in his youth were spectral forerunners . . . a premonition of the men and women that he would kill for money as an adult.

He did not believe the dead could hurt him. But he knew the living could, and would, if he ever let his guard down. Physically. Psychologically. Emotionally.

The only people on the planet Oasis he could be said to love, with his parents and two siblings all living on Earth, were Indigo, Hans and Brass. But even then, he knew he would kill any one of them, even Indigo, if they betrayed or endangered him in any way, and without hesitation. And they had the same understanding in regard to him. This mutual feeling, in a way, only strengthened their dependence on loyalty, and thus strengthened their affection.

In a way, the only person Jasper Conch regretted killing—though on occasion he had seen the sobbing relatives or spouses of his victims on VT—was the frightened little boy he had once been, who only wanted to bury his head in sleep.

Beside him on the bed—now that the soothingly humming screen was in place—covered under his blanket, was a two-handed assault engine that could fire just about every type of destructive beam, gel rounds filled with highly corrosive plasma, and a variety of solid rounds including mini-rockets. A pistol could even be detached from its belly. This was the only bed companion he could always trust. With him also in bed was his palmcomp, and he rang up each of his men in turn on a scrambled frequency. He woke Brass, sleeping like a baby with his war paint scrubbed off for the night, apologized to him, reminded him tomorrow the duel officially began though this reminder was not necessary, and told him to go back to sleep. Hans was awake and shirtless, his Yakuza tattoos showing brightly, polishing a mean-looking Ramon dagger. He had given a similar dagger to Conch as a past birthday gift and Conch often wore it in a boot sheath. Hans saluted him with the dagger. Lastly he checked on Indigo.

"I'm going to stay up reading," his slender, soft-spoken friend told him, the room around him dark but for a single greenish fluorescent lamp glowing on his pate through the bristles of his closely cropped head. "Tomorrow begins for us at dawn. But for some people, tomorrow begins at midnight."

"We're all on our guard," Conch reassured him. Indigo's unwillingness to sleep didn't disturb him. Thanks to a combination of drugs and will power, Indigo rarely slept, in any case.

"Maybe we should sleep in the basement until this is over," he suggested. The so-called basement was their office, and more like a bunker, and Conch doubted there was a police precinct even in the worst sector of Punktown with a more impressive armory.

"Scattered targets are harder to hit."

"Still, I get a black vibe from the Devils. Together, our team could sleep in shifts. We could guard each other."

"We'll be fine. You don't sleep, anyway. I've got my canopy. Hans' girl is there with him and she can fight nearly as good as he can. And Brass is living inside that big dead robot outside Forge Park and even if someone suspected it they'd never get in through its armor. Go read your book, Gramma."

Indigo flickered a small smile, nodded, and signed off. Conch lay the palm-comp down beside him. He then turned on his side, buried his head in his pillow, and covered his face with his arm.

As a boy, he had begged his parents in vain to let him sleep with the light on. Now that he was a man, no one could tell him not to. He left the light on.

. . .

In his dream, the air of his bedroom became suffused with a misty blue-green illumination. It glowed through his closed lids, and oddly it made the veins in his lids stand out vividly black against the phosphorescent flesh. There was a hum in the air, soft but louder than the mother's lullaby hum of his force screen. The door in his room must have just been opened. The zombies must have begun filing through . . .

Conch's lids flashed open. His hand flashed to the assault engine covered like a lover beside him, and he rolled onto his back to see the Vlessi as it swung in a vicious arc a sort of black metal tomahawk with a blade at one end of its head, a cruel spike at the other, the bottom of the handle tapering into another, thinner spike.

The Vlessi's blow was repelled by the force screen, the blade skittering off to one side as if off a sheet of smooth metal, a bluish static illuminating the surface of the field for one moment. The physical shock through his body and the shock of surprise rippled through the offworlder's tall, thin frame. Before he could recover himself for a second blow, or for escape back into the blue-green glow which was fading away behind him, Conch reached his left arm up to his headboard, fingered open the hidden panel, thumbed the control button, and opened fire with the assault engine gripped in his right fist and braced against his knee. If he had fired a moment sooner, before he opened the screen, the ricocheting emerald bolts from one of the beam barrels would have killed him where he lay. Instead, he saw two of the short lances of energy disappear into the Vlessi like crossbow quarrels. One of them was lost inside him, but the other emerged out his back. The Vlessi dropped, still clutching his war hammer, and when Conch leapt to the floor he had to dart back as his enemy swung the axe at his legs. He managed to kick it out of the warrior's grasp, and then he stomped hard on the being's twice-punctured chest to keep him still.

Pointing the assault engine down at the pelvis-like face full of empty orifices, Conch demanded, "How did you get in here?" He knew how, vaguely—that misty blue-green light, which had now entirely faded—but he didn't know what the light had been. The afterglow of some method of teleportation he was unfamiliar with?

The Vlessi stared up at him, his six tiny lidless eyes revealing no pain, and Conch wondered if the Vlessi were indeed capable of feeling pain. Pain was a fluke of evolution, after all. An alarm system to warn one of danger, the touch of fire, it could instead increase the danger through distraction or immobilization. Conch hoped the Vlessi were not more evolved in that sense.

It was the Vlessi with the lime green scarf. Their leader. In his translated voice like that of a dead man speaking underwater, he said, "You were lucky."

"And you're lucky I haven't killed you yet."

"You intended to when you shot me. And you will, you must, if you are to fulfill your contract with Ziggurat."

"You're right. I am going to kill you. But it can go quickly or it could go on for a week. The decision's yours." Not taking his aim off the bony head, Conch backed up just a few steps so he could grab his palmcomp off his bed with his left hand and flip it open. Thumbing it to audio command, he told the device to ring up Indigo.

It tried. The two enemies waited. No one answered.

Conch rested the device on the edge of his bureau. "Keep trying," he ordered it. Then to the Vlessi he snarled, "How did you fuckers do this?" He aimed his engine at the Vlessi's left leg. "I'll take you apart a limb at a time, believe it."

"I am not a coward."

An emerald streak. There were two thin bones which comprised the bottom half of the Vlessi's leg. After the bolt of energy had spent itself, only one of these two bones still held the leg together. No blood oozed from the black, cauterized edges of any of the three beam wounds. Did the alleged blood-drinkers even have blood?

"How did you get in here?" Conch repeated. He watched the alien spasm briefly, writhe more slowly, get itself under control again though it maintained a steady vibration. He doubted this trembling was out of fear. So they did feel pain; they were just good at controlling it. The voice remained deep and steady when the Vlessi answered him.

"Wherever you are, I can will myself. Within a certain radius of you. Not much larger than the extent of this room."

"What do you mean by that?"

The palmcomp beeped, and Indigo was there. He was alive. Despite his relief, Conch didn't take his eyes off his prisoner to turn toward the screen.

"One of the Vlessi came to my room," Indigo said calmly. "It's dead."

"How'd it get there? Did you see?"

"I looked up from reading, saw this light, and then it stepped out of the light swinging a hatchet at me."

"It didn't live long enough for you to question it, I suppose."

"No," said Indigo simply. "It didn't."

"Check on Hans and Brass and call me back. I've got my Vlessi alive but wounded."

"All right." The vidphone feature went silent.

Conch gestured with his bulky weapon. "Tell me more. Are you teleporting yourselves into our apartments?"

"No."

"What, then?"

The Vlessi hesitated a moment too long. Conch shifted his gun slightly, and a second later black smoke tendrils curled out of a hole just below the knotty knee of the Devil's other hoofed leg. Again, the being fought briefly to rein in and corral his agony. Again, his voice did not betray the strain of his struggle.

"We make our home on another plane."

"So you are extradimensionals, then. Are you some kind of alternate versions of the Anul people, like they say?"

"Not just the Anul people."

"What's that supposed to mean?"

A few beats of further hesitation. Conch pointed his gun at an arm and raised his brows meaningfully. The Vlessi replied from his nonexistent mouth, "I can come and go from my plane to this one most readily on Anul, because that is where the broadest and most stable rift exists. Other than that rift, I can not come and go between planes except in the immediate vicinity of one of my doubles."

"Explain doubles."

"One of the infinite alternate versions of myself, one in each of the countless realities. My double on this plane could have been an Anul or it could just as easily have been a Choom female or a Tikkihotto infant. I am . . . we are . . . all the facets of one great soul, which despite its many eyes can not see its own entirety. We Vlessi have found that we are one of the only races that are aware of these other facets of our souls."

"So what you're trying to tell me is . . . that you are me. And I'm you."

"Yes. We are each other. And that is how I could will myself close to you. And how my team members could will themselves close to your team members. When Rescue learned that Ziggurat had contracted you four to settle their conflict, we four were contacted and hired as well. We are more alike than you suspect, Mr. Conch. On our plane, we four are friends—and assassins—as you four are. Not all aspects of our lives run in parallel. But you will find that often, the major characteristics follow fairly similar directions. I hoped one day . . . I knew one day . . . we four would gather to test ourselves against you other four. I perceive something else you do not. An unfathomable web, a design, that you might dismiss as fate, or destiny."

Conch lowered his gun muzzles only the most imperceptible degree, unconsciously. "God," he whispered to himself. To his *human* self, that is.

"Do you not believe me?"

Now that he was conscious of the truth, he could feel it. Feel their connection quite clearly. As if obscuring cataracts had been removed from his vision. It was as though he recognized at last his own eyes plainly reflected in the Devil's six asymmetrical eyes.

"Yes," he muttered. "But how . . . how could you come here to kill me, knowing that we're part of the same . . . the same . . . "

"Soul? Spirit? Essence? The particular entity you and I share is infinite, as I say, Mr. Conch. Facets of its existence wink into life and blink into death on planets and in dimensions and in far gulfs of time past and future, every fraction of every second." His voice, though monotonous, nevertheless sounded oddly amused as he educated this less enlightened, inferior version of himself. "You are not some precious and singular soul. You are a mere single cell in a being beyond what your primitive mind can encompass."

"Then you aren't much of anything, either," Conch told the Vlessi, aiming his weapon more pointedly again. "You won't be missed much, either."

"Can you do that, Mr. Conch? Can you kill yourself?"

Conch was about to say something, but he wasn't sure what, when Indigo came back on the palmcomp's small screen. "Brass is dead," he said in his flat voice. "So are Hans and his girl. No one saw anything except someone in Hans' building heard screaming."

"Fuckers," Conch hissed, and he kicked the Vlessi hard in his skeletal ribs like those of a wasted, reanimated zombie. "Get over here, Indigo. We have to decide what to do with my captive."

"Be careful, man, in case the other two materialize there, too."

"That isn't possible. Come over and I'll explain." Conch addressed the Vlessi again. "How come you haven't escaped back into your own plane?"

"I would have if I could. I have been trying while we talked. I am too badly injured. I may be dying."

Conch pumped the slide on his assault engine's shotgun feature, his lips curling back from his teeth. "Maybe I should put you out of your misery, huh?"

"Why don't you, Mr. Conch? Do you find it difficult, now that you know we are essentially the very same being?"

"I didn't say I was convinced."

"Then kill me. Kill me now. I am most likely dying anyway . . . "

"Why should I do you the favor, then? Maybe I like to see you shake."

"Be honest with yourself, Mr. Conch." The Vlessi made a very unpleasant approximation of a laugh at his own joke. "You *are* primitive, aren't you? You with this narrow, limited scope of your own being? This flat mirror you perceive as the only aspect of yourself? You are afraid to kill me now. It is so easy for you to end another's life. You can not empathize properly with another's existence. But you can't help seeing the killing of me as a kind of suicide. As if suicide should be more difficult than homicide. Mr. Conch, you fear the consummation and obliteration of self, of your supposed unique existence. You fear something I do not, because I can perceive the infinite, the eternal. You fear death."

"You're one to talk about empathy. You don't have empathy with me. With *this* version of me."

"We find it easier to kill aspects of ourselves rather than those of other souls. In that way, we consider ourselves more advanced than you."

"That's some pretty lame moralizing, Jasper." Why shouldn't he give the Vlessi that *nom de guerre*? He hadn't started out with it, himself. "Don't lie to yourself." He chucked the Vlessi's own joke back at him. "We're both up to our necks in blood and it doesn't matter whose it is, in the end.". . .

Indigo arrived, and when Conch let him in he already had a black pistol drawn. Conch had his Decimator .220 in one hand but he held it loosely. He led Indigo into the bedroom, where his friend stared down at the Vlessi unfazed. "It's the leader," he noted. "When did you kill it?"

"He died right before you came. From the wounds he got when I opened my bed shield."

"Good thing you had that."

"Good thing you don't sleep."

"Two are dead. Now we need the ones that killed Hans and Brass. I want to skin those wankers alive."

"They won't be as dangerous to you and me as they were to Hans and Brass," Conch mumbled somberly. "They won't be able to surprise us like our doubles surprised us."

"Doubles?" A few beats, and then Indigo said, "Doppelgangers?"

Conch would explain. And he didn't doubt that now with the Vlessi having lost their best weapon, the unexpected, he and Indigo would defeat the two survivors with their affinity for crude weapons pretty easily . . .

But he did doubt that he would be able to skin their opponents alive when they caught them. He thought he would want to kill them as quickly and mercifully as possible . . . knowing that, in a way, one of them would be Hans, and the other Brass. Maybe Brass' double would even prove to be the female Vlessi he had pretended to lust after in the club the night the eight men met, when they had stared across at each other as though into a distorting carnival mirror. Even without his war paint, the one being would be Brass in some mysterious way. The other Hans, even without his tattoos. Where once Conch believed he could have killed his own friends if he thought they might prove a risk to his safety, now he dreaded seeing them both die a second time . . . in another incarnation.

Who would have thought that he would have learned a lesson in empathy in this way?

Who might have guessed that, in a way, he would learn it from himself?

"We should melt the body," Indigo said. He nodded at the assault engine on the bed. "Does that have blue plasma rounds in it?" Blue-colored plasma would dissolve only organic matter . . . wouldn't eat into the carpeting or floor.

Conch lifted his weapon from the bed and pressed it into his friend's hands. "You do it," he said softly, and left the room so he wouldn't see the obliteration of himself. He was afraid that if he saw it, his childhood terrors would return that night.

And this time the force field around his bed would not function properly. And this time, the walking dead would eat him at last.

ABOUT THE AUTHOR

JEFFREY THOMAS is the author of the novels *Boneland* (Bloodletting Press), *Everybody Scream!* (Raw Dog Screaming Press), *Letters from Hades* (Bedlam Press), and *Monstrocity* (Prime); the collections *Aaaiiieee!!!*, *Honey Is Sweeter than Blood*, *Terror Incognita* (all from Delirium Books); and the novella *Godhead Dying Downwards* (Earthling Publications). Forthcoming books include *The Sea of Flesh and Ash* (with brother Scott Thomas, from Prime), with the collections *Punktown: Shades of Grey* (Necro Publications) and *Unholy Dimensions* (Mythos Books), on the horizon as well. Anthologies featuring his work include *Whispers and Shadows* (Prime), *Leviathan Three*, *The Thackery T. Lambshead Pocket Guide to Eccentric and Discredited Diseases*, *Warfear*, *Frontiers of Terror*, *New Mythos Legends*, *Quick Chills II: The Best Horror Fiction from the Specialty Press*, *Octoberland*, *Strangewood Tales*, *The Dead Inn Volume 1*, *Dark Testament*, and Daw's *The Year's Best Horror Stories XXII*. He is the editor of the anthology *Punktown: Third Eye*, also from Prime, which collects tales of Punktown written by a variety of authors. When not visiting Oasis, Thomas lives in Massachusetts.

Printed in the United States
29093LVS00001B/262